Hushed

Tales of Ryca, Volume 2

Shereen Vedam

Published by Shereen Vedam, 2018.

This is a work of fiction. Similarities to real people, places, or events are entirely coincidental.

HUSHED

First edition. April 10, 2018.

Copyright © 2018 Shereen Vedam.

ISBN: 978-0995344754

Written by Shereen Vedam.

This fantasy novel is dedicated to all my friends. They, too, are my family.

Chapter 1

"PUT YOUR CLOTHES BACK on!" her mother said.

Eighteen-year-old Princess Tamara's ears still rang from the door slamming shut. Left alone with her daunting mother in this torch-lit chamber, a tremor of dread swept down her spine.

How could her first time in a man's bed have ended up with castle guards carting off her would-be lover and leaving Tamara at her mother's mercy? And where were they taking Thyel?

Buck up! She straightened her spine. This was no time to show weakness. She defiantly dropped the bed sheet. Retrieving her shift, she dragged it over her head, then put on her discarded amber silk gown that Thyel had passionately flung off not fifty heartbeats ago. Her fingers fumbled with the ties at her back. It was hard to focus when she wanted to rip the gown to shreds. She controlled her temper before speaking.

"How did you find me?" Was that her voice, sounding so flippant? *Well done, Tamara.*

Mamosia, Queen of Ryca, slowly raised one elegant eyebrow. Tamara's mother was not fond of flippancy. Then again, she was not fond of Tamara at all, lately. "Do you realize what almost happened, child?"

"I'm not a child."

"Your actions suggest otherwise." By torchlight, her mother looked every inch the royal monarch. Her red velvet gown formed a close v-shaped bodice, extended over wide sleeves, and fell in a full skirt. The circlet of gold over her burnished blond hair finished an attire that was simply elegant.

Tamara usually admired her mother's casual grace. However, since the queen set her ultimatum a week ago, only fury burned up Tamara's insides. Yet, like vanishing mist, all her machinations to counter that challenge had dissipated. She took a deep breath. "I almost found myself a husband by the deadline you set."

Her mother came around the bed and plucked the loose cords at her back out of her fingers. "It is beyond me to understand your thinking. Or perhaps thinking is too much to ask of you these days."

"I was trying to protect myself. If you hadn't forced me into this situation, I wouldn't have had to resort to such a tactic."

"Do not blame me for your sad lack of comportment, young lady."

"Your ultimatum ends in days, Mother. What did you expect?"

"If you wanted to marry this fool - and I'm not saying I would have agreed, for he is too ambitious for my liking - why not simply tell me you favored him?"

That was rich. The man her mother picked, vile greedy and intolerant Gideon, only saw Tamara as a gateway into the royal family. Her mother seemed oblivious to his true nature. So, Tamara tried to explain her thinking in choosing Thyel instead. "I couldn't tell you. Not until..."

"Until what?"

The moment stretched. Finally, unable to stop the words that gnawed away deep in her heart, Tamara said, "You decreed no man may touch me until my wedding night. That gave me the perfect way to test Thyel's character."

Her mother's cool fingers stilled on Tamara's warm back. "How?"

"To see if he had the strength to oppose your will. He did! That suggests I can trust him to bend to my wishes above all others, even you, which makes him the best choice for my husband."

"Tamara...why do you distrust my judgment?"

"I've learned otherwise to my peril, Mother. Or have you forgotten your time spell?"

"That saved our lives!"

"I would gladly have given mine up to have avoided those horrible decades." *Shut up.* Too late. The words she'd swallowed for five years had erupted like a volcano.

Her mother swung her around to face her, holding her in place with fingers tight on Tamara's upper arms. "What do you mean? We were unaware of the years passing. One moment, we stood in the woods with your uncle's Horsemen surrounding us. The next, we were in the castle and my little Saira, all grown up, was unraveling my spell."

Tamara pulled out of her mother's painful hold and turned to hide her torment. *Hush! Cover up. She mustn't find out the truth.*

Over two decades ago, in one devastating night, her mother had lost her husband, her kingdom and almost lost Saira, her favorite child. Seeing the horror in her mother's eyes, Tamara made a solemn silent promise. For the rest of her life, she would protect her mother from further anguish.

After the time spell was cast, her brother and mother's lives had indeed paused. Not so Tamara. She'd been miserably awake during every excruciating moment that followed. Frozen in place. Her cries unheard. Listening to the ravings of her murderous uncle and his mad wizard cohort.

The knowledge of her daughter's endless torment during those lost decades would destroy what remained of her mother's shattered heart. So, since Saira broke their spell five years ago, Tamara carefully hid the trauma she had undergone from her mother, from her family, from everyone. She planned to take her horrific secret to her grave.

She would not be the cause of further harm to her mother.

However, everything had changed for Tamara. She was no longer the eldest and much-loved daughter. Now she was treated as no more than an encumbrance. Someone who needed to be protected, cared for, sheltered. Yet, it was her mother who most needed protecting.

To distract the queen now, she said, "I don't care for this new life. Everything feels odd."

Queen Mamosia gently stroked Tamara's hair. "We all have people and things we miss."

She meant her beloved husband. Tamara's father. Her throat clogged with old sorrow. "I don't want to talk about Father. You need to forget him, but not by setting yourself to torture me for the rest of my sorry life."

"Marriage doesn't have to be torture, Tamara."

"It will be, if you insist I marry Gideon."

"He is a rich merchant who is kind, thoughtful and admires you greatly. He has also promised that if he were privileged to become your husband, he would take exceptional care of you, always." The queen's fingers returned to Tamara's ties, pulling them tight and her next words came out hard and implacable. "You will not see Thyel again. I've expelled him from the kingdom."

Tamara swung around and glared at the queen. "How could you?"

"Pick another," the queen said implacably. "You have five days to present me with your choice, or I *will* choose your husband."

"I won't marry Gideon!"

"I've given you an opportunity to chart your own destiny, Tamara. If you are unable to do so, I will do it for you."

Tamara swallowed to soothe the dryness of her throat. There had to be a way out of this mess. The walls pressed in.

"Your sisters never gave me half as much trouble."

She turned her back to the queen. "I'm sorry I'm not as good as Saira or Anna."

Her mother's fierce tug on her gown's ties tipped Tamara backwards. She stumbled until she found her balance. Rolling her eyes, she tilted her head back far enough to stare up at the two-story-high domed ceiling of the guest chamber.

Breathe. You need air for clear thinking. Take what you can before Mother wrings out your last breath.

Faltering footsteps hurrying along the stone floor of the corridor outside alerted them to a newcomer. The interruption saved Tamara the shame of begging a reprieve for air.

The door opened and her sister Saira entered. Her younger sister looking older, still startled Tamara.

Thirty-eight-year old Saira's limp had been completely healed by their talented sister, Anna. Yet, when excited or surprised, Saira still walked the old way. A poignant reminder of that terrible night.

Tamara was thoroughly grateful for Saira's unexpected arrival. Anything to distract her mother from Tamara's transgression. She nodded a welcome.

Her sister studied her state of dress – no doubt noting her missing hair covering, bare feet, and crumpled gown – but then, thankfully, she shrugged these facts aside and addressed the queen. "Mother, we've trouble. Bevan's missing."

Bevan, her sister Anna's nine-year-old son, was another of the Queen's favorites. Likely because he was fast growing up to be as strong a sorcerer as her late husband.

Which is why Saira's news did not concern Tamara. The boy was more than capable of taking care of himself. She glanced behind to check on the queen's reaction though.

"Are you sure?" her mother asked, concern darkening her gaze.

A shadow of her mother's fears flit across her face. Tamara resisted the urge to put an arm around her in comfort.

Saira stepped further into the chamber. "Tom and I returned home to find a note from Bevan asking to meet. When I went to his quarters, a shield surrounded him. It had a strange look to it, not the Light shields I've taught him to build, but something with a sparkling green tinge. I approached and the shield fell away, and he was gone. I did a spell to trace his whereabouts, but I sensed no trail at all."

That stirred Tamara's curiosity. Saira could trace and dismantle most any spell. Could Bevan have grown stronger than his aunt? Possibly. The boy was brilliantly talented at wielding Light magic.

Saira shook her head, as if confused and worried. "I've sent a runner to inform his parents, but Anna and Marton are halfway across Ryca. It'll be days before they return."

The queen came around the bed to speak with Saira. "Where could he have gone?"

"More like taken, I think," Saira said, looking angry.

"Taken? How?" Alarm rose in her mother's voice.

Tamara's heartbeat skipped with worry, but she shook it off. Bevan was probably practicing a new spell. She almost said so but realized both women had forgotten her. Her glance flew to the half open door. Escape beckoned.

"Who could have taken him?" her mother asked.

"No one in Ryca is that powerful." Tamara cursed the instant she spoke her thought out loud.

Saira finally seemed to take in her surroundings, her gaze wandering over the warrior tapestries on the wall to the watercolor paintings before settling on Tamara. She took in her barefoot state, standing with a hand gripping the door handle.

"What are you two doing in here?" Saira asked. "I thought it odd the guards directed me to the guest wing."

"Never mind that," their mother said absently.

Tamara breathed in relief. *Yes, never mind, Saira.*

A curt tilt of her mother's head and Tamara reluctantly shut the door and stepped back into the room. Soon enough, she was forgotten again.

Familiar bitterness overtook her relief. Unlike the rest of her family, Tamara was considered useless during a crisis because she had no magical ability. Another thing to blame her father for. His extraordinary abilities had passed to all his children and grandchildren, all except for Tamara.

If she'd been born with the ability to wield Light, to weave magical spells, she would have faced down the sorcerer Tamarisk, and made him pay dearly for destroying her family. Her mother certainly wouldn't be forcing her to marry against her will. The queen wanted to ensure her helpless daughter would be protected.

Gideon would shield her, all right. Making sure she had no freedom, doing exactly as he bid for the rest of her miserable life. Meanwhile, he would gain all the power and prestige of marrying into the royal family.

She shivered, remembering his cruel possessive look earlier today. Ever since his merchant vessel docked in Tibor's harbor two months ago, he'd been playing on her mother's concerns about Tamara. Well, she would have none of it. No one would trap her. Not again.

Silently, she skirted the canopied bed and stepped onto the tiny balcony attached to this opulent guestroom. The cold out here was preferable to the oppression inside.

If only the queen hadn't found her out. She should have known better than to think she could fool her mother. Everyone in this castle acted as her mother's eyes and ears.

At least this new dilemma about Bevan gave her breathing room.

Staring at the star-strewn night sky, she took a deep breath of the cool salty sea air. Being outdoors always gave her a subtle sense of freedom. How little time she had left to enjoy this precious sense of autonomy. Leaning on the railing, she clenched her fingers around the cold iron balustrade until the sharp edges bit into her palms.

Their castle was built on a hill. Far below stretched the sprawling coastal city of Tibor. Along its eastern edge, vessels hugged the shoreline. They were all sizes and shapes, from barges and tugs, to merchant carriers and fishing vessels.

High above it all, the three moons, called the Three Sisters, were perfectly lined up. Their full, brilliant glow bathed Tibor's rooftops, masts, and booms, and rippled over the Sea of Tyver.

Such an alignment of the moons is rare, Bevan had told her this morning. *One that portends grave danger.*

Had Bevan said that? The memory proved as elusive as the wind that embraced and then abandoned her. She tried to remember and an ache instantly throbbed beneath her eyes.

Wait! Bevan had told her that he'd gone off like this before, and then returned to his bed perfectly safe. How could she have forgotten that? She hurried into the room, shaking her head at her mother worrying unnecessarily. She should know better than to be concerned about that talented boy. "Bevan will come home soon enough."

The two women turned their angry looks her way.

The dungeon suddenly seemed a safer place. Manacles and a rat-infested cell weren't as frightening as the queen's ire.

"Do you not understand the situation, Tamara?" Saira asked. The only royal child with red hair, her sister often reminded her of a hearth fire – warm, but dangerous. "Someone's taken Bevan. We must get him back."

"He's gone off like this before and returned." Tamara shrugged to display nonchalance. "So, why worry?"

"When?" her mother asked. "When has he gone off like this? And why didn't you tell us before?"

The question sincerely surprised Tamara. "But it shouldn't be news, Mother. If he told me, he surely had already confided in you, or Saira." Her quiet nephew had never been close to Tamara, and he thought of Saira as a second mother.

Her sister and mother approached. At their close proximity, her old terror of being confined jabbed her. She inched backwards but a wall halted her escape.

"Did he say where he went?"

"How long has this been going on?"

Tamara slid past the two questioning women. "Give me time to think!"

The hairs on her arms prickled with tension as she hurried away. *When did this become my fault, too?* She strode past a writing table, chair, and an intricately decorated oak chest pressed against a wall. In her haste, her bare foot struck the heavy chest, jarring it. She hopped on one foot cursing silently, until an iridescent ribbon stuffed behind the chest caught her attention.

A little tug released the pretty scrap of fabric. Earlier tonight, Thyel had lovingly draped this around her shoulders. She'd instantly felt constricted. Tamara hated anything close to her neck. When he began to disrobe her, she tossed it off. The silky thing must have slid behind the chest. Missing Thyel now, she tied her loose hair back with it. A wave of dizziness struck.

"Tamara," her mother said. "What's wrong?"

"Nothing." She rubbed at her temple, but it continued to ache abominably, and now green sparks fluttered behind her eyelids. With irritation, she pulled off the silky band and threw it back toward the chest, where it fluttered out of sight.

Stupid ribbon!

With her hair untied, her headache improved. Her mother and sister sent her worried looks.

"Are you sure you're well?" her mother asked.

"Yes, please stop fussing." This day was worsening at a gallop. If only she could remember what Bevan had said at breakfast. He was normally the quietest of lads. So, why hadn't she paid attention when he came in for a chat?

In fact, now she thought of it, most of this day felt unusually shadowy. Strange, since she normally had an excellent memory, unhappily so. Of course, this morning she'd been distracted, planning her evening with Thyel. When Bevan showed up, Tamara had even momentarily wondered if the queen had sent her grandson to spy on her truculent daughter.

Concentrate. What had Bevan said about those times he went away? Something about meeting a stranger, yes, that was it. She turned back. "I remember now. Bevan said a being visited him and told him of a foreign land. You know how fanatical he is about seeing new places. He probably went to see for himself what it was like."

That caught their attention.

"What did this stranger look like?" Saira asked. "And where is this foreign land situated?"

Tamara rubbed at her forehead. The throbbing had returned with a vengeance. Then in a flash she saw the person Bevan described. As clear as if she gazed at his portrait. "The man has a narrow face, icy blue eyes, pale white hair and skin. Oh, and he spoke with a soft musical voice." Of its own accord, her arm shot up until her hand hovered high over her head. "And he was this tall," she said, though she felt as unsure of that fact as her arm seemed certain of it.

It had green skin, stood knee high, and was nasty tempered, Tamara. It was very rude.

She frowned, confused. Had she imagined Bevan saying that last bit? The words swept by in the whisper of a cold, north wind. The latter description was so different from the picture that stayed glued to the forefront of her mind. She delved deeper into the memory and the hammering in her head thundered. She cried out.

Saira was at her side, her hands covering Tamara's head. "Let me look at you. You're flushed."

"I'm fine!" Her sister's fingers burned. She pushed Saira away and stumbled backwards. "Leave me alone. You're making my head hurt more. Why must everyone crowd me?"

Tamara edged away. The further she went from Saira, the less her head hurt until she could finally look around without squinting with pain.

"I've never heard such an odd description," her mother said, thankfully keeping her distance.

"Neither had I," Tamara agreed readily. "Truly, Mother, I thought he'd dreamed it or I would have spoken sooner."

"What else did Bevan say?" her mother asked.

Did he say something was green? The memory faded. "Nothing I recall."

Her mother turned to Saira. "The Erovians were a myth until you introduced them to Rycan society. Could this tall, white-haired stranger be real, too?"

"I don't know, Mam."

The pet name surprised Tamara. It was an old nickname Saira had used as a child because she couldn't pronounce Mamosia. The slip showed how upset her sister must be, for she was always careful to refer to the queen only as "mother" these days.

The queen approached and gently took Tamara's fingers. "Try to remember, dear. What else did Bevan say?"

Tamara trembled within her gentle hold. Could her nephew truly be in trouble? Had she made a terrible mistake in not listening to him? Looking into her mother's worried blue eyes, Tamara's guilt spiked. Could Bevan die because she had allowed Thyel to distract her? The large room shrank, crowding her. "I don't remember anything else."

The disappointment in her mother's eyes brought a lump to Tamara's throat. She freed her hands. Maybe if she had some privacy and space, all what Bevan said would come back. "I'm going to my room to rest. If I remember anything else, I'll send word. I promise."

"Should we contact Garren at the university to let him know what's happening?" Saira asked.

"No," Mamosia said. "You've contacted Anna and Marton. That's enough for now. Let's leave Garren be. I don't want your brother troubled as he focuses on his studies."

Tamara ran out before she burst into tears. Two guards stood watch outside. She was half way down the corridor when she remembered Thyel had heard Bevan, too. He might remember what her nephew said. She ran back to the two guards. "Where has Thyel been taken?"

The men remained silent.

"Tell me!"

"I'm sorry, your highness. You are not to see Master Thyel again. Queen's command."

With a frustrated shout, she stormed off. Further down the corridor she halted a female servant passing by. "Do you know where Master Thyel was taken by the guards?"

"Out of the castle, your highness," the young girl said, voice quivering. "To the docks, some say. I'm so sorry."

It was too late for a ship to set sail tonight. Without sunlight to guide the way, a vessel could never navigate safely past the rocks that surrounded Tibor's harbor. That could mean he was being held on board a docked vessel, awaiting a morning sail.

If so, for once, time was on her side.

Realizing she still held the shaking servant girl, Tamara released her with a muttered apology and thanked her for the valuable information. She hurried along the twisting corridors. Picking up her skirts, she sprinted down the curved stairs that led to the front entryway.

She had to find Thyel. Talk to him about Bevan.

The guards posted by the heavy front doors lowered spears to bar her way. Furious, she pivoted and sped back up the stairs. Other doors led to the outside. Surely not all would be guarded. Footsteps pounded behind her. A shoulder check showed a guard in pursuit.

Could her mother have ordered her confined to her quarters? She sped up, racing up to the second floor. She ran past a courtier and several startled servants. Around another corner and she came across the servants' stairs. She headed up to the third floor. What she needed was a safe route to the outside and she knew exactly where to find it.

It sounded as if the guard was gaining ground so she slipped behind a heavy wall-length tapestry and held her breath. Her pursuer flew past where she hid. She was about to go in the other direction when her palms skimmed past a hidden catch along the rough-cut stonewalls. A smile of triumph spread her cheeks wide.

As a child, Tamara had used the castle's secret passageways many times to evade her governess. She pressed two depressions on the wall and a panel at her back slid open, sweeping out cool air. She fell backwards into the passage and then instantly regretted her rash action. Before she could run back out, the door slid shut on her face and the lock clicked closed. A frantic search with her hands in the dark confirmed no handle or latch on this side.

She covered her mouth tight to stop her scream releasing. Getting caught by a guard would be worse than being stuck in here. There was a way to escape, but was she capable of doing it? She had run down these hidden corridors enough times to know where the next opening was.

Fears born of her long entrapment in the time spell, however, were creeping closer. Her legs quivered in the drafty corridor. Her knees buckled and she slumped onto the cold stone floor, knuckles scraping along the walls. Anger, frustration, and horror engulfed Tamara.

Years of being held immobilized returned with a vengeance. Then, her mother cast the charm to protect her. Now, Tamara's mind cast its own spell of terror, one her body unconditionally obeyed.

How could she have been so foolish as to put herself in this position? Her heart raced as if it planned to tunnel out of her chest. Her palms and forehead grew sweaty, and her throat closed in so tight, she couldn't have screamed even if she wanted to.

Minute by minute she became as immovable as the stone walls that surrounded her. All the while, her body stayed frozen in place.

Chapter 2

TAMARA STAYED CROUCHED in the dark, trembling, her mind shouting at her to, *Get me out of here!*

But time stood still.

Again.

In the silence, drums sounded a call inside her head.

That's what Bevan had said this morning. Something about hearing drums. Her nephew needed her. He could be in danger. What if he was killed because she didn't help?

Along either side, the corridor stretched the length of the castle. There were other openings with handles on this side of the wall. All Tamara had to do was get up and find one.

Sobbing, she forced herself to stand and move along the musty enclosure, one forced step at a time. Little things scuttled away from her bare feet in the dark. She tried to ignore the sound of skittering nails in the darkness ahead. Palms flattened against the wall, heartbeat thundering, she repeated, "Breathe, Tamara, and take a step. You are free."

An interminable time later, her hand brushed across a lever. She slammed her weight against it and a panel slid open. Crying in relief, Tamara tumbled in and fell to the floor. A glance up confirmed this was Saira and Tom's bedchamber. At least neither of them were here to witness her breakdown. As she lay there, every wasted moment ticked by at an excruciatingly slow pace.

Tamara managed to crawl to the bed but once on it, she had to lie still while her head settled from its spinning motion. A rustle brought her alert. She squinted in the faint moonlight and noticed a man standing in the middle of her sister's bedroom.

Was that Tom? Had her sister's husband come in?

The outline of the intruder showed a tall spare-framed male wearing a floor-length robe cinched at his waist and clutching a fat book. His skin was dark enough to blend into the shadowed room, but his distinctive white robe proclaimed him as none other than Jarrod of Erov. That's why she hadn't heard the door open.

An Erovian had the ability to pop in and out of places, and only Jarrod carried that silly tome wherever he went.

Jarrod's interest had always been allied solely with her sister Saira. He would never come to see Tamara in the middle of the night, without warning, and in an obvious fluster about something. Her eyes narrowed with displeasure. Surely Tom wouldn't approve of a handsome single man invading his wife's bedroom in the middle of the night. She disregarded the fact that she'd invaded her sister's room uninvited.

Jarrod came around the side of the bed and knelt. He was about her age, perhaps a year or two older, but where her skin was ivory, his was ebony. She might have never seen him in the darkness if not for his white robe. "Saira, I have urgent need of your help."

He was here for Saira. Always, Saira. At all royal functions, he ignored Tamara. On rare occasions when they found themselves face-to-face, he avoided eye contact.

Tamara gave a curt nod. "Good evening, Jarrod."

"Princess Tamara. Where's your sister?"

A quick succession of pictures flashed through her mind. Saira fast asleep by a camp fire in the woods, waking up inside a hut, speaking formally to long-robed Erovians in a multi-colored tent city.

Saira had said Erovians could share their feelings without saying a word to each other. They were circumspect with outsiders, never intruding unless invited. It surprised her that she could sense Jarrod's thoughts in this instance, and so clearly. Did he realize he projected them? Even more intriguing was the idea that these images were how Jarrod viewed her sister.

The scenes fit Saira's adventures to rescue her family. Seeing the story through this quiet, studious man's dark gaze brought those stories to life. Except, her sister had looked frightened in Jarrod's memory. How strange. Tamara had always thought Saira was the bravest of her family.

"Where's your sister?" Impatience gained ground in his normally calm tone.

She didn't care where Saira was. Tamara needed to find Thyel and ask him what Bevan had said this morning. She swung her legs to the floor. Could Jarrod be of help with her need? "There's a problem with Bevan. My sister's helping with that matter."

"Perhaps I can help her."

Ah, Jarrod to Saira's rescue, not Tamara's. With an irritated sigh, she jumped off the bed and then regretted it as the room shifted as if she were underwater.

"Are you all right?" he asked, steadying her with a hand at her elbow

"No time." She waited for her sight to settle and then shook off his hold and ran to the door.

He hurried after her. "I must find Lady Saira-Gilly. It's imperative."

Tamara stopped to turn and say, *She's busy,* when she noticed Jarrod's gaze transfixed to her shoulder.

Was he avoiding eye contact again? She itched to slap him to relieve a bit of frustration. Then she noticed that because of his earlier hold on her, her already loose gown had slipped to reveal a generous glimpse of her pale shoulders.

Well, well, well. Could it be that the strikingly aloof Chief Councilor of Erov was not as immune to her charms?

She lowered her shoulder and her dress obligingly slipped to the edge of her bosom.

A delightful frown appeared on his forehead.

"Jarrod, would you mind tying my gown in place?" She turned, to give him a clear view of her bare back.

His precious volume dropped to the floor. Tamara bit her lip to keep her laughter in.

His fingers fumbled as he pulled the cords tight to tie it. His hands were warm on her cold back and she leaned into his touch. "Please stand still, Tamara."

She thrilled at the tremor in his voice. He'd forgotten to address her as princess. All too soon he was done and he picked up his book, shuffling loose pages together.

She turned to observe him, her mind running rampant on how she could use his attraction of her to her advantage.

He straightened, his precious book clutched like a shield. Sending her a frowning glare, he opened the tome and followed a line of script with a finger. "Where Saira is should be marked in here," he muttered. "I don't understand why I can't find the notation."

It was Tamara's turn to squint at what he looked at. He couldn't possibly see anything in the dark. The bit of moonlight from the window barely highlighted his handsome dark face. Erovians were intrinsically magical, so perhaps the script was spelled to allow him to read even in the dimmest chamber.

A useful talent, if one was a scholar. Useless to her. Jarrod had another talent that could work on her behalf. His ability to pop in and out of places without anyone noticing.

To gain time to plan her next move, she allowed him to read in peace as she lit a candle and then deliberately, brushed by him on her way to set it on the hearth's mantle.

He practically jumped at her touch.

Priceless! Hiding her jubilant grin, she set the candle down and swung to confront him. "I'm curious, Jarrod, how did you get into this room?"

The glance he sent her way was filled with deep intensity and an odd appeal. A shiver spiked along her spine in reaction. So, this was what it felt like to have him look directly at her. Her stomach fluttered and heat rose up her cheeks. Of their own accord, her bare toes curled on the sheepskin rug.

Tamara noted all these reactions with a sense of dismay. All of Thyel's love talk and kisses had never stirred her like this. Jarrod had done it with one glance? How? He was a tedious young man who was in love with her sister.

She enjoyed having a sexual impact on him, but her reaction was unacceptable. She took a few breaths to slow the blood rushing through her veins like a flooding river and to quiet that odd music ringing in her ears.

"Jarrod," the word came out breathless. She cleared her throat and adjusted her next words to sound coy, instead of captivated, "How do you travel from place to place?"

He went back to looking at his tome. "We're born with the ability, Princess. Now I must find your sister. There's no reference to where she might have gone. Unusual. All royal events should be recorded here and that includes Saira's movements. She was due to return to the castle this evening. Even stranger that I cannot sense her presence anywhere."

"She'll be back soon," Tamara said. "While travelling, can you take someone with you?"

He shook his head, his soft black curls swinging. "I don't have time to explain. Where could Saira have gone?"

"If you agree to take me, I can guide you to where Saira is." A lie, but it might get her transported out of the castle. She moved closer and leaned in to pick up one of his long strands of hair. It felt as silky and light as she'd always imagined. He smelled faintly of ink, parchment and fresh air. Odd that such ordinary scents could seem so alluring.

He stepped back until she released her hold. "Tell me where she's gone and I'll find her myself."

"Take me with you, or you may wait here for her return." She gave him an inviting smile, twirling her own hair and watched with hidden triumph as his gaze followed the movement. "I believe she said she might be several hours."

He ignored her and turned a page.

Her annoyance peaked. With Bevan's life on the line, she didn't have time for this. She slammed the tome closed. "Stop looking at that ridiculous book."

His finger barely escaped, uninjured.

"Your choices are simple, Jarrod. If you wish to see Saira, allow me to guide you." Already regretting her show of temper, she soothed her face into a teasing smile. She raised her chest, and while his gaze went there, she reached back unobtrusively and loosened the cords at her back. A dropped shoulder and her gown obligingly slid to reveal what her mother would consider a shocking amount of bare flesh. "Or we can wait here for Saira, together."

• • • •

IN GREAT DISTRESS, Jarrod couldn't tear his gaze from Tamara's pale smooth bare shoulder. His hands holding Falcon's Tome turned clammy. His heart pounded as if someone knocked with great urgency inside his chest.

His thoughts slowed and his logical reasoning became as sluggish as walking through quicksand. *Think!* Could Tamara truly know where Saira was? If so, why was she being so difficult?

"We only ever transport apprentices," he said at last, deciding to humor her. "To teach them the ways of our magic. They are always fellow Erovians."

"But you could take me, if you wanted."

He sighed, breathed deep and kept his gaze anywhere in the dimly lit room but on her. She was so young. Barely eighteen. Yet, she had the kind of beauty that made men want to please her. Already his mind played with ways he could grant her wish.

"You are going to take me!" she said.

He glanced flew back to her in surprise. He hadn't projected that thought. Had he?

She wrapped her arms around his neck and then wilted. He instinctively supported her. "What's the matter?"

"Nothing." She sounded cross, and pushed away. "Now, hurry. We haven't a moment to lose."

Why the rush? "Where do we go?"

"To the docks, to find a man named Thyel."

"He knows where Saira is?"

"He can help us." She sounded evasive.

Jarrod's suspicions ballooned but he squelched them. At the moment, finding Saira overrode all other concerns. If helping Tamara aided his cause, how could that be bad? If nothing came of this, he could always return Tamara here and seek out the queen to ask for her help in finding Saira.

So, with Falcon's Tome tucked to his side, he drew Tamara closer. Her scent invaded his body like a heated, mind-numbing, floral infusion. Instinctively, his arm tightened its hold on her. He wove his travel spell. "Close your eyes."

She obeyed, lifting her face up expectantly. With her golden lashes fanning her cheeks, she looked more vulnerable than ever. He took a moment to study the most difficult of the Rycan princesses. This was the softer, delicate side of herself that Tamara hid from the world.

Seeing her like this, reminded him why he normally avoided her company. Already, with her pliant in his arms, without a struggle, his defenses against her charms crumbled. He straightened her gown, tightened his hold around her slender waist, and breathing deeply of her lovely scent, was about to transport them both to where he sensed this man Thyel was when someone knocked on the door.

"Ignore that," Tamara ordered.

The *rap-rap-rap* now sounded urgent. "Aunt Tamara, are you in there?" Skye's voice. She was Tamara's niece, Bevan's sister. A ball of Light popped into the room, hovered in front of them and then popped back out the door.

"I know you're in there," Skye said. "Please let me in. I need your help."

Jarrod released Tamara.

She silently cried out, *No!* The word rocked him. Beneath it, he sensed a terrible sense of guilt within Tamara. What had she done to Skye?

"I'll speak to this Thyel while you attend to your niece," he said and transported himself from the room. He heard her shout his name and his spell wavered. Afraid he might accidentally trap himself in the *between* places, he focused hard, willing himself to move through time and space.

In a blink, the world re-righted itself and he gave a profound sigh of relief. That was close. The spell should not have taken such a turn. Was his magic feeling the effect of whatever was harming his people? Or merely the result of him being so distracted by the princess?

He'd never transported anyone but another Erovian and couldn't believe he'd almost attempted it, and with Tamara of all people. What a disaster that would have been if his spell had failed while she was with him. Her greatest fear was being trapped and he might have done exactly that.

He found himself on board a vessel and a lone watchman looked in his direction. "Who goes there?"

The sailor had been sorting through a pile of reef fish, squirming eels, and squids scooped aboard in a net. He stopped what he was doing and came over. The closer he approached, the more he reeked of a strong, fishy odor.

"Teacher," the sailor said, referring to an Erovian's most common role on Ryca. "How may I serve you?"

"I'm looking for a man named Thyel."

"The prisoner below deck?" the sailor asked.

"Prisoner?" Unease stole over Jarrod. What had Tamara not told him?

• • • •

TAMARA TOOK A DEEP breath and shut her eyes as she leaned against the wall. She couldn't do it – ignore Skye's call for help after she'd let her brother down so badly. She opened the door and found her niece on the other side with her hand raised as if she'd meant to pound on the door again. "What is it?"

"Have you heard what's happened?" Skye asked.

"Yes. Mother and Saira are searching for your brother. He's sure to be found soon." She went to shut the door and Skye blocked the action.

"What are you doing in Saira's room?" At thirteen summers, Skye was young enough to go without a head veil, so her unbound hair fell forward as she leaned in to look into the room. "Aunt Tamara, do you really think we'll find my brother?"

"Don't give up." Tamara spotted the guard who had been following her loitering in the corridor, so she reluctantly stepped aside to allow her niece to enter. Then she shut the door with a defeated sigh.

If she couldn't get out of the castle, it might have been nice to at least head for the parapets. Even that wasn't allowed her now. She enjoyed being in the open and up high. Sometimes, when she felt really low, she liked to look down and picture herself jumping over.

It would put a quick end to her sorry life. What use was she anyway to her family? Just another encumbrance. Right at this moment, ending it all sounded like the best alternative to being married off to greedy Gideon.

"Why are you in Aunt Saira's room?" Skye asked again, interrupting Tamara's downward spiral.

"Why are you here?" she countered.

"I sent my Light ball to seek you out and it led me here."

Ah, explained how the guard found Tamara. Skye had brought him straight to her. She eyed her niece with displeasure and, walking over to Saira's bed, flopped down. With Jarrod gone, she'd lost her last best hope of getting out of this castle.

"Did Bevan seek you out yesterday?" Skye asked, following her.

Tamara cringed. How to answer? *Yes, he did, but I wouldn't listen, and now I can't remember what he said.*

"Um...did he speak to you about your dreams?" Skye asked, sounding cautious.

Tamara's roving gaze returned to the young girl with startled interest. She sat up. "Why would Bevan want to speak to me about my dreams?"

"He told me a beast's been bothering you at night."

Tamara's heart pounded in shock. "Bothering *me*?"

"Yes. Isn't that what we're talking about?"

Was she losing track of her conversations now, along with her memory? "Skye, what exactly did Bevan say to you?"

"He said, 'A beast's visiting Aunt Tamara at night through her dreams. It's in dire trouble and only able to reach her to call for help.' He said he'd tried to contact it, himself, but couldn't, so he was going to talk to you, even though you hate him."

"I don't hate him." Tamara's defensive response came out automatically, but Skye had reminded her of her recent vivid nightmares. A frightening creature, larger than anything she'd ever encountered had been haunting Tamara's dreams.

She couldn't see all of it, just felt the flap of leathery wings brush her side. Then she would hear a horrendous, mournful howl filled with abject helplessness and fear. A surprising match to her own feelings these days.

She usually woke up, eyes snapping open, to find herself already on her feet ready to defend the beast from whatever tormented it. Dripping in a cold sweat, her arms would be raised and her bare feet planted in a fighter's stance on her cold stone bedroom floor.

She shivered thinking about those nightly visitations. She pushed her hair behind her ears and realized the fingers trembled. She clenched her hands into fists and then hid her arms behind her back.

She hadn't spoken about her strange nightmares to anyone, afraid those tormented years trapped in the time spell were finally unraveling her mind. How could Bevan have found out about them?

She stood and, skirting Skye, she strolled around the room. "Did Bevan tell you what kind of beast this was?"

"A dragon," Skye said from behind her.

The answer settled within Tamara like a missing puzzle piece. Yes. That's what visited her each night. Why would a powerful dragon seek her for help?

If she weren't so confused, she'd laugh at the idea. *Her*, defend something that wild and ferocious? And with what? Against whom? She shook her head at her absurd dreams.

What truly intrigued Tamara was the question, could her strange dreams be connected to Bevan's disappearance?

Skye now slumped down on Saira's bed looking defeated. "Aunt Tamara, what are we going to do about Bevan?"

She turned to her niece with resignation. "I don't know. Have you told the queen any of this?"

Skye nodded.

Of course. The queen doted on Skye, so she would have listened to her. Tamara shelved her resentment. *Think!* Dragons. What did that remind her of? *The towers!* "Skye, there's an abandoned temple in Tibor. That might give us some answers."

"What temple?"

"You know, in the center of the city with its tall, crumbling twin towers overgrown by vegetation."

Skye sat up on her elbows. "The Quinlin Temple?"

"Yes, that one. It used to belong to a dragon sect. Father said that...never mind." Nothing he said mattered anymore. "Could Bevan have gone there to see if the temple was related in any way to my dreams? In fact, that could be where mother sent Saira."

"I'll ask." Skye jumped up and ran for the door.

"No." Tamara caught up to her and pulled her back. "Mother's probably busy and wouldn't want to be disturbed with triviality. We don't really know anything yet."

"Then I'm going to the temple to find out more," Skye said.

"How? Did you notice the guard outside? I doubt either of us will be allowed to go anywhere or do anything useful."

Skye took Tamara's hand. "Please, will you help me? I'm afraid for Bevan's life."

Tamara sighed. "There is a secret way out of the castle."

"Tell me where this passageway is and I'll go."

Great. Sending Skye off to a forsaken temple in the dead of night looking for her brother would probably get Tamara married to Gideon by morning's light. "You can't go to that temple alone."

"If you came with me, I wouldn't be alone," Skye suggested tentatively.

Tamara shook her head. Enter those cramped hidden corridors again? *Never.* She pulled out of Skye's hold. "No."

"Please." Tears flooded Skye's big blue eyes, and all her fears surfaced in the look she gave Tamara. "I don't care if you don't like Bevan or me. Please help me find him."

The comment annoyed Tamara as much as Skye's obvious emotional plea. "When have I ever said I didn't like you or Bevan? Never mind. My advice is to let Saira find your brother. This is the type of rescue she's famous for. Now, good night."

Tamara opened the door but Skye slammed it shut and stared at Tamara with a mutinous expression. "With or without your help, I'm going to find my brother. I don't care what danger it puts me in."

"I do," Tamara replied. "Just let this go."

"Tell me the way to leave the castle," Skye said. "I'll be fine on my own."

If Skye stopped to think about it, she'd realize the Light balls that she used to find things could probably lead her to the passageway without Tamara's help. Yet, how could she, in good conscience, allow Skye to go off into danger alone?

"All right, all right, I'll help," Tamara said. "But we'll have to find another way to leave the castle unobserved." Wasn't this where she started this night? Life was spinning in circles.

"All the doors are guarded. The secret passageway sounds like the best route."

"No."

"Why not?"

"It's confining in those corridors."

"Oh! I didn't know you were afraid of closed-in places. I could help," Skye gently suggested.

"How?" Tamara asked with suspicion.

"I could lead you through, if you tell me where to go."

Tamara shook her head. She wasn't going into that confined passageway ever again.

"You could shut your eyes," her niece said in earnest, "and pretend you're outside." She took Tamara's hand again. "Trust me and I will lead you safely through."

Tamara shook off the hold. "No!"

"Aunt Tamara, please."

"How can I guide you with my eyes shut?"

"I'll use my talent," Skye said. "Oh, I should have thought of that. I can cast a spell to find a way out."

And there it was. Too late to back out now.

Chapter 3

"YOU CAN'T GO ALONE to that temple," Tamara said to Skye, stalling for time. Then an intriguing thought popped into her head. Could she solve two problems at once? If Thyel helped to rescue Bevan, would her mother see the wisdom of Tamara choosing him?

"Skye, maybe we should take Thyel with us. It would be good to have a man accompany us, for protection."

"All right. Where is he?"

"Locked aboard a vessel by the docks."

Skye nodded, seemingly not surprised by that news. "I wondered where grandmother sent him after she found you in his bed." Gossip traveled faster than mice inside a castle. "Let's go free him."

Tamara's conscience nudged that she was about to get Skye into trouble. Her niece had realized her finding spell could lead her outside without Tamara's help, so what choice did she have? She couldn't let Skye go off by herself into danger. She'd already put Bevan in trouble's way by not listening. There was strength in numbers. That still left the problem of using the passageways.

She shuddered thinking about it. Yet, this plan could garner her a greater prize later, for a little discomfort now.

Skye put her arms around her and whispered, "I won't let you go, I promise,"

Tamara clenched her jaws. *I have to do this. For Bevan. For Skye, and for myself.*

"I want to change out of this gown first." She broke free of Skye's hold and hurried to Saira's cupboards. If they were going into that corridor again, eyes shut or not, she wanted clothing that wouldn't drag on the floor or impede her progress. She also wanted a solid weapon.

Tom's tunic, trousers, chainmaille and sword immediately caught her attention. Thyel would get a good laugh if she showed up in that attire.

．．．．

JARROD ARRIVED IN THE throne room for an audience with Queen Mamosia deeply troubled by Tamara's state of mind. After his visit to the vessel where she had sent him in search of Saira, he discovered not only was Saira not there, but the prisoner Thyel knew nothing of Saira's whereabouts.

During his discussion with the man, Jarrod gained an unsettling impression of Thyel and Tamara's developing relationship. Tamara used that man to wriggle out of marrying someone her mother deemed was best for her – merchant Gideon. She didn't love Thyel. She couldn't. He was a self-serving, underhanded, scoundrel.

"What brings you to Tibor, Jarrod?" Queen Mamosia asked.

He bowed in the Erovian way; deeply, with elegant arm gestures. "I come seeking Princess Saira's help, Your Majesty. There's trouble in Erov and we have urgent need of her wisdom and talent."

The queen invited him to be seated beside her on a marble bench. "Trouble abounds everywhere tonight, my friend. What's touched your wandering city?"

He indicated his tome. "The news is grave indeed. I begin to suspect that history itself is being affected, and, along with that, people from Erov have been disappearing."

"History? Is that possible?" Mamosia asked. "Once events have happened, how can they be reshaped? And is the absence of your historians related to Bevan's disappearance?"

"I'm unsure. I intend to find out. Do you know where Princess Saira has gone?"

"Yes. After some discussion, we decided to have her cast a seeking spell. She sent her spirit soaring in search of my grandson. The spell took her to a land called Melak."

"Melak? Surely, that's a child's tale? The place doesn't exist. We've no record of it in Falcon's Tome."

Mamosia gave him a tolerant smile. "Just because something isn't written in your book, Jarrod, doesn't mean it doesn't exist. Besides, I've heard that your history is based solely on Ryca. Legend suggests Melak is not a landmass on our world, but another world entirely. Now Saira has visited it, we know it exists, somewhere. If I weren't so worried, I'd be excited by this discovery."

Everything of importance was recorded in Falcon's Tome. If this other world truly existed, that would have been noted inside its pages. Some in Erov even believed the book came into existence before time itself. Falcon, the first Erovian, had this book in his grasp when he came into being.

"What is this world like?" he asked, for despite his lingering doubts on the validity of this discovery, news that Saira thought she had visited another world intrigued him.

"Saira says Melak is a green water world, thick in vegetation with oceans covering much of its surface. After she returned to her body, she and Tom left to seek Bevan in person."

"How does she hope to find this mythical world?"

"She believes Melak can be accessed from a magical boundary on the southern end of Ryca. No one ventures past that point for fear the world ends there, but Saira now believes it may be a gateway to other worlds."

"A dangerous supposition," Jarrod said with a frown. "What if she's wrong and that is where the world ends?"

With a shake of her head, the queen stood and paced away. She looked torn by his words. The idea of losing Saira again would be devastating.

He rose, unhappy to have upset her majesty with his brash question. The possibility had to be considered, however. Saira and Tom may be heading into harm's way.

Mamosia roamed the circular room, going in and around the eight matching red columns bordering the chamber. The numerous lit torches added a misty glow that trailed her shadow.

Jarrod opened his tome, searching for a reference to the southern reaches of Rycan. "History merely notes that area as unexplored and avoided by folk. Strange disappearances have occurred at sea near the Tavda plains, which is why sailors believe the world ends there."

"These are not normal times, Jarrod. My grandson's missing and if that is where he's been taken, Saira will not stop until she finds him." She leaned tiredly against one of the columns before sending him a slight smile. "My Saira has grown into a determined woman. I suspect she has been unable to forgive herself for not seeking me out in the past. She will not repeat that mistake with another member of her family."

"The Defender of Light is indeed remarkable," Jarrod agreed, his mind frantically trying to connect dots. Might his people be disappearing into this strange world, too? If so, he wanted to go to her. "She may need assistance on this dangerous quest. May I have your permission to join her?"

"Yes, please." Mamosia sighed in relief. "I know she has Tom, and soon Anna and Marton's company, too, but your presence would give me great reassurance."

Jarrod couldn't shake his fear that his world was shifting out of control. The odd effects on his magic were an indication of its worsening state. Before he left, he'd arranged for every elder in Erov to start researching what bits of history were being erased, while others contacted as many Erovians as possible spread across the breadth of Ryca. That he hadn't been able to locate his friend, Daniel, still worried him.

Given Saira was about to attempt stepping off the end of the world – was going off to find her his best move? Should he instead return to Erov to coordinate matters without Saira's magical help?

"Your Majesty, is there no possibility of finding Bevan other than through this gate to another world?"

Mamosia gave him a quizzical look. "Not unless Skye's stories of dragons are real."

Jarrod's heart thumped in surprise. "Dragons? But the dragon sect was eradicated during your brother-in-law's reign. Their temple lies in ruin." He flicked through his book as he spoke, excited by the possibility. He would have said that dragons were as mythical as Melak except there was a record of such beings in Falcon's Tome.

"From what my husband once told me, dragons are as unsociable as Erovians," the queen said. "They mingle with humans even less than your people. They're unpredictable. Keegan used to say dragons did not care for humans because we are much alike in our ambitions. Both want to rule the world."

Jarrod pointed to a notation. "It says here they can transport themselves as my people can," he said, excitement raising his tone. "Skipping from place to place at the blink of an eye. An Erovian's movement is confined within Ryca. What if a dragon's magic is not so bound? Allowing them to travel between worlds as easily as I could go from here to Nadym?"

"The possibility is immensely intriguing," the queen agreed, "but there are no more dragons on Ryca."

"It wouldn't hurt to check the temple," he said.

"I already did, as soon as Skye spoke to me," Mamosia said. "My guards questioned the keeper there. He said no one but himself has crossed the two thresholds of the towers in decades. There were certainly no signs of any dragons about. Their size alone would make them difficult to miss."

"You have a point." The note in Falcon's Tome agreed with the queen's supposition. No dragons sighted on Ryca in decades. He shut the book with a snap. With no other leads, following Saira seemed his best course. That would also give them a chance to discuss what was happening to his people.

He couldn't bring himself to leave, however, without addressing one last matter with the queen. Right or wrong—and his people would definitely label his interference with royal court affairs as wrong—he had to say something on Tamara's behalf.

His discussion with the prisoner Thyel had left Jarrod greatly disturbed. If the queen persisted in her ultimatum to marry her off to the merchant Gideon, he feared she might do something drastic. This Thyel character was apparently quite willing to go along with whatever the princess proposed.

After speaking with Thyel, Jarrod suspected the real reason she wanted to go to the vessel was to break Thyel free. Not to reunite Jarrod with Saira. What if she succeeded in her next attempt?

His people's role on Ryca was to be the land's historians, recorders of important events, not instigators of actions that could have repercussions on the natural evolution of history. Yet...

"Your Majesty, before I leave, may we speak about Princess Tamara..."

"Jarrod, did you know that she said Bevan's gone off like this before, but she never bothered to tell any of us?"

"I'm sure she had good reason. She's..."

"I don't know how to get through to her."

His throat closed up. Years of training constrained his voice, but he spat the words out anyway. "About this ultimatum you've placed on her."

The queen silenced him by slicing a hand in the air. "I don't wish to discuss that, Jarrod."

"But this Gideon–"

"Is a fine, honorable and trustworthy man. He cares deeply for Tamara, and for her future welfare. He tells me he's as worried as I am of what will become of her without a strong hand to control her."

Jarrod cringed at that, knowing it would be the worst possible way to deal with Tamara.

"He's right, Jarrod," she continued. "Tamara almost allowed that serpent Thyel to seduce her tonight!"

"I heard." The prisoner had gloated about it.

"As if I haven't enough to worry about."

"What do you really know of this Gideon? He's new to Ryca. Who are his parents? His family?" Again, he flicked through Falcon's Tome. "I don't even see any mention here by Daniel about Gideon's arrival to this city."

"Daniel?" The queen raised an eyebrow. "Who's Daniel?"

Jarrod went cold as if he had accidentally transported himself inside an iceberg. How could the queen not recognize the name of the Erovian historian who had spent the last several years in her company recording every royal decision she made?

It was the queen who had specifically requested his second in command when Jarrod was unavailable for the duty of court historian. Now she didn't even remember the man?

Heart hammering in real panic, he realized his decision was made. "I had best find Saira," Jarrod murmured, tucking his book to his side.

"She and Tom have set out to sea. Saira magically guides the vessel to navigate the rocky shoals near the harbor in the dark. They are to pick up Anna and Marton along the southern coast of the Tavda plains. We felt it would be faster to travel by sea."

Ah, that explained why he couldn't sense Saira's presence in Ryca. She was not connected in any way to Rycan soil, where his magic was centered.

"I shall join her in Tavda, then," Jarrod said. He checked his book. "Princess Anna and her husband have reached Nadym. The meeting place is about an hour's journey south from there. When the vessel stops to pick them up, I'll be there."

The queen nodded. "Thank you for helping, my dearest friend. You have been a true boon to Saira, and to me. I shall not forget your service."

If things continued to evolve as they were, she may forget him as easily as she had Daniel.

He bowed and stepped back in preparation to depart when the doors to the throne room burst opened.

A guard ran in. He knelt on one knee. "My queen, Princess Tamara and Skye cannot be found."

"Why not?" Mamosia asked in a panicked tone.

"I followed them to Princess Saira's quarters, but when it became quiet inside, I knocked. Hearing no answer, I entered and found the chamber empty."

"Do not worry," Jarrod interrupted, "I sense them. He clearly saw them coming out of a castle passageway and into the stables. "If you will permit me, Your Majesty, I will fetch them before leaving for the Tavda coast."

"Oh, thank you, Jarrod," Mamosia said with fervent relief. "That girl will be the death of me yet."

Jarrod had no doubt she meant Tamara and not Skye.

With a low bow he left, still troubled by the queen's forgetfulness. He arrived inside the royal stables in time to see the two young princesses ride away on a pair of horses.

With a sigh, he let them go, for he guessed exactly where Tamara was headed with her niece. He went straight to the vessel where Thyel was imprisoned.

Jarrod materialized inside the hold this time, avoiding the necessity of explaining his presence to the sailor guarding above deck.

Thyel gave a startled nod of greeting through the floor grate. "You're back."

Jarrod ignored the man and lit the lantern, placing it on the floor before leaning against a nearby barrel.

"Why?" Thyel asked, apparently not offended by silence. The man had the audacity to grin. "Tamara's coming for me, isn't she?"

Jarrod doubted Tamara truly loved this rouge. She might consider marrying him for her own reasons, but her heart was untouched, of that he was certain.

He restlessly circled the tiny chamber. He should be on his way, not waiting for a recalcitrant princess. This matter of Thyel and Tamara was none of his business. What if he inadvertently altered Tamara's destiny?

Ironic that, for Saira often chastised him for adhering strictly to his role of historian and not helping her enough. Now, here he was, wanting to help Tamara.

Running footsteps on the wooden stairs above alerted him to the arrival of the two accomplices. Skye and Tamara came to a crashing halt at finding Jarrod in the hold.

He gestured a welcome.

Skye wore a long blue gown, beautifully embroidered at the hems with silk thread. Tamara had thankfully changed out of her indecently loose gown, though he was unsure he preferred her new manly garb any better. Her trousers outlined a pair of long divine legs. Why did she carry a sword? What mischief was she up to?

Skye spoke first. "Jarrod, have you come to help us?"

"Don't be foolish." Distrust flashed in Tamara's sparkling blue eyes. "He's here to take us back to the queen as if we were misbehaving children."

"Your mother worried that you might have disappeared as Bevan had," Jarrod said.

Tamara's eyes lowered and her cheeks flushed with guilt.

"I offered to see you both safely home before departing."

Her blue gaze flashed back to his at that. "Where are you off to? Did my mother tell you about Saira's whereabouts?"

"Your sister is on her way to a world called Melak, to retrieve Prince Bevan," he said quietly. "I hope to speak to her about what's happening in Erov. Some of our people are disappearing, too. If the two events are connected, it would be prudent that I accompany her."

"You are rushing off on another adventure with Saira!" Tamara sounded accusatory.

"Melak!" Skye interrupted. "Is that where Saira thinks Bevan is? Jarrod, where is this place? I've never heard of it."

"It's a myth," Thyel answered before Jarrod could.

He spared the prisoner an annoyed glance before turning his attention to Skye. The young girl was truly apprehensive about her little brother's whereabouts and he wished he could offer her solace. The bit of information he'd gathered would have to suffice. "It appears there may be other worlds besides ours."

"Jarrod." Skye grabbed his sleeve. "Are you sure Bevan's in this other world?"

"Saira did a seeking spell and found him there."

"Oh," Skye sounded disappointed. "We thought he might have gone to the dragon temple." Then she brightened. "Could there be a portal from the temple to this Melak?"

"What type of portal?" Thyel asked.

The man's voice grated against Jarrod's already raw nerves. He wished they could take this conversation elsewhere but one glance at Tamara told him that hope was a waste of time.

"We have no idea if there is such a portal there, Thyel," Tamara said. "Bevan mentioned dragons to Skye yesterday. Now he's nowhere to be found. The Quinlin Temple seemed a good place to begin our search for Bevan."

Tamara then surprised Jarrod by turning Skye toward her. "Do you wish to join your mother and Saira? That seems the most certain way to reach Melak." She gave a rueful grin. "Saira is good at finding what she goes after and your mother could use your comfort. Jarrod can transport you with him. He can jump from place to place."

"It's not been tried with anyone but an Erovian," Jarrod warned.

"Can you take me to Melak?" Skye asked.

"Only within Ryca," both he and Tamara spoke together and then glanced at each other with surprise.

"I think we should check out the temple instead," Thyel put in. "It sounds as if Princess Saira is capable of finding Melak all on her own, Tamara. Wouldn't our time be better spent following up on any other clues you find?"

"Good point," she replied.

"The queen has already checked on the Quinlin Temple," Jarrod said. "The keeper insists no one came there this day."

"There are two towers," Tamara said. "If the keeper was in one, he might have missed something happening in the other."

"There are wards on both entrances," Jarrod said, reading from his book. "If anyone had entered, the keeper would have known it."

"But Prince Bevan is reputed to be powerful," Thyel said. "He could have devised a way to bypass the wards. This is talking around the issue. Why don't we follow both clues? Jarrod and Skye can join Princess Saira and Anna, while Tamara and I go to the dragon temple."

"You're not going anywhere with Tamara," Jarrod swiftly replied, completely repulsed by the thought.

"I'd be safe with Thyel, I'm sure of it," Tamara said.

"No."

"Jarrod." Skye tugged gently at his sleeve. "I know what I want to do. Aunt Saira doesn't need my help. Mother can do without worrying about me while she's on another quest. I want to go to the dragon temple."

"That's decided then," Tamara said. "Jarrod, you might as well settle to it and join Saira. Thyel can watch out for us."

"I promised the queen I would bring you both home."

"I'm not going back to the castle," Skye said. *There's nothing you can do to stop me.* The threat was clear.

The idea of Thyel going with them alone churned Jarrod's stomach like a meal gone bad. He did not trust this prisoner. Worse, his mind plied him with enticing reasons why he should accompany them. If Bevan had found a way to get to Melak through the dragon temple, they could, too. Could there really be dragons in Ryca? If so, he wanted to see one and record its presence in Falcon's Tome.

Above all, he wanted to be there for Tamara this time, if she got into trouble. Except, Tamara wouldn't leave here without Thyel. The stubborn tilt of her chin proclaimed that clearly enough. With a resigned sigh, Jarrod tucked Falcon's Tome under his arm, pulled the key off the wall, and bent to unlock Thyel from his cell.

Out of the corner of his eyes, he noted Tamara watching him with astonishment. "I think Jarrod's coming with us," she whispered in an awed voice to her niece.

Skye whooped with joy.

Jarrod pulled up the heavy metal grate, hoping he would not regret this choice.

Giving him a look of curiosity, Thyel climbed out and held his arms out for his manacles to be unlocked, too. That done, while Tamara commiserated with Thyel on his bruises and scrapes, Jarrod took out his quill and wrote a quick message in Falcon's Tome to his new second in command.

In the book Aaron carried, the pages would glow gently as an indication a message awaited his attention.

Send a Master Seer to meet Princess Saira. She travels to a world called Melak in search of Prince Bevan. Since the prince may possess knowledge about why our historians are vanishing, we must assist her to locate the prince.

Also assign a novitiate to list the names of all Erovians, their level of study, and where they are currently assigned – in the event even our memories begin to fade as the people of Ryca's appears to have done.

I go to assist Princesses Tamara and Skye to find the prince. We head this night to the Quinlin Temple.

"Come along, Jarrod." Skye ran up the stairs. Thyel followed close behind.

"Yes, recording of history can wait," Tamara said. "If you're worried you'll forget what events just transpired," she gave him a mischievous look, "Skye can remind you. Her memory doesn't seem affected." Giving him an over-the-shoulder teasing grin, she raced after her niece and Thyel.

Despite her cheeky tone, Jarrod was pleased to see Tamara's mood improve. Her anticipation enveloped him in a warm glow and surprisingly stirred his own, long-denied, thirst for adventure.

· · · ·

DESPITE HAVING POKED fun at Jarrod, Tamara was immensely relieved he had decided to join her, Skye and Thyel on their journey to the Quinlin Temple. They rode double on the horses, with Skye sitting in front of Jarrod, and Thyel securely holding Tamara. She shivered, remembering the horror of her second trip through the castle's corridors.

To her niece's credit, the girl had held onto Tamara's hand as tightly as Tamara gripped Skye. Their mutual hold had given her an odd sense of comfort. Something she'd not experienced since she was a child and her mother held her hand as they fled the castle.

Admittedly, she had not been so confident about her and Skye going to the temple alone with just Thyel for company. With Jarrod along, she felt lighter, as if a burden had rolled off her shoulders.

There was also the added benefit, that if anything dangerous happened, Jarrod could whisk them away to safety. That is, if he could transport four as easily as he could himself.

What pleased her most was that Jarrod had chosen to accompany her instead of Saira. That warmed her through to her toes and made her view him with a more appreciative gaze.

Jarrod was quite handsome, in a dark, studious, and absentminded way. Not the usual type of man who attracted her. Yet, when they'd been alone in Saira's bedroom, he'd aroused her more than any man she'd ever met.

She gave him a backward glance. She'd never considered Jarrod as a possible mate, deeming him unsuitable. He was the leader of a mysterious, magical race that disdained mingling with regular pale-skinned Rycans. She'd assumed his people only married other Erovians.

A pity, considering his deliciousness.

He was also her mother's trusted advisor and Saira's closest friend and devoted follower, which added a dark mark against him right there. She smiled thinking that might be hard to see against his smooth ebony skin.

Oddly, she often sensed the solid, strong, and purposeful Jarrod tended to avoid being anywhere near her.

Until now!

Chapter 4

CLOSE TO DAWN, TAMARA'S group arrived at the base of the Quinlin Temple. Ancient trees, giants with outstretched branches, had begun to crowd in the open square clearing. Immense steps led upward to the base of the towers. From there, as if aiming for the sky, the twin towers carried the line of sight high up into the clouds.

Once dismounted, Tamara gave into her worry that she had overly upset her mother by running away with Skye. She requested a blank page from Jarrod and using his magic quill, penned a note about their purpose for this visit and promised to return home soon.

She tucked the note under the saddle and slapped the horse's rump. With a startled neigh, it took off. She shouted after it, "Home."

The second horse bolted after the first, whipping its reins out of Thyel's hold. He shook his hand as if it stung. "Why'd you do that?"

"Sorry for the burn," she said. "We're within walking distance of home, so don't need the horses. Also, if my mother didn't hear from me, she would slay me."

Skye gave her hand an approving squeeze before racing up the steps.

Tamara estimated there were at least a hundred or so to climb and groaned. Since this place had fallen into disrepair, the stone stairs were covered with moss and overgrown vines. Great chunks of stone were broken and had crumbled in places forcing her to sidestep gaps and turned-up stones.

A third of the way up, Tamara stopped and rested her hands on her aching thighs. Taking deep breaths, she looked back toward the city. Tibor's torch-lit streets lined up toward the temple like long arrows of light. That explained why people often said all roads in Tibor lead to Quinlin.

Some eight hundred years ago, when the city was first built, dragons had served as the central focus of people's lives. They were the guardians of the city, the keepers of peace, and some even believed the giant creatures helped transport those who died to the Land of Eternal Light.

As a child, she'd always been curious about the past, pestering her father for stories. After he died, and they were on the run, her mother discouraged talk of the past. Afterwards, while she was trapped in the time spell, she'd overheard her uncle ordering all the castle's old records to be burned, especially anything to do with Ryca's magical heritage.

"Jarrod," she said, "when we have time, would you allow me to look up the history of Tibor in Falcon's Tome?"

"If possible, you may," he said but sounded grave, as if he doubted that time would ever come.

"Keep up, Tamara," Thyel called. He and Skye had gone up a dozen steps.

Her steps lagging, Tamara continued on, disappointed at Jarrod's lack of enthusiasm. He was protective of his tome but she wouldn't hurt it. Just read from it.

A few steps up, movement to the side had her swinging to her right. A lizardy thing was slithering up the trunk of a nearby tree. It stared back at her. It had wild green hair on its head and a long tail, but its body was covered in green-tinted scaly skin. What startled her most was its malevolent glare.

When it looked as if it would leap toward her, she called out in panic. "Jarrod, Thyel!"

Skirts held up, thirteen-year-old Skye was the first to run back down the giant steps until she reached Tamara's side. "What's the matter?"

Jarrod was there a moment later, his arms wrapping protectively around Tamara. He looked at where she indicated, but the green thing had disappeared into the darkness.

Tamara turned to insist she'd seen something. The instant their eyes met, she guessed he already believed her. Soothing emotions eased into her mind and a sense of immense safety calmed her nerves.

How does he do that?

"What was that thing?" she asked him, for she guessed he'd picked up the picture of the creature from her thoughts. Did he read everyone as easily as he did her?

He shook his head. "I don't know."

"You saw it, too?" Skye asked.

Tamara had to grin as his startled glance took in Skye. *Go ahead*, she urged him silently, *explain your way out of this.*

He released his hold of Tamara and stepped away. "I meant, I hadn't seen anything."

"Oh," Skye said.

Liar! Tamara scolded him silently, starting to enjoy this bizarre, silent communication between them.

Jarrod opened his book to write something, deliberately ignoring her.

Thyel joined them then, jumping down the last two steps with a thump. He squinted into the surrounding woods. "Don't know how you can see anything in this darkness."

Whatever that green thing had been, it was gone now. "Perhaps it was a lizard." She tapped Jarrod's book as she walked past him. "Be sure to note that down. Tamara saw a lizard."

She ignored his scowl as she proceeded up the steps. Thyel, chuckling, shadowed her.

At the top, they all stopped to catch their breath, slumping onto the cold stone floor. Tamara nursed a stitch at her side while taking in the wide landing that housed the pair of identical gray towers.

A flat open bridge connected the towers at the top. Two stone dragons, tails curling around the bridge and wings unfurled, peered at those wandering below.

From her seated position, Tamara looked up at the towers with wonder. Had the dragon riders of the past used that wide bridge to dismount before they entered the temple? She pictured herself up there, her dragon's feet spanning the bridge, claws grasping the edges. She'd pat the beast to indicate she was descending, and then slide down the scaly body until her booted feet thumped onto the landing.

"The queen said an old keeper guards the temple," Jarrod said, startling Tamara out of her daydream. "He must live in the left tower. The vines and brush are cleared away from that one the most."

Skye the youngest of them, had recovered first, and now raced up to the tower door and knocked. Receiving no answer, she tried the handle. "It's locked. What do we do now?"

"Is there a bell chain to announce arrivals?" Tamara asked, reluctantly getting to her aching legs.

The men joined Skye to search on either side of the door among thick vines.

"Found it," Thyel called out and pulled a cord.

A hollow gong sounded within but they heard no sign of anyone responding.

"If I climb to that narrow window using those plants for handholds," Thyel pointed to where sinewy vines grew along the walls, "I could get in and open the door."

Before he'd taken a step, though, an iron latch screamed in protest on the inside. The large wooden door scraped the stone floor as it creaked open.

A thin young lad about Skye's age, maybe a year older, poked his head around the opening. Sleepily squinting in the dark, he raised his lantern. "What do you want?"

"We're looking for Prince Bevan." Thyel stepped up to the doorway. "He's nine years old, with shoulder length blond hair. Have you seen him?"

"We already told the queen's guards, he didn't come here." He began to close the door.

Thyel stopped the motion by jamming his shoulder against the heavy door. "We'd like to look for ourselves."

"No outsiders are allowed inside the temple towers," the young lad said.

"It says that here," Jarrod said over Thyel's shoulder. He was busy flicking through the pages of his book. "I don't have anything about you being at the temple though. When did you come here? Where's the keeper?"

The young lad leaned past Thyel, and raising his lantern he stared at Jarrod. His mouth hung open at seeing one of the fabled Erovians at his temple doorstep. Then he snapped out of his shock and repeated, "No one's allowed in the temple, Teacher. I'm sorry." He put his weight into closing the door.

Thyel took exception and shoved the door open wider.

The doorkeeper tumbled onto the dusty flagstone floor. His lantern clattered as it crashed and the light died. He scrambled to get back on his feet in the dark entryway. "You'll be in trouble if you come in!"

"Will you set your dragons on us?" Thyel asked with a mocking grin as he strolled inside.

"What's your name?" Jarrod asked, quill in hand.

"Fane, sir."

Skye stepped forward. She held out her right hand, palm up, and opened her fingers. A ball of Light appeared. It rose and expanded until the room shone as if lit by a hundred candles.

Fane gasped and staggered backwards, his wide-eyed gaze swinging between Skye and her Light ball.

Tamara entered last and also stared in silent awe at her niece's magic before turning her attention to the young lad. "What do you do here, Fane?"

"You're...one of the magical princesses!" Fane said, his gaze still glued to Skye.

Tamara refrained from saying she was a princess, too, if not magical. Wearing Tom's tunic and trousers probably detracted from her feminine allure. Her glance flew to Jarrod, wondering if he no longer found her as attractive in this garb as he had in her half-untied gown.

While Skye made introductions, Tamara strolled around the entryway under the glow of her niece's Light ball. The place was in terrible condition. Someone had attempted to clean up the debris, but the room lacked furniture, carpets, or chandeliers and the hearth wasn't lit. Despite Skye's Light, the whole place felt dark and dreary.

From the size of the tower outside, she'd expected it to be bigger. Then she noticed the two staircases curving up in concentric circles, rising ever upwards. They gave way on occasion to doors positioned along the walls.

No tapestries or pictures adorned the walls, which looked as if a battering ram had been taken to them. Great big holes let in a cool breeze.

The two staircases caved-in part way up, with most of the railings torn off. The whole structure had a forsaken feel. Not something she'd want to climb.

This entryway was like the bottom of a well, with a domed ceiling. Panels of glass topped it. Through the dirty panes, the day looked about to break.

Her steps took her by Jarrod, who was busy with his book. The page he worked on was easy to see, even though he stood in a shadowy corner. He was busy outlining the inside of the tower. He was a good sketcher.

"You missed a doorway," she pointed out, in hopes of annoying him.

He refused to respond.

Fane was speaking to Skye, his expression earnest. "I'm sorry but your brother did not come here. The master checked the wards. If anyone had crossed our threshold, he would have known."

"Shall we get on with searching then?" she asked.

"No!" Fane gave her an exasperated look that said, *Haven't you heard a word I've said?* "The wards were disabled after the palace guards came here earlier, or the keeper would have known that you've intruded and come to throw you out. Might be too late already." He glanced nervously up the stairs before turning back to them. "You should all leave."

"But Bevan said he had a vision of a dragon visiting Tamara in her dreams," Skye said. "He could have come here to learn more."

"I may have spoken to him about hearing the sound of drums," Tamara added.

Fane stared at her with a stunned gaze. He was deathly pale and swayed as if he might faint. He'd finally noticed her, but not with admiration.

"That's impossible," he finally sputtered. "You couldn't have heard drums, for there are no more dragons or summoning ceremonies that require it."

Summoning ceremonies? Drums summoned dragons?

"Looks like this was not where Prince Bevan came after all," Thyel said. "We might as well leave."

"No." Skye's mouth was set in a stubborn line. "I need to know for certain if Bevan came here or not." Looking at her ball of Light, she chanted, "If my brother's in trouble, in this temple of rubble, show me the way, don't keep me at bay!"

The Light reduced in size and lowered to circle her head. For a moment, it flickered, as if about to go out. Skye cupped her hand around the ball until it strengthened.

The searcher Light then swept toward Fane. He ducked and swatted at it.

The Light ball easily evaded his touch and sped toward one of the curved stairways.

Skye ran after it, shouting in triumph for the rest to follow. "It's found a trace of Bevan!"

Thyel raced up after her.

"Come back," Fane called. "You're not allowed to go up there." Giving Tamara and Jarrod a frustrated glance, he sprinted after the other two.

Jarrod shut his book and, gestured for Tamara to go first. Then he followed.

When they reached a landing, a closed door carved with obscure symbols led off to one side.

Tamara didn't particularly like the confined feeling she picked up the higher they went. She repeatedly glanced down the long barrel of the tower to see the open entryway door below and whispered, *We're not trapped.*

She was also getting royally fed up with all this climbing. First to reach the towers, and now this curving stairway leading ever upwards. A third of the way up, a stitch pulled in her right calf, making her steps falter.

Skye raced ahead, following after her Light.

Tamara stopped. If she took another step, she would collapse.

"We need to go in here," Skye called down. Her Light had finally stopped by a door. As Tamara came up, the ball expanded to encompass the wood in a white glow and then disappeared inside, leaving them in semi-darkness. Skye produced another Light ball to see by as she tried the door.

Locked. She turned to Fane and held out her hand. "Key. Hand it over."

He shook his head. "I don't have it. Only the keeper has keys to any of these rooms." He, too, was panting. "I've never come this high before."

"Then find the keeper," Skye said.

"Is he in the other tower?" Jarrod asked, leaning against the wall beside Tamara to catch his breath.

"His room's off the second landing below us. He's old and hard of hearing, as well as blind. I'm being trained to take over, but it's not yet my time."

"Jarrod," Skye said, suddenly, "can you transport yourself to the other side and let us in?"

"Of course, he can." Tamara straightened away from the wall, thinking resentfully that he could have transported them all up here and saved them a climb.

Jarrod glanced at Tamara with disapproval for revealing that secret.

"Oh, please," Skye said. "Bevan might be in there. Why else would my Light have marked the door?"

"My magic is not as reliable as it once was," he murmured looking at the door with a frown. "Something's been affecting it."

"It worked sweetly before when you left me in Saira's room," Tamara said. "Surely you'll try?" She extended her arms. "I'll hold your book."

"Unnecessary." He disappeared in a whirl of wind that slammed her against the railing. It buckled under her weight.

Thyel caught her and pulled her into his arms. "Careful."

"Thank you," she whispered, thinking she'd made a good choice in picking this man.

"I hope nothing went wrong," Skye muttered, looking at Tamara with concern.

The idea that Jarrod might be hurt had Tamara pulling away from Thyel and hurrying to the door. "Jarrod? Are you in there?"

A lock clicked on the other side. Jarrod opened the door and invited her in with an elaborate bow. When he rose, his eyes were alight with triumph, but also a shade of worry.

A great wash of relief flowed over Tamara at seeing him safe. She impulsively hugged him tight, startling them all. With a laugh Skye joined in the embrace, turning the awkward moment amusing.

"May we all enter?" Thyel asked, a definite peevish note in his tone.

They all hurried into the unkempt room. It must have been a study. Empty open shelves lined one wall with tall windows bordering it. In the middle of the room, writing tables, chairs and stools had been toppled, books scattered on the floor. Pages had been ripped out. Shredded and torn maps, charts, and paintings hung haphazardly on the walls.

Dust motes floated in the air. Tamara drew a finger along a table top, disturbing layers of dirt. Bevan had obviously never been in here; else his footprints would have been as distinguishable as theirs. Skye's Light was nowhere in sight either. Had it died after entering?

"This room has the Horsemen's stamp imprinted all over it," Tamara said with disgust. Wrinkling her nose at the stale, moldy scent, she moved to a window where rays of morning light struggled to enter through dust-streaked panes.

Opening it, she breathed deeply of the fresh air and enjoyed the feel of complete openness.

"Now what?" Thyel asked.

"I told you," Fane still stood by the doorway, shifting from foot to foot. "No one's allowed here except for the keeper. The prince did not come here."

Skye looked like she was about to cry.

Sympathetic sorrow tightened Tamara's chest.

Jarrod seemed the most excited. He shifted around the room, picking up books and scattered papers. He straightened a table and rested his tome on it. Then he pointed to a painting on the wall. "What's that in the corner?"

Everyone except for Fane crowded over to see what he'd spotted. Hanging half tilted was a slashed painting of the Rycan landscape. A small hand-drawn map peeked out of a cut corner. It looked to be a sketch of Ryca.

Jarrod carefully eased out the drawing and laid it on a table for all of them to study. Overlying the western shores of Ryca, the word 'Melak' was printed in bold script. Above that, Skye's Light ball was hovering.

No wonder none of them had seen the Light earlier. Not only had it been hidden by the painting, but it had also shrunk itself into a tiny spark, barely visible.

Tamara glanced at Skye with a smile. "Why did we ever doubt Saira? She's always right. Your worries about Bevan are needless, Skye. If anyone can bring him home in one piece, even from a mythical world, it's my sister."

"Jarrod." Skye turned to him. "Can you take me with you to meet my mother after all? I've changed my mind and want to travel with her and Saira to Melak."

He closed his eyes a moment and when he opened them, his dark brown eyes were shaded by sadness.

"I'm sorry, but I can no longer sense either your parents or Saira and Tom on Rycan soil. I would guess they have been picked up and are well on their way by sea. Saira may have used a spell to speed her vessel's passage."

The longer Tamara stared at Melak, the more her head ached. She focused instead at the other end of the chart. "What are these other places?" She pointed to two circular land masses. "Isa and Ashari. I've never heard of them."

From the doorway, Fane leaned in so far, he was in danger of falling over. Reluctantly, he came forward. Once he had an opportunity to study the map, he nodded sagely. "Those are worlds the dragon riders have traveled to."

He pointed to the one called Isa. "That's the dragon realm. I've dreamed of returning there for years."

"Returning?" Tamara said. "You've been there?"

"I was born there, Princess," Fane said, surprising them all. "I'm an apprentice of the last dragon rider. He brought me here five years ago. My village raised eleven children who were picked as potential dragon riders. My family had high hopes I would be the third in our family to ride one. That's why a dragon rider chose me to train."

Skye looked at him with narrow-eyed speculation. "So, it's true that dragons can travel between realms?"

"Yes."

"If you acquired a dragon, would you take us to Melak?"

"Skye," Tamara said gently, "that's a bit of a stretch. How are we going to get to Isa for Fane to acquire a dragon? Even if we could travel between realms, wouldn't it be better to bypass Isa and head directly to Melak where Bevan is?"

"We cannot go to Melak," Fane said. "There's no corresponding gateway there. Only on Isa. It matters not, the gateway stones on Ryca are lost to us."

"What are gateway stones?" Thyel asked.

"They allow for travel between realms." Jarrod said, reading from his tome.

"Yes," Fane said, "but when King Ywen, the usurper, banned all practice of magic, his sorcerer, Tamarisk, ordered the tower's Quinlin stones to be destroyed. Without one of those stones, we cannot access the dragon realm, or any other world."

"Uncle Ywen had much to answer for," Tamara agreed in a grim tone.

"Yes." Jarrod pointed to a page in his tome. "It's written here that all of the dragon riders, clan members, and apprentices in the temple were put to death."

Fane nodded. "Except for me because I hadn't been brought to Ryca yet."

"Bevan's clever," Skye said, with a stubborn turn to her mouth. "He could have found another way to the dragon realm and from there to Melak."

"It wouldn't matter," Fane said. "I tell you, without a Quinlin stone, or a dragon, no one can travel between realms."

"You said a dragon rider brought you here. What happened to him and his dragon?" Jarrod asked, quill quivering with excitement.

Tamara rolled her eyes.

"When the royal creed was executed," Fane said, seemingly as happy to relate past events, as Jarrod was to record it, "two dragon riders were scheduled to return here. The first, left his dragon on Isa and came through the gate. Tamarisk's men killed him on entry. The other, who returned on his dragon, saw what was happening and escaped back to Isa."

Fane's face was bathed in enthusiasm as he retold these exciting events. Tamara suspected that since he lived here alone with an old blind keeper, a chance to interact with people and talk about his passion, even if it involved a retelling of gruesome events, must be a rare joy.

"That last dragon rider returned now and again to Ryca to check for news. He was aging and waited for the chance to return home for good. After King Ywen and Tamarisk were killed five years ago, the rider searched for a new apprentice to bring with him, and picked me. Together, we arrived at the tower in secret, for the rider no longer trusted those in Ryca."

"Wise," Tamara said, thinking she didn't truly trust anyone on Ryca either.

"He's now the blind keeper, isn't he?" Skye said. "And you're his apprentice."

"Yes, Princess. He wanted to continue the tradition of protecting this temple."

"Where is his dragon?" Thyel asked, skepticism in his tone. "Why has no one on Ryca seen it?"

"The dragon had been ailing, sir, and it died shortly after our return to Ryca. My master would have perished, too, for the bond between dragon and rider is compelling, but he lived on. The day his dragon died, he lost his sight, and is often in much pain. He lives to train me to follow in his footsteps. He says legend speaks of a new age to come when a queen dragon will return to Ryca with a rider matched to her for life. Together, they will resurrect the Cult of Dragons."

"You hope to be that other rider, don't you?" Thyel gave a laugh. "You think yourself strong enough to control a dragon, lad?"

Fane frowned. "Riders don't control their dragons. When a rider and dragon bond, their purpose becomes one."

"Then I would not care to ride one," Tamara said with a laugh. "I would never surrender my needs to another."

"Well spoken, my love," Thyel said, casually draping an arm around her shoulders. "I, too, would balk at such an arrangement." His gaze stayed glued to Fane. "If I rode a dragon, it would be completely under my control."

His words sent a shiver down Tamara's back. Not only did the notion of controlling something else not appeal, but the idea Thyel saw the world that way bothered her.

This was the man she had almost chosen as her future mate, someone she took as malleable and who would bow to her wishes. Now he sounded harsh and domineering.

She stepped back toward the window pretending to look out, but in truth it was to remove his hand from around her shoulder.

Who was this Thyel?

Chapter 5

WITH TIME SLIPPING away between Tamara's fingers, the possibility of her mother commanding her to marry Gideon loomed.

Jarrod's hand touched her shoulder gently, and she glanced at him in surprise. The open sympathy in his eyes brought tears to hers and she looked away, stepping out of his reach, too. She didn't want him focusing his talent on her, feeling sorry for her.

"If there was a chance to acquire one of those mythical beasts," Thyel was saying, "I would certainly accompany you, Princess Skye, but Tamara's correct, this is a foolish dream. We've done all we can here. We might as well leave."

Skye turned desperate eyes to Jarrod. "Can you not transport us to Isa?"

"Isa is outside Ryca, so no."

"Can you go anywhere within Ryca, sir?" Fane asked.

Jarrod gave the young lad a curious look. "If I have something to focus on. What did you have in mind?"

Fane's eyes shone bright with renewed enthusiasm. "We might be able to acquire another Quinlin stone with which to travel to Isa."

"From where?" Thyel asked. "You said they'd been destroyed."

"The one from the second tower wasn't lost," Fane said. "When the edict came about no magic, the keepers feared for the portal stones' safety. They were in the process of dismantling the large stones when King Ywen's men arrived. They only had time to save one."

"They hid it," Jarrod said.

Tamara spotted him reading from his book again. What an amazing tome. "It says that there?"

He nodded. "Of course. All history of Ryca is recorded in Falcon's Tome. I only need to think of what I wish to search for and then I can find the information."

"Where was this second stone taken?" Skye asked.

"And why have you not brought it back?" Thyel added.

"We don't know where it's hidden," the young man admitted. "The one entrusted to ensure the stone's safety was slain by King Ywen's men."

"And the stone was taken?" Thyel asked.

"We don't know," Fane admitted. "It could have been destroyed or it might still be safe in its hiding place."

Tamara had an answer to that. "Its location is probably recorded in Jarrod's book." She leaned to read over his shoulder. "Isn't it?"

"I thought you didn't care for the tome?" he said.

"That was when I thought it was useless." At his frown, she pasted an apologetic smile on her face. "Now Jarrod, you're not going to let our little disagreement about the book keep you from telling us where the stone is, are you?"

"Of course, he isn't." Skye approached Erov's Chief Councilor with a determined stride.

He closed the book, and took Skye's hand. In a flutter of his long white robe and her blond hair, they both vanished, leaving the room in a swirling chaos of papers.

"Jarrod!" Tamara called out. How could he have taken Skye, when Tamara had been standing right beside him? She would have cheerfully hit him if he re-appeared.

"Ahhhh!" she screamed to relieve her frustration and shook her arms in fury at the empty spot where Jarrod had stood.

Fane took a cautious step away. "Where did they go?"

"To fetch us the stone, of course," Tamara said in a bitter tone. "Where else?"

"I doubt it," Thyel said. "With such a powerful jewel in his possession, we may never see him again."

"He'll be back." Tamara gave Thyel a dark look. "He would never betray us."

Thyel looked skeptical but then turned to Fane. "Where is this keeper of yours? Why has he not found us yet?"

"He's an old man," Fane replied. "He spends most of his time sleeping. I usually shake him awake to give me my lessons."

Tamara, who still felt distinctly disgruntled by Jarrod's desertion, barely listened. All of a sudden, she was exhausted and hungry.

Sunlight poured in through the high narrow windows. She pointed to them and said, "It's morning and I haven't eaten in too long. Any chance of getting food, Fane?"

"I can fetch some." Fane bit worriedly at his thumbnail. "Maybe my master won't blame me for letting you stay after I tell him you're helping us recover the Quinlin stone."

"Good thinking." Thyel turned Fane about and gave him a shove toward the doorway. "Go get us food."

He then turned to Tamara with a thoughtful expression. "It might be useful to see this portal room. To make sure we'll be able to use the stone, if your Lord Jarrod ever returns with it. If you're tired, Fane and I can go."

She didn't want to be here by herself so she shook her head. "I'll come. Sleep can wait."

Luckily, she didn't have to wait long. In short order, Fane returned with an armful of bread and cheese, and a cask of water to wash it down. Thyel instantly set to convincing him to show them the portal room.

"Absolutely not." Fane backed away still clutching the provisions. "I'm in enough trouble for letting you in here."

"What harm is there in checking to see if the Quinlin stone, if recovered, could effectively transport us to Isa?" Thyel tossed the loaf of bread to Tamara. He then extracted the block of cheese wrapped in cloth but kept a hold of it. It smelled as tempting as the bread in her hands. Her stomach grumbled in anticipation of breakfast.

"We could eat our meal there while we wait for Jarrod," Tamara suggested to Fane with a pleading smile. "What difference does it really make, Fane, if we wait here or there? And there, brings us closer to dragons."

At the mention of dragons, the lad's eyes lit up.

Tamara couldn't imagine the slight hesitant young boy ever riding a ferocious beast like the ones depicted in stone on the tower bridge or like the one swooping toward her in her dreams, but that's what he apparently craved.

Thyel gave her a nod of approval from behind the boy.

"All right," Fane finally said. "I suppose waiting there is no different. We have to go down first, then up using outside stairs. King Ywen's Horsemen destroyed the inner stairway that reaches to the top of the tower."

With the water cask in his grip, Fane led the way. Thyel waved for Tamara to go ahead of him. She tucked the bread under her arm to avoid the temptation to take a bite. Her stomach grumbled at having to wait to eat.

"Hurry," Fane whispered from down the first flight of stairs, "but be quiet as we pass by the keeper's quarters."

Two stories down, they crossed a landing that had a plain wooden door, scarred and cracked with age. Fane looked back at them and held up a finger to his lips.

Tamara crept past that entry. Every scrape of boots on stone, her every breath that hushed out, seemed to echo loudly inside the long central tower. One step down past the landing and Thyel cursed softly behind her. The cheese was slipping out of the cloth wrapping.

Tamara, who was right in front of him, deftly caught the smelly cheese. It squished within her nervous grip. The aged scent drenched in brandy invaded and overwhelmed her senses, making her salivate.

Unable to resist, she tore off a little piece and ate it, relishing the strong creamy flavor.

Thyel shook his head, giving a tolerant smile before he grabbed the bread from under her arm and kept going past. Fane flapped his arms, urging them to hurry.

Before Tamara could heed his instructions, the wooden door on the landing creaked open.

"Who goes there?" a shaky male voice called out.

She froze and slowly looked over her shoulder.

A bent old man looked out the open doorway, his nose raised and sniffing. His hair was white and waist length, looking stringy and knotted in places. His beard, too, was long, hanging down to the middle of his chest. What caught and held her attention were his eyes that matched his white hair.

He shuffled out, bringing with him the stale odor of unwashed body and clothes that threatened to make the cheese she had eaten come back up.

Her heart thumped so loud the blind keeper might hear it even if he couldn't see her.

The old man's fingers reached out blindly straying close to Tamara. Another inch and his fingers would graze her hair. She leaned back as far as she could.

Fane ran up the steps, his sandals clacking loudly on the stone steps. "Master. It's only I."

"Fane?" the keeper sounded surprised, his hands thankfully retreating from near Tamara. "Why do you scurry about? Is it time for your lesson?"

"No, Master." Fane passed the cask of water to Tamara who grabbed it with her free hand. He took the old man's hand and turned him back to the open doorway. "I merely meant to check on the portal room, to make sure it has not been disturbed."

"Foolish boy," the old man said, blindly patting Fane on his head and disarranging Fane's carefully groomed brown thatch of hair. "Of course, it's not disturbed. No one's been there since Ywen's men destroyed the Quinlin stone. Come inside and we'll begin your lesson."

"But, Master..."

"Come along, Fane. Don't tarry," the old man said. "Odd, I thought I smelled cheese."

Fane gave them a shrug over his shoulder and followed the keeper in and shut the door.

Thyel and Tamara sat on the stairs and waited. After several minutes passed and Fane did not return, Thyel suggested they carry on to the outside stairs. The boy could find them when his lesson was over.

Tamara agreed. Her legs had stopped shivering in fear. They made their way to the outside stairs and headed up. At the top of the flight of stairs, the portal door was locked.

"Now what?" she asked.

"Now we could use your Lord Jarrod's help," Thyel said with a frustrated sigh.

. . . .

JARROD ARRIVED AT THE foot of a mountain with Skye beside him.

"How..." she began. "What happened?"

"We're at Mount Jama in the Makakala Range." He glanced at the barren rocks and sandy soil with intense interest. His travel spell had brought them half way across Ryca without a single mishap, which suggested the interference with magic was localized near Tibor.

Skye still gaped at their abrupt shift from the tower room in the Quinlin Temple to this wide-open expanse.

"Oh!" the thirteen-year-old exclaimed in awe and turned in a circle, taking in the land that stretched up behind them for quite a height. On the opposite side, below, a river wound through a valley. Broadleaf trees sheltered a riverbank covered in brush, grass, and wildflowers.

"Why are we here?" she finally asked.

"It was recorded in the tome that the keeper with the last Quinlin stone was killed here."

"Does your book say where the stone is hidden?"

"There's no mention of the stone's whereabouts." Just then the sun peaked over the mountain range and its golden glow spread downward. Warmth flooded over the darkened landscape, blinding his sight. He shielded his eyes as he glanced up. "If that keeper had hidden the stone before he was caught, it should be nearby. I hoped one of your finding spells might locate it."

"That's why you brought me along!" Skye exclaimed. "I wondered." She held up her hand and a Light ball formed. *"Find me the Quinlin stone, to place upon its rightful throne."*

The spell ball rose and was immediately lost in the blinding glare of the sun.

"Where did it go?" Jarrod asked.

"I don't need to see it to sense its path." Skye started up the mountainside.

Jarrod tucked his book into the satchel strapped onto his back and followed her. Finding a safe route past boulders, sage bushes, and sharp drops sometimes required a bit of backtracking. There were many openings and cavities that Skye ignored, determinedly forging upwards.

Jarrod had to smile at the young girl's wild state of excitement. No mere mountain was going to halt her from rescuing her brother. Still, perspiration dotted her forehead. She was tiring, too, even if she would never admit it.

He called a halt saying he was thirsty. He had water and a bit of flatbread to offer to keep up their strength.

"Okay, but we're really close." She took a deep swallow from his cask before returning it. "Jarrod, that's ice cold! If you don't take it back this instant, I'll finish it."

He chuckled. "Drink as much as you want. It replenishes itself."

"It does?" Skye took another swallow and then swished the remaining water around until she felt the weight increase. "It's full again!" She took a deeper drink before returning the cask.

"Being constant travelers," he explained after taking his own fill of the icy water and strapping the rapidly filling container back to his belt, "my people carry casks that can magically refill when the level of the water falls below half full. Also bread." He passed her a piece.

"Useful magic! And tasty."

Once they were rested and full, he indicated the path back up the mountain but she shook her head. "I said we were close. Over here." She bent to enter a shadowy portion at the back of an overhang.

Jarrod caught up to her and pulled her back. "Let me go first."

A small round opening near the ground in a dark recess invited him in. He crawled inside on hands and knees until the opening grew large enough to allow him to stand.

Skye followed him into the larger opening, and checked around the cave.

"Let's stop here for a minute," he said. "I know you're anxious but we've been travelling for over an hour. We need to gain our strength back for whatever we face in here. It will also give us time for our eyes to adjust to the darkness." He slumped to the ground beside the opening before she could argue.

Skye sighed, but mimicked his action without protest. She pointed to the far side of the cave. "My search spell went through there. There's another opening."

"We need light," Jarrod said.

She nodded but looked worried.

"What's wrong?" he asked.

"My magic has been erratic lately. When Tamara and I were in the castle passageway, for a while I couldn't connect to the magic of Ryca. I didn't tell her, because I didn't want to worry her, but Light wouldn't come to me when I reached for it. Thankfully the magic flared after a bit and we could keep going. Then again in the Quinlin Temple, my Light spell was hesitant. The seeker spell I sent here after the Quinlin stone feels stronger."

Her words confirmed Jarrod's own worry that magic was indeed being blocked in some way closer to Tibor.

"Give your magic another try," he said.

She held out her hand and a ball of Light formed in a blink, glowing gently, painting the cave in golden shades. She gave a delighted laugh and tipped it into the air. "That was easier. It is stronger here than even in the Quinlin Temple."

"I've been having similar problems," he admitted.

"Oh, that's right," Skye said, sobering. "You said so before but I didn't connect your problem with mine, since they're such different forms of magic. What does this mean, Jarrod?"

"I don't know. We could definitely use your brother's magical help right now, which makes me suspicious that he, of all people, is the one that's missing. Now Saira, the second strongest sorcerer in Ryca, has gone on a chase to locate him."

Into the silence that followed that troubling statement, Skye asked quietly, "Do you think we will ever find Bevan? Does your book say anything about the future?"

"Falcon's Tome only records Ryca's history. It does not foretell the future." He gave her a wry, sideways glance. "Are you going to call it useless, as Tamara seems to see it?"

She chuckled. "Not at all, Chief Councilor. Unlike my aunt, I value history. Without the aid of Falcon's Tome, and the true history it had recorded and kept safe for decades, we would never have learned of all that Uncle Ywen had done or even found a way to stop him."

"I suspect Tamara wishes her history had never happened," he said, thinking of the time spell. He stood, shaking off his brooding thoughts. "Shall we continue?"

Skye nodded and rose, too. The passageway was narrow but tall enough that they could walk upright. Skye's Light ball led the way. Jarrod took the lead, in case they came across anything dangerous.

"Do you find Aunt Tamara's wish to forget her past hard to accept, Jarrod?" Skye asked from behind him.

"The past is part of us. It defines who we are. Trying to forget what happened is like trying to make a piece of us disappear."

"I know how highly Erovians value the past," Skye said, in a thoughtful tone. "You said earlier that Bevan's disappearance and your magic being affected might be connected."

"As are the recent disappearances of Erovian historians." He explained about being unable to communicate with several of his people. "I'm hoping your brother might be able to find them."

"He just might. Magic is an instinct with my brother. Like Saira, he can do anything."

"Yes. Finding him will also free up your Aunt Saira, who might be of help to me. Light runs deep in your family."

"For all except Great Uncle Ywen and Aunt Tamara."

They came to a fork in the passageway and Jarrod paused. Skye pointed to the left without hesitation.

Nodding, he headed that way.

"We know how the inability to tap into Light warped Great Uncle Ywen's character," Skye continued. "I worry sometimes that Aunt Tamara's lack of magical ability may be warping her thinking, too."

Shocked she would say such a thing, Jarrod stopped to look at Skye. "Tamara is nothing like Ywen!"

She backed up a step, as if startled by his vehemence.

Heat raced up to the tips of Jarrod's ears, as much from embarrassment at having shown his emotions so clearly as with a simmering frustration that Skye could be so mistaken about her aunt's character. "Your Uncle Ywen never understood how Light worked and hated anyone who could wield it."

"Is that not the case with Aunt Tamara, too?" Skye challenged, an eyebrow rising with skepticism.

"Not at all." He paused and took a deep breath, realizing he was on the verge of ranting. Even after all these years, the memory of what Ywen had perpetrated still haunted him. Forbidden to interfere, his people could only record what was happening. It was Jarrod's rebellious father who had taken the first step to returning Ryca's rightful heir to the throne, and that interference had cost him his life.

Skye watched him with a worried look. She seemed convinced her aunt would eventually go the same route as mad, twisted Ywen.

"Skye," he said in a calm tone, "Tamara may wish she had a talent for wielding Light. She may even resent you for possessing it. She also admires your abilities and would never wish any of you ill for having it. Her hurt runs deeper than merely yearning for a magical talent."

"You sound as if you have insight into her heart, Jarrod." Skye looked at him intently. "If she doesn't hate our ability to use Light, why is she always angry and distrustful of us?"

It was time her family understood at least a part of what upset her, for it was obvious, five years on, that Tamara would never speak of her years of torment aloud.

"She feels deeply the loss of her father," he murmured. "She has been mourning his loss for decades." A large part of him was shocked he said that aloud. He thought he was nothing like his father. Yet, he, too, was trying to alter people's lives instead of simply watching and recording events.

"Decades?" Skye said in shock. "But Aunt Tamara was suspended in time for most of those years."

He'd said too much. Jarrod could not bring himself to spill any more of Tamara's secrets. He carried on moving forward and Skye followed in thoughtful silence. The passage they traveled through narrowed and soon they had to drop to hands and knees again in order to keep moving forward.

Jarrod was glad to have an end to this topic. Whenever he thought of Tamara, he invariably felt restless. She was perplexing, intriguing and, all too often, entirely alluring. Like when she changed out of her gown and into those revealing trousers. Every time he glanced at her, he could clearly picture her limbs beneath. Worse, she had the uncanny ability to make him forget his duty to Erov, as he had when he agreed to accompany her to the Quinlin Temple.

Yet, he hated her treating Falcon's Tome as a joke. Why couldn't she see the book was a symbol of his people, their work? More importantly, of his life and future.

Chapter 6

UNABLE TO SIT SIDE by side on the narrow outside stairs, Tamara and Thyel sat three steps apart with the food spread out between them. Occasionally, Thyel would try to pick the lock but each attempt resulted in him more frustrated than before. They had finished most of the bread and cheese and all of the water by the time Fane raced up to greet them.

"Sorry," he panted and came to a breathless halt. "My master would not let me go. I'm glad I had one more lesson though. If we actually make it to Isa, I shall be ready to summon a dragon."

Thyel looked at him with interest. "What exactly did you learn?"

"It's not easy to summon a dragon, sir," Fane said. "They are contrary creatures who by nature are solitary and prefer to be in control rather than join with another to make shared decisions. It makes bonding with one truly difficult and dangerous if not done correctly."

"I see," Thyel said and stood.

"That's why there are so few riders in each generation," Fane continued. "My master says that if the connection isn't done properly, it will only last a year and then..." He stopped.

"What happens at the end of the year?" Thyel asked before Tamara could.

"For humans, the break in bonding can have a devastating effect. In my master's case, although the bond was true, when his dragon died, the break left him blind."

"A dangerous relationship," Tamara murmured, handing him the last piece of bread and cheese.

"Thank you." Fane took a big bite.

The lesson must have built up his appetite. She was glad they'd saved him a little. "How does a broken bond affect a dragon?"

"It's worse for them," Fane said around a mouthful.

Thyel indicated the closed door. "Shall we continue this discussion inside?"

Fane fished out a key ring with his free hand and headed past her. "I took this from my master after he fell asleep."

Tamara laughed at his self-congratulatory expression. "Hard to believe you've never stolen in here before this."

"I had asked my master if we could come up here, but he always forbade it." He gave her a sheepish smile. "It never occurred that I could do it without permission. Until now."

"I see," Tamara said. "I'm sorry for having subverted your morals, Fane. Oh, wait a moment, if you didn't have the key all along, how did you expect to enter the room before?"

"I thought I'd pick the lock," the boy said in all innocence.

Obviously, once subverted, he had gone all the way. "I doubt it would have been quite so easy," she said with a laugh. "Thyel has been trying that, on and off, since you left."

"I was close to gaining entry," Thyel protested.

If he had been that close, why had he been doing nothing but stretching out on the steps for the past half hour?

After a bit of fiddling, Fane unlocked the door, but then he couldn't seem to budge it.

Thyel moved the boy aside and put his shoulder to the task. The door scraped forward an inch. Fane added his efforts to the cause. Tamara stayed where she was. There was barely enough room on the landing for two let alone three.

Suddenly, the door slid forward and with a shout of triumph, Thyel wedged himself between the frame and door and forced his way in.

She and Fane heard Thyel swear from inside.

They looked at each other in concern and then Fane hurriedly squeezed through the slim opening.

Hearing the boy's shocked intake of breath, Tamara muttered, "Move aside," and slid through next.

Dust and cobwebs shrouded a room littered with shattered wood. If the map room had been in sad shape, the portal room was a hundred times worse.

On the far wall, a shattered doorway stood where the grand entry from the inner stairs to the room had been. Timber lay scattered on the floor and parts of the surrounding walls were smashed, leaving huge gaping holes through which the wind blew.

"My master mentioned this wreckage," Fane said, "but I never imagined such utter destruction." He touched the side of the wall that held the impression of where a large gem must once have rested. "Even if your friend finds the stone, how can we make the portal work now?"

Tamara walked to the gap in the wall and looked across to the opposite tower where a matching hole was in that portal room. The bridge between the two towers looked to be intact but in bad shape. She would never risk crossing it.

Up close, the statues of the dragons on either end of the bridge were more battered than they had seemed from below. The King's Horsemen had been thorough in their work.

Years after his death, her Uncle Ywen still managed to make her tremble at the destruction he had perpetrated on Ryca. Could being trapped in that time spell have been preferable, after all, to being alive and helpless when he was in control?

She slid to the floor, her back against the wall adjacent to the opening, breathing in the rush of fresh air. Despite the falling-to-her-death danger, the opening made her feel less confined. Now that she had time to rest, the need for sleep deserted her.

Still in a fit of temper, Thyel paced around the round tower room, kicking aside fallen timber, showing no concern for precious books and artifacts that littered the floor, or for Fane's distressed mutterings.

Fane looked so despondent, Tamara decided to ask about the dragons. Talk of his favorite topic might improve his mood. "You said dragons fared worse if the bonding did not take." She stretched out her legs. "What did you mean, Fane?"

He stopped picking through the rubble to glance at her. Then, with a sigh, he came over and sat beside her, leaving Thyel alone to disturb the remnants of the room.

"If the bonding isn't done properly, it causes a drain in the dragon's energy. Within a year, the males become sterile and the females unable to conceive."

"Then why risk it? The consequences seem too harsh for both participants."

"If the bond is done properly, it makes the dragons more fertile and gives humans the ability to travel between realms."

Fane's eyes glowed with excitement. "I have only experienced such traveling once, when my master brought me to Ryca. It is the most remarkable passage, Princess. As if we flew through a warren of lights. It's said, a dragon rider saw the Lighted Ones during one such passage."

"That's impossible," Thyel said, for the first time taking interest in Fane's story.

"My master says not," Fane replied with a stubborn tilt of his chin.

Thyel shook his head. "If you could see the Lighted Ones, then you would also be able to see souls that have passed from this life to the next, and I know that is impossible."

Fane shrugged. "Where do souls go when they die but back into the Light? Where does the Light in our world, the magic of Ryca, come from if not from the Land of Promise where the Lighted Ones are said to reside? My master says that Ashari is the Land of Promise where Light was first born out of the Well of Darkness."

"Children's tales," Thyel scoffed, but Tamara noticed a frown on his forehead that suggested Fane's words had a deeper impact than Thyel wanted to admit.

Fane's tale intrigued and disturbed her, too. If he were right, and if this Land of Promise, this Ashari, existed, would her father be there? The thought brought a chill that was colder than the wind blowing through the hole.

"If humans gain the ability to travel between realms," Thyel said, "what do dragons gain? I cannot imagine they bond merely to breed more."

"On Isa, dragons who can successfully bond with a human and survive the year, rule their world. A true bond is a sign of a dragon's strength, vitality, and power."

"Simply because it makes them more fertile?" Tamara asked in astonishment.

Fane shrugged. "Without that bonding, a female dragon normally only conceives once every ten years, and then only produces one egg. They are long lived but not a prolific breed."

"How is that changed when a dragon bonds with a human?" Tamara asked, her interest piqued.

"When a female dragon mates with a male while properly bonded with a human, she can often lay several eggs, up to a dozen."

"That many?" Tamara said, shocked.

"Yes, and because it strengthens her clan, they can rule all of Isa. Even the giants will not bother the ruling dragon clan."

"Giants?" Tamara asked. "There are giants on Isa, too?"

"Does the bonding have any effect on the males?" Thyel asked, seemingly fixated on the dragon talk.

"His virility increases and he is able to impregnate as often and as many dragons as he wishes."

Thyel laughed. "An exceptional benefit indeed. I wonder what happened on Isa when this temple was shut down and humans no longer went there?"

"Isa, too, has human villages. I was born in one. My people are not like yours. We do not have cities like Tibor or magical guilds. Most of us rarely survive to adulthood."

"Because of the dragons or the giants?" Tamara asked.

"Both. The giants dislike humans as much as they do dragons. They stomp through our villages and savagely murder all who are too weak to get out of their way. They steal our produce and take our young people to work as slaves in their homes. Our only protection is the dragons. They may not particularly like each other, or us, but they especially hate the giants."

"Why?" Thyel asked.

"Because the giants take great fun in throwing boulders at them when they fly by."

"A most dangerous place to live," Tamara said, rethinking going to Isa at all. "I'm surprised any of you survived."

"We stay far away from the plains where the giants live. We prefer the foothills by the mountain ranges which the dragons call home. All the human villages vie to produce a child that could bond with a dragon. For then they can be assured of the protection of the dragons and their riders."

"As your village was," Tamara was starting to understand the cultural dynamics that troubled Isa.

"Yes. Though before the Rycans came, most of us hid from the dragons, too. It is rare among my people to be able to dragon speak. It was the Rycans who built temples on Isa, organized the calling ceremonies, and formalized the bonding rites with the dragons." He paused and silence settled onto the shattered room like falling dust. "We were returning to those dark times," Fane finally said in a quiet voice, "with dragons turning their backs on us and the giants raiding our villages when my master came for me."

Tamara didn't pursue the topic further. She could imagine what might have happened on Isa since Fane left his home. He had been on Ryca now for a good five years. In that time, would his home and family have survived without the protection of dragon riders?

• • • •

THE LOW TUNNEL JARROD and Skye travelled through finally opened into another cave. Able to stand, he turned to help her rise.

"Watch your step," he warned, holding her back when she would have gone forward. Her Light ball swerved in front of them to show that not two feet from where they stood, the ground dropped off sharply. The Light ball then flew across the deep chasm.

"It's a good thing you didn't pick my aunt to come with you." Skye shook dirt out of her long blond hair. "Tamara would never have survived that last part of the journey. Even I felt trapped in there."

"Without you along, we wouldn't have found the Quinlin stone." Jarrod pointed across the cave where Skye's seeker Light had come to rest against the wall. A large golden gem rested in a depression near it, its edges glinting in the darkness.

"Oh, it's beautiful," she breathed.

"And unreachable. There is no pathway to that ledge where the stone rests. Even if I could transport myself over, there's no outcropping for me to stand on."

"Then what do we do?"

"The keeper of the stone must have somehow managed to get over there to place the stone in its spot," Jarrod murmured. "Perhaps there's another way to get across."

He indicated the oppressive darkness and Skye obligingly sent a second ball of Light speeding up to the craggy ceiling above to highlight the pit of darkness below.

"There's no way to get to the stone," Skye said, disappointment deep in her tone.

"Look over there." He pointed to a hole well above where the stone rested. "I can transport myself into there, and reach the stone from above."

Unhooking his pack, he set it down, and willed himself to the higher ledge. Once over there, behind him, a tunnel led off down a side corridor. This place was a maze. They might eventually have found their way here, but his special ability to travel where he pleased had helped bypass any traps laid on the way here.

He lay flat on the floor, waved a hand to Skye to show he was fine, and leaned an arm down, feeling along the wall for the opening below.

"To your left," Skye shouted. "Lower."

Jarrod inched forward, bracing his feet against the walls and slipped a little more out of the opening. A stone brushed past his arm and tumbled down. He listened, waiting several heartbeats before it crashed to the ground. A long fall.

His left foot slipped and he slid forward.

Skye shouted a warning.

Jarrod held himself in place with his free hand. Once he was steadied, he shouted, "I'm fine."

"Be careful!"

As if he needed that reminder. "I can't see the stone. Guide my hand."

"Jarrod, maybe I should be there with you, to hold onto your feet, so you don't fall into the chasm."

The soil slipped beneath him. He didn't have much time before the whole floor disintegrated and swept him and the Quinlin to the bottom of the abyss.

"Is my hand close to the stone?" he asked.

"Yes."

"Which way?" The soil beneath his right foot gave and sent him sliding far enough for his head and shoulders to jut out of the opening. He braced both feet apart again to stop the movement.

"Jarrod!"

"Be quick. We've little time."

"Directly to your left. Yes, there!"

As his fist clenched the stone, the entire shelf he rested on gave way. He tumbled face first, heading down.

"Jarrod!" Skye screamed.

He fell faster than he expected, unable to turn himself about to get his bearing. He couldn't remember how many counts before that stone had hit the ground. It seemed far too few as he was speeding toward the chasm's floor. Heart in mouth, he pictured Skye and willed himself to her side.

In a whoosh, he reappeared by Skye's side, with solid ground under his feet. Dirty, disheveled, and surprisingly delighted, he adjusted the neckline of his robe that had slid up to tangle around his ears.

"Oh," she sighed, hugging him tightly. "Don't ever scare me like that again."

He hugged her back, heart still racing. He couldn't remember the last time he had experienced such sheer exhilaration. Perhaps Tamara was right. Spending his time with books, and recording the daring deeds of others, could he have missed a vital part of what life had to offer? He laughed out loud at the idea that almost getting killed might be a worthwhile life experience.

"We have the Quinlin," he said, releasing Skye to show her the stone. He'd clutched at it so tight, it had left indentations on his palm.

"It's smaller than I imagined." She fingered the jewel's sharp edges. "Hard to believe it has the power to open portals to other worlds."

"Let's find out if that's true." Jarrod picked up his pack and gave it to Skye. Then he closed his eyes to sense Tamara's whereabouts. She'd moved from where he'd left her. He transported himself and Skye directly to her new location.

This room was more elevated than their previous location – the air felt thinner, similar to what he and Skye had breathed at the top of the mountain. Here, the air was stale and dusty. The far wall, battered open to the outside, gave a clear view of a hawk flying by the opposite temple tower.

Her back to them, Tamara was on the floor and peering out of the opening, Thyel was beside her with Fane curled on the floor, asleep.

"Aunt Tamara?" Skye called out.

His heart skipped a beat at the panic in her voice.

Tamara swung around and Jarrod breathed in relief. She was safe.

Skye handed Jarrod his pack and stepped toward her aunt.

"You're back," Tamara looked relieved.

"You found the stone." Thyel's gaze was fixed on the small plum-sized jewel in Jarrod's right palm.

Fane scrambled to his feet and hurried over to touch the stone with trembling fingers. "The Quinlin." He breathed out the name in an awed voice.

"Almost lost Jarrod while fetching it," Skye said.

Tamara gave him a quick look. Was that a hint of concern? The thought warmed him.

"What's happened in here?" Skye indicated the disastrous room.

"Horsemen's handiwork," Tamara said, standing with Thyel's help before they both came over to admire the stone.

"Will we be able to use this?" Jarrod asked, looking around the rubble with grave doubt.

"There's a depression in what's left of the wall over there." Tamara pointed to the area near where the wall had been bashed open. "We can see if it still works."

"Halt!" a voice boomed.

"Master!" Fane said in alarm, turning to stare at a white-haired man squeezing through the doorway.

Tamara, tiptoeing over to Jarrod's side, whispered, "The keeper. I can't believe he navigated those outside stairs totally blind."

"What means this, Fane?" the keeper demanded. "Who are these people? How did they gain entry to this sacred space?"

"Master," Fane approached the old man. "I've excellent news! We have visitors. Two princesses and two men accompanying them. They're looking for their brother."

"Tell them to leave immediately," the keeper said.

"But these people have found the lost Quinlin stone for us, Master. If only you could see it. It is breathtaking. All golden and glinty. I touched it and I shivered as its power coursed through me."

Jarrod looked at the Quinlin with a frown. He'd felt nothing but the cold, smoothness of the stone. In his excitement, had the boy imagined the trace of power?

"Silence," the keeper said. "You have defamed the temple by allowing strangers in. Have I taught you nothing?"

"But Master," Fane began.

"Out. Everyone out of the tower. This instant."

"We're not leaving, old man," Thyel said in a hard tone. "Not until we test the stone out in its crevice."

"Master, please, listen to me," Fane said.

"I will not. This action makes it clear that you cannot be trusted to show sense." The keeper shook loose of the young man's grip. "Take these infidels and leave the temple. That's an order. Don't bother to return. You've forfeited your right to your apprenticeship." He flailed at the boy, landing sharp slaps accurately on the back of Fane's hands. "Be gone, I tell you."

Fane withdrew his bruised hands, and shrugged at them. There was hopelessness in his eyes that he might have lost everything he valued.

"Ignore him." Thyel held out his hand to Jarrod. "I'll test it for us."

Jarrod hesitated. "This place is the keeper's home. We're the trespassers." He held the stone close, protectively. "Even this rightfully belongs to him. If we explain our dilemma, he might understand why we need to use it."

"Fools," the keeper shouted. "You must not use that stone."

"Let's find out," Thyel snatched the jewel and ran to the indentation in the wall. He placed the stone in its place and stepped back.

"What's happening?" the keeper asked.

"Master," Fane said, with excitement. "When one of the men placed the Quinlin in its hold, the most amazing thing happened. The stone glowed."

"Take it out, quickly," the keeper shouted.

"No! Wait." Thyel blocked Jarrod's path to the stone. "It's working."

"Jarrod, he's right," Skye said. "This might be our only chance to enter Isa and find Bevan." There was desperation in her voice.

Tamara slid her arm around her niece's shoulders. "Skye, Isa may not be as safe a place as you believe."

Jarrod was both pleased and surprised by her practical view on the matter.

The glow from the stone continued to expand, filling half the broken wall. The air vibrated, and a sense of connectedness to another place invaded the room. A circular glow expanded from the stone, like a door opening.

The keeper grabbed and shook his apprentice. "Stop, you fools! You don't realize what you're doing."

Light filled the entire wall, swirling in colorful circles.

Jarrod's gaze fastened on the sheer terror in the keeper's white-glazed eyes and the man's fear invaded him. Jarrod shoved Thyel aside and plucked the stone from its place.

The circle collapsed, flinging Jarrod across the room. He lay stunned, clasping the Quinlin to his chest as its glow slowly faded.

• • • •

TAMARA CLUNG TO SKYE as waves of disturbed energy lashed out at the room. Then all went quiet. The portal had closed.

Beside the tower room doorway, the keeper lay on the floor and moaned. Fane scrambled over to help his master.

"Why?" Thyel got up from where the energy burst had tossed him. His hands were clenched into fists.

Afraid he intended to attack Jarrod, Tamara released Skye and placed herself between the two men and faced Thyel. "Let's talk about this first."

Skye was close to tears. "I want to know, too. Why did you do that, Jarrod?"

Jarrod spoke directly to Skye. "We must hear what the keeper has to say about the stone." His voice was gentle but firm. "If we risk walking into danger ourselves, Skye, we may end up dead and be of no use to your brother." Jarrod knelt by the keeper's side. "Sir, what was your fear when the Quinlin was placed in its resting place?"

The old man pushed Jarrod away. "Fool! Leave me be."

"Master," Fane said. "Why would you deny others what you were once privileged to experience?"

The old man reached toward Fane, his hands shaking. "Take me...to my room." His chest rose and fell rapidly, his breath coming out in tiny whips. "Medicine..."

"Herbs," the boy said. "They help him breath."

Jarrod nodded. "Once he regains his strength, he may tell us what we need to know."

"What a waste of time," Thyel muttered.

"The keeper needs our help," Tamara said.

"Yes, he does." Jarrod assisted Fane in getting the old keeper to his feet. He then took his tome out of his pack. Opening the book, he put the Quinlin inside, and snapped it shut. Instead of bulging, the tome lay flat, as if it did not encase something round.

"How did you do that?" Tamara asked.

"Never mind." Jarrod called Skye over and putting the book into the pack, he gave it to her to hold.

Tamara watched that trusting exchange with an uncomfortable flare of envy.

"Fane, I can transport him to his room, but I'll need you to guide me there. Think of his room."

Before Tamara could say, "What about us?" the three men disappeared.

Chapter 7

SKYE, TAMARA AND THYEL took the long way down the treacherous stairs to the keeper's room. They arrived in time to hear the old man mutter to Jarrod, "Too dangerous, too dangerous."

Jarrod was squatted before the old man. "Keeper, calm yourself." He gently rubbed the old man's slender, veined white hands in his smooth dark ones.

She had to admire Jarrod's persistence. She would have given up on the keeper by now.

The keeper grabbed Jarrod's shoulders and shouted. "Too dangerous!"

Tamara jumped in fright, and then sighed. "Old fool."

"Explain yourself, old man," Thyel said.

The keeper's fingers pinched into Jarrod's shoulder enough to make the Chief Councilor visibly flinch. "You must not leave through that doorway."

"Master." Fane knelt to speak with him. He placed a container of water between the keeper's shaking hands. "Drink. I've put your herbs in it."

The keeper flung the goblet away. Uncannily, it sailed straight for Thyel and Tamara. She instinctively ducked. It missed her and sailed by Thyel's head, barely an inch away.

He gave an angry oath.

"Foolish boy," the keeper shouted.

"Why?" Fane asked, his own anger stirred. "Why am I foolish? You've trained me for five years for this moment. I've been a good student. I can discipline my mind enough to embrace a dragon's mind-touch without panicking. I have practiced on dogs and cats and birds. I know I can do it. Now I have a chance to fulfill my destiny and you pluck it away."

Fane took his master's hands. "Don't you understand, Master. I want to be like you. I want to soar across the sky on the back of a dragon. Travel between realms. See wonders I have only imagined from your tales."

"Keeper." On the other side of Jarrod, Skye, too, bent to speak to the old man. "We must use the stone. My brother is in trouble and I must go find him. The only way I know how, is through that opening to Isa."

The old man shook his head. "Too dangerous."

"Why?" Fane asked.

"Because there's nothing left to focus the stone's energy, to keep it whole," the keeper said. "Boy, if you go through that portal, there will be no returning home. Not ever. To use the portal in its current state will destroy the last remaining Quinlin stone on this side and the other, denying you the ability to return if all is not as it should be on Isa."

Never able to return? Tamara staggered back, and sat on a bench. *What had they almost done?*

"Not if we find a dragon," Fane said. "If I bond with a dragon, I could travel back and bring these people with me."

"If you don't bond? If no dragon is willing to try anymore? They were becoming more quarrelsome with the humans the last time I visited Isa. Or what if you're killed before you find one? Isa is not a place for the unwary. You know that, Fane. Do your friends?"

"I would face any peril to save Bevan," Skye said.

The keeper's quivering hand came to rest unerringly on her shoulder. He turned his blind eyes to her. "Would you, girl? Even if it meant you may never return? That you could be trapped on Isa for the rest of your life?"

Skye's face turned ashen and her gaze swung toward her aunt. Her blue gaze filled with compassion met Tamara's. It held a determination to carry on, no matter the risk.

Her niece had a plan. Tamara saw it in her eyes. She would enter Isa, find a way for Fane to bond with a dragon, and then fly them out of that realm in search of Bevan, marauding giants or difficult dragons notwithstanding.

Even the possibility of being trapped on Isa did not faze Skye. The possibility expanded in Tamara's mind.

Silently, she pleaded with Skye to not go. She couldn't stand to lose her, as well as Bevan. Her mother would never forgive her. Tamara could never forgive herself. She shook her head, hoping to discourage Skye.

Her niece stared back, and then mimed the words, "I'm sorry," and turned back to the keeper.

Tears flooded Tamara's eyes. She had nothing left now but to go home and tell her mother that without lifting a finger to help, she'd allowed Skye to walk into danger, as she had Bevan. The first time, she'd done it from a sense of impatience. This time, it would be sheer cowardice.

Jarrod came over to Tamara's side and sat beside her, taking her hand. There was such profound understanding in his gaze that a long dead part of Tamara woke up with a start.

Her spine firmed, stiff as an ancient oak. Shaking off his hold, she stood and approached the old man.

Don't think.

Don't plan.

Don't worry about what's to come.

Live for this moment. One breath at a time. For once, do what's right.

"We are going to Isa, Keeper," Tamara said. "You can either help us reach there safely, or stay out of our way."

Everyone in the room gazed from her to the keeper.

Silence rang like a thunderclap.

The keeper raised his hands blindly toward Tamara. "Come here, girl."

She looked at his foggy eyes and shivered. What was she doing? *Don't think! Just breathe.* She knelt by the old man.

The keeper put his shaky, clammy hands on either side of her head. He leaned forward until their foreheads touched and brought his uniquely, gagging scent. Whiffs of it invaded her lungs. *No, don't breathe, hold your breath.*

Just as she thought her chest would explode, dragons flew at her. At least a dozen. In the air. Chasing her. Screaming in rage.

The keeper released his hold and she fell onto her hind end. She was back in his smelly quarters.

Tamara's tight chest deflated like a pricked bubble, air gushing out. Which was when it dawned that when those dragons chased her, she'd been airborne.

The keeper laughed.

"What's so funny?" she asked.

The old man shook his head. Tears streamed down his wrinkled old cheeks. He hacked, trying to catch his breath between chortles. "Fane!"

"Yes, Master? I'm here."

"Take my blessings with you to Isa." He caught the boy by his neck and, still in great humor, brought him down to his level. "You've done well, boy.

Beyond my wildest expectations. Now go. The queen of the dragons has spoken." Then he laughed again, hacking and wheezing.

"He's gone mad." Thyel said.

Tamara cringed at that, afraid if she said she'd seen dragons in her mind, he'd call her mad, too. Instead, she stood and gave Skye a nod and then walked out the door, heading for the portal room.

Queen of the Dragons, indeed. Somehow, he must have tapped into one of her nightmares and the old fool was making fun of her. Face hot with embarrassment, she wanted to get away from the keeper before he said anything else rude.

Skye raced to catch up. Her niece's slender fingers gripped hers, the only indication she appreciated Tamara's support.

Tamara squeezed back and made another silent promise to her mother. *I will take exceptional care of her, Mother. I won't lose her, too.*

• • • •

IT TOOK FANE A WHILE to send a homing pigeon to request and receive confirmation from a neighbor that he would look after the old keeper while Fane was away.

Finally, all but the keeper convened in the portal room and Jarrod retrieved the Quinlin stone from his tome. He stepped up to the depression in the wall and gently laid the stone in its proper resting place.

The Quinlin started to glow.

He stepped back as the circle of light expanded. The stone's vibration increased as the portal built, growing taller and wider, until it covered the gaping hole in the wall.

"Are you sure you want to come with us?" Skye asked Tamara.

"Wrong question."

"Right." Skye squeezed Tamara's fingers in understanding.

She would never be ready for this. Tamara requested to be the first to step through. If the stone didn't work and she stepped off the edge of the tower, it wouldn't matter. She'd often imagined such an event occurring. At least this way, her sacrifice would save Skye. It was the least she could do for letting Bevan down when he needed her.

At Skye's worried look, Tamara lied and said, "The less time I have to think about it, the better."

She moved into the golden light and her body shivered and shook like the Quinlin stone in its resting place. Fear swamped her and she would have backed away except Skye, the foolish child, was right behind her. She hadn't waited to see if her aunt was about to fall to her death.

Tamara shut her eyes and mind to her fears and imagined walking through a lighted corridor. With each measured footstep, her heartbeat hammered like a summoning drumbeat.

The walk seemed endless, filled with whispers, hundreds of voices speaking in tongues she couldn't make out. A clear, oddly familiar voice asked. *Tamara?*

Leave me be! Had she shouted that aloud?

An explosion thrust Skye stumbling into her back.

"What was that?" her niece asked.

Tamara opened her eyes. They were inside a small crude temple made of wooden walls and a thatched roof.

Fane, Jarrod, and Thyel came through next pushing her and Skye further into the room. The amazement on her friends' faces mirrored her awe.

"We made it!" Fane shouted. "This is Isa! This temple is exactly as my master described it."

To their right an altar constructed of a large flat stone held various implements carefully lined up. Fane ran to pick up a bowl and then a candle. He muttered in excitement over each find until, finally, his trembling fingers touched an iridescent scale the size of his chest.

Tamara remained rooted as her friends and Skye wandered about, exploring various corners of the room. Her heartbeat continued to thud like the beating of a giant drum.

Even as her surroundings skewed alarmingly, Tamara recognized the distortion for what it was. A clear sign of her fear, her world encompassing the space of her body, standing still, her right hand clasped safely within her mother's left. Back then, she'd been unable to move a muscle, her thoughts skittering around the edges of her confinement like a panicked rat in a miniscule cage.

Now, although she had all the freedom she could hope for inside this foreign realm, deep inside she knew there was no clear avenue to return home, which left her as trapped as she had been by her mother's spell.

She hugged herself as her blood cooled, then heated, and cooled again. Her legs shook so hard, she feared she might collapse. She headed for a bench on the far wall and sat. Bending, she laid her head on arms crossed over knees and allowed the swimming sensations to sweep through her.

Finally, the queasiness stilled and she sat up and looked around. Straight ahead, Thyel studied the area they had just come through. The wall looked like a circular carved gateway. Within her hazy thoughts, she realized the tower room would have looked like this had it not been destroyed.

Thyel ran his hand over an indentation. He picked up a handful of crumbly dirt. The remains of the Quinlin stone on this end? Had their use of the unstable receptacle at the other end destroyed the stone here, too, as the keeper predicted?

Was that the flash that occurred when they came through? If the stone at this end had splintered a few moments earlier, while they were still inside the lighted tunnel, would they have been trapped there with those incessant whisperers?

Jarrod strode in front of her, blocking her view of the depressed shelf where the Quinlin should have been. He knelt until his face came surprisingly close. Taking her cold hands in his warm ones, he murmured, "We're fine, Tamara. We made it through."

He'd read her thoughts again. She willed herself to remain tranquil. She did not want to visibly panic. It was bad enough he could read the darkest recesses of her mind.

"Once we find Bevan," he said, sounding not in the least concerned about that improbability, "we will fly straight home on a dragon."

Skye exclaimed then, pointing to a wall. "Look, a map!" She ran to study it.

Jarrod looked over and his eyes widened with interest.

History was recorded on that wall. Instead of being resentful of his distraction, Tamara softened, smiling indulgently at his keen interest.

Skye's find also gave Tamara the excuse to seek privacy, time to gain some self-control. "You'd better see what she's found. Could be a map that shows us where the dragon nests are located."

"Will you be all right?" he asked.

"Quite fine, Chief Councilor," she replied, but with a tolerant smile. "Don't let me keep you from your study."

He hesitated, then gave into his curiosity. With a nod, he went over to where Skye followed a route on the map with a forefinger.

Fane and Thyel, too, joined Skye.

Tamara was glad. She preferred to be alone. Her head had started to spin again. The room closed in on all four sides and made perspiration drip down her forehead to sting her eyes. Her heartbeat, while slower than earlier, still pounded away like a runaway horse.

She spied a doorway at the other end of a corridor. Standing on shaky legs, she headed toward the sliver of light highlighting the edges of a door.

"The map shows all of Isa, including the villages dotting the countryside," Skye said in an excited voice.

"Look! I know this village," Fane replied. "My uncle lives there. He could tell us about the state of the dragons."

"Why not head straight for the dragon hold?" Thyel pointed at the map. "It's closer."

"Because that would take us through giant country," Fane said in a firm tone. "We don't want to do that."

Her companions' voices faded into the background. Their chatter seemed inconsequential compared to finding a way outside so she could see the sky.

What did it matter where they were headed? They would still be stuck on Isa. For now, all she wanted was to get out of this cramped little temple and see daylight, breathe fresh air. Hands braced against opposite walls, she followed the light that promised a sense of freedom.

She pulled open the door and stumbled out into blessed openness. Fresh, cool air assaulted her face. She squinted into the bright daylight.

The sky was painted in an unaccustomed grayish-blue hue. Thankfully, it was still high up and did not press down. The knots in her shoulders loosened. The land behind the temple stretched far into wide-open, grassy fields. By any measure, this new world was definitely not a tiny cage.

Her teeth unclenched, and her sore cheek muscles thanked her. To the right were low-lying hills on the horizon, like freckles. A pretty sight. To the left, about a league away, a forest made up of strange spindly trees spread out in front of a mountain range whose tips were hidden by gray clouds.

Among all this unfamiliar terrain, the three moons that hovered low on the horizon were pleasingly familiar. The sight gave her a warm reassuring embrace. She could as easily be standing on the castle gardens, looking at the horizon. This soil may be red instead of brown, but she felt sure those three moons were the same ones she'd seen last night from the castle balcony.

Had it only been last night that her mother barged into Thyel's room and berated Tamara on her conduct? The event seemed a lifetime away.

Her perspective shifted. Had she approached her troubles with her mother in the wrong manner? Instead of rebelling against the queen's every order, she should have proved to her mother that she was now an adult. One who no longer needed the queen's protection, or anyone else's.

Perhaps this journey wouldn't be a complete disaster. They might yet make it back home. A possibility that had seemed incredibly unlikely a few moments ago, now grew new wings.

If they found Bevan and brought him home, her mother might believe that Tamara didn't need a caretaker. She could not only see to her own needs, but to those of her family and friends as well. Even without having a shred of magical talent.

She rejoiced that she'd shown the courage to join Skye on this daring journey. Not only was she not trapped, she was in the midst of her very own adventure.

She raised her arms and twirled, shouting, "I'M FREE!"

"Munno!" a voice rumbled high overhead.

Something plucked her up and raised her until air swept by painfully, plastering her hair across her face.

Tamara screamed, fearing her nightmare had come to life. Eyes tight shut, she shouted, "Dragon!"

"Dragon?" the voice above her mimicked her startled cry. She was spun around until she was dizzy and couldn't make out what had her in its tight grip.

Only once the spinning finally stopped did Tamara open her eyes and realize it wasn't a dragon who held her in its fierce grip, but a giant man.

Her assailant's gaze remained focused on the sky above, the arm holding her swinging about with his continued frantic search. "Kanda? Kanda filty? Kanda dragon?"

Her eardrums shuddered at the loud voice calling out practically in her ear.

"Tamara!" Jarrod shouted in a tiny hollow voice from below.

The world thankfully came to a stop as the giant stopped turning to look downward. Tamara's head kept spinning for a moment more and she wondered if she was about to throw up all over the giant's fingers.

"Let her down!" Skye shouted up at them.

Her head finally settling, Tamara leaned as far as she could over the giant's fingers and craned her neck to look down. Far below, her friends and Skye had gathered outside the temple.

"Kanda dragon?" the giant asked again.

"I...I thought you were the dragon," Tamara said.

"Y?" the giant asked, turning his astonished gaze to her. "Y, filty?" Then he chuckled. "Y gulta, human." He shook his head as if she'd said a silly thing, and with her still in his grip, he walked away from the temple.

"Put me down," Tamara shouted.

He came to a halt and brought her up to eye level. "Cho?"

"Because I don't want to go with you."

"Ta munno," he said matter-of-factly, pointing to his chest, and kept walking.

"My friends will make you give me back," she warned as his large legs ate up miles, leaving her group far behind.

The giant looked back at the four tiny humans running after him. He gave a rumble of laughter and kept going, heading further into the plains.

Tamara's heart did a flip-flop of terror. He had a right to laugh. How would her friends ever find her if he kept going at this pace? She squirmed to get out of his grip, but he only tightened his hold, until she cried out in pain.

The giant pointed a finger at her in warning but then thankfully, loosened his hold enough to let her breath, and then he kept walking.

Tamara took a grateful breath. For a moment, she thought it wouldn't matter if her friends ever found her because she would be dead by then. Then Jarrod appeared on top of the giant's hand and Tamara let out a startled squeal.

He pried at the fingers confining her, and she wiggled to get loose, whispering a heartfelt, "Thank you!" How could she have ever thought he didn't care about her?

The giant shook his fist and Jarrod went tumbling off.

"Jarrod," Tamara cried out, but he vanished midair. She breathed a sigh of relief. Thanks to his intervention, she'd almost freed herself. Then the giant moved his fingers until she was firmly back in his grasp.

Jarrod re-appeared beside her.

"Nee da," the giant yelled, flinging the hand that held Tamara, but this time Jarrod hung on to the large thumb.

Tamara worked her sword free and used it to stab at the closest finger holding her.

"Ahhhh!" the giant bellowed and sent both Jarrod and her flying through the air.

Jarrod grabbed her dress and the two of them reappeared back by the temple.

Tamara sheathed her sword and clung to Jarrod, afraid the giant would pluck her up again. If he did, she wanted Jarrod with her.

"Cho?" the giant called. "Cho human? Ta munno!"

The rest of her group ran up to them and they hid at the side of the temple.

"Don't make a sound," Fane whispered. "Giants have great hearing."

The large man hurried back toward the temple. Jarrod encircled his arms around all of them, pulling close, and in one swoop, they found themselves on the far side of the encroaching forest.

Tamara turned to thank him and found Jarrod pale and shaken. That had cost him more energy than he could spare. She hadn't thought Jarrod's magic had a limit. Obviously, she'd been mistaken. She put her arm around him in silent support and he sagged against her. His forehead burned hot to her touch.

They looked back and saw the big man lift the little temple and look beneath it.

Giving a "harrumph" of disappointment, he gave up. He set the temple down and walked away, scratching at his head with one hand and looking back every once in a while.

"Thank you," Tamara said once the giant was lost to their sight and it seemed safe to speak.

"Yes, we all owe you our lives, Jarrod," Skye said.

Fane agreed and even Thyel reluctantly nodded in acknowledgement of Jarrod's effort.

"You're welcome," Jarrod said, "but let's not do that again. I may not be able to transport all of us a second time." He straightened beside her, seeming to have recovered a little.

"Yes," Fane added. "Everyone stay close." Though his words addressed the whole group, his eyes were trained on Tamara.

"Sorry," she said in a contrite voice.

"Isa is not like Ryca, Princess," Fane said. "You cannot walk around unprotected."

She shuddered at the understatement, remembering the enormous fist holding her. If not for Jarrod, who knew what might have happened to her? Silently, she laughed at her earlier assumption that she could not only take care of herself but her friends and family, too. She glanced at her group and realized she was glad every one of them was with her.

"Now, what?" Thyel asked.

Fane took out a map he'd squirreled away inside his tunic and unrolled it on the ground so they could all see. "We follow this route to my uncle's village."

"How long will it take?" Jarrod asked.

"Are there likely to be more giants on the way?" Tamara added.

"Not long, maybe a day, and no giants. Too close to the dragon stronghold. Except during raids, they mostly respect each other's territory."

They set off, staying close and keeping a careful watch all around. Oddly, this part of the forest seemed familiar to Tamara. She had seen skeletal trees like these before. In her dreams. Had she just woken up and walked into the landscape of her nightmares?

Soon, they came across a path that led deeper into the forest. A sign was carved into a flat plank and nailed to a tall stump, marking the beginning of the pathway. She didn't need to read the words to know what the foreign script said.

Still, as Fane translated the words, a shiver went up Tamara's spine. "All Who Enter, Beware! For There Be Dragons Here."

Chapter 8

ON THE GLOOMY WALK through the forest, Tamara listened for a loud "thud" that would indicate the giant was back on her trail. It didn't help that for the past hour, she'd also been hearing someone whimpering.

When it got really loud, she stopped and whispered, "Did anyone hear that?"

"What?" Skye asked from beside Fane, who was leading them.

"Someone's crying," Tamara said.

Everyone stopped to listen. To the occasional scurrying of small birds. To the wind in the leaves. To silence. Thyel was the first to glance at Tamara with a question in his eyes.

"I could have sworn someone was in trouble," she said.

"We're probably in more trouble than anyone else in these woods," he said with a grim smile.

"Maybe we should walk faster," Fane suggested, looking around with fearful eyes.

Their lagging steps picked up speed. Tamara glanced to the side in time to see a familiar green lizardy shape scurry under cover of leaves. She jerked in alarm.

"What?" Skye asked from right beside her.

When had she moved back here?

Jarrod, too, came up to Tamara. "What was it?"

She shook her head. "You wouldn't believe me if I told you."

"Try us," Skye said.

"At this point, I'd believe anything," Fane added coming up to them.

"It looked like that green lizardy thing I saw on our way up to the Quinlin Temple."

"How could it have got here?" Thyel asked. "It wasn't in the portal room with us. Was it?"

"No," Tamara said. "I said you wouldn't believe me."

"I believe you saw something," Jarrod said.

"But why only her?" Skye asked. "Why are we not seeing it, too?"

"Let's stay close," Fane suggested, "then if Princess Tamara sees something odd again, we're more likely to spot it, too."

"We're all long past formalities, Fane," she said, absently. "Just Tamara, will do." She glanced around the forest for that lizard-like creature.

Skye took her hand.

She would have snorted at that unnecessarily protective gesture from the thirteen-year-old, except, in some odd way, her niece's hold of her trembling fingers did provide comfort.

Jarrod flanked Tamara's other side. Fane led the way and Thyel dropped a pace behind. Though she appreciated their support, she didn't like this arrangement one bit. She felt trapped again. What could she do? They wanted to help. As the hour progressed and nothing unusual crossed her sight or her hearing, she felt a complete idiot.

They passed an old oak with an intricate knot in its trunk. Then the knot began to whirl. She jerked in fright.

Skye gently squeezed her fingers. "What's wrong?"

She pointed to where the green lizard had appeared by the knot, its claws clinging to the bark while its head turned so it could boldly stare at her. "Don't you see that thing?"

Everyone peered at the knot.

Thyel came around to stroke the trunk. "Is something here?" The doubt in his voice rang in her ears.

Tamara turned away. "Not anymore."

Jarrod's look was filled with concern and then she sensed the gentlest touch of soothing calm brush past her.

She pulled away, mentally and physically, shutting him out. *Don't read me. I'm not one of your books of strange tales to be dissected and probed.*

She shook off Skye's hold, too, and fell back. "I want to follow behind. You're all crowding me."

One little encounter with a giant and she began imagining things. Only no one wanted to admit to it. If she had a smidge of magic, they might have thought what she saw was real. She didn't. She was as ordinary as a piece of grass or a grain of sand.

As their trek continued, Tamara wondered about that problem. She didn't have any special gift to offer in support of this journey. Now it looked as if she were also losing her mind. How would she fare during the rest of this dangerous trek? Would she be of help, or end up a hindrance as always?

Jarrod opened his book and took out his quill.

She could just guess what he was going to write down. *Tamara is acting strange again. She seems unstable. I worry she may break down completely before we ever find Bevan.*

"Must you record everything?" she asked.

He ignored her scoffing tone and shook his quill. A drop of red appeared, covering the tip like a bead of blood.

Despite her family's ease in using magic, appreciation of Jarrod's unique talent bloomed within her like that droplet. A glance over his shoulder at his book showed no blotches of ink, just neat script as he added a note about where they were currently headed. Amazing! She could barely write legibly while sitting with her elbow steadied, let alone while walking.

"That reminds me, Jarrod," she said. "I meant to ask. How is it your magic works here? Isn't it confined to Ryca?"

He stopped and she stumbled into his back. "You're right. My magic shouldn't work, and yet it has, many times."

The others gathered close to listen.

Jarrod shut his eyes a moment and then opened them, gazing at her with regret. "No teleportation off this world."

"Perhaps your magic works for the same reason we can see the Three Sisters in the sky," Skye said.

Jarrod gave her an approving nod. "Yes, exactly. We're still on Ryca, or where Ryca should be. This world must be overlapping it. I can move by magic within it but not between the overlapping worlds."

Resting his quill in the middle of his book, he took out his water cask strapped to his hip. "Anyone thirsty or hungry?"

"Yes, please," Skye said.

He passed it to her and then tore up a flat bread and shared it with everyone. Skye drank and gave the cask to Fane who passed it to Thyel. When it finally reached Tamara, she shook it. It was completely full!

After drinking her fill, she returned the cask to Jarrod who then drank last.

"I wonder how everyone is doing back on Ryca," she murmured. Her mother would have received Tamara's note but if she then sent someone to the temple and found them missing, her worry would have spiked.

Jarrod frowned and said, "Let's keep going."

Remembering the problems with his people disappearing that had first brought him to the castle, she regretted reminding him of his troubles. By the time they returned home, all of his people might be gone. The thought made her worries seem miniscule.

"Fane, how did the first pairing with the dragons happen?" Skye asked as they set off again.

Tamara was glad for something more cheerful to think about. Fane's next words, however, brought her good spirits crashing.

"The giants were to thank for that."

Of all the topics to discuss, why must their conversation keep returning to giants? An involuntary shiver speared through her.

"While we feared them stealing our children and wrecking our homes," Fane said, "the dragons hated them most."

"Why?" Thyel asked. "Presumably dragons are of matching or larger size. Not easy to intimidate."

"From the time they're young, giants take great sport in throwing boulders and trees at dragons that fly too low. They steal their eggs...to eat." Fane added that last with utter disgust.

"I take it they're tasty?" Thyel asked with an amused quirk to his lips.

"Worse," Fane said. "They think if they eat one a day for a score of days, it will make them as light as the dragon and therefore able to fly. After a raid of the dragon caves, they even have competitions to see which giant gets to eat all of the stolen eggs. Fools!"

"Over the years, that must have dangerously reduced the dragon population," Tamara said in a thoughtful tone. "From what you said before, dragons don't lay many eggs to begin with, do they?"

"No, they don't," Fane agreed, "and the giants stealing the few that were laid drove the dragons close to extinction. The elders say that in the ancient days, a villager saw perhaps one dragon in a month. Now they're as numerous as the giants. That's mainly because they befriended humans."

"How did that come about?" The question leaped out of Tamara's mouth without conscious thought. She was curious about the answer. Making friends wasn't easy. She should know. She had none. For two such vastly different species in size and power, to trust each other enough to form an alliance, even befriend each other, seemed improbable.

"There is an ancient story of a villager who found a dragon trapped beneath a boulder, and left to die. The villager went to help and was astounded to find he could mind-speak with the beast." Fane's eyes were bright as he gazed at them. "It led to the first ever natural pairing on Isa."

"Natural pairing?" Tamara asked. "What other kinds are there?"

The light died from Fane's eyes and his gaze skittered past hers like a mouse that had stumbled across a snake.

"It's a saying." He went on with his story, leaving Tamara wondering, *What is he not telling us?*

"From that first encounter," Fane said, "the collaboration between humans and dragons was born. Now, once a village acquires the protection of a dragon, that dragon's cluster will patrol the skies and we in turn send warnings of any swarms near the Dragon Mountains."

"Swarms?" Skye asked.

"That's when the giants travel in family groups, sometimes as many as fifteen or twenty, all scaling the mountains in search of dragon eggs."

"How does warning the dragons help?" Thyel asked. "In those numbers, the giants could still pound away at any dragons that fly by."

"When a swarm approaches the mountains, the dragons do not defend themselves, sir. Instead, the queen and all the young ones take the eggs to safety while the males fly to the giants' terrain and burn everything to the ground. Over time, that's helped reduce the number and frequency of swarms."

Skye chuckled. "Clever beasts."

Her encounter with a giant still fresh on her mind, Tamara grew tired of this conversation. Her steps lagged and soon put her two lengths behind her group. Sound of nails frantically scrabbling against rock had her hurrying forward again. Ducking under a low hanging branch, she skirted a large tree to rejoin her companions.

"Fane," she asked, "how did the Quinlin stones come to play into all this?"

"When the dragons carve out their caves in the mountains, they collect the stones and hoard them in their nests. The stones are fed to newborns and old ones to help ignite a deep belly fire."

Tamara perked up at that news. "We should try to acquire one of those stones then. We could use it at the temple we came through to return home."

Skye sent her a worried look.

"I only meant if we don't find a dragon that's willing to bond with Fane," Tamara added quickly. "It never hurts to have a backup plan. Father used to say that." Not that he'd followed his own advice.

"The dragons don't give them up easily," Fane warned. "They consider the Quinlin their treasure. However, it's also a ritual gift they present to a human after bonding. So, we're sure to acquire at least one."

"Not that we need one," Skye said. "I've every faith we will find a dragon Fane can bond with. Then we'll be able to travel to where we can rescue my brother. After that, we can all return home on the dragon, with or without a Quinlin stone."

"It would still be prudent to take a few stones back with us," Thyel said. "They're obviously powerful in and of themselves for traveling between realms."

"Only one," Fane warned. "And we can't steal it. It must be given as a gift."

"Agreed." Jarrod said, busy writing in his book.

"Fane, tell us more about the pairing," Tamara said. "Is there something you haven't told us?"

"What do you mean?" Thyel asked. Then he grabbed Fane by his arm and brought him to a stop. "What does Tamara mean? Have you kept something from us? This journey is dangerous enough without any of us keeping secrets."

Fane looked worriedly from him to Tamara. "It's nothing important."

"We'll decide what's important," Thyel said.

Fane shuffled under his grip but he refused to release the young man. Finally, Fane sighed and spoke in a rush. "I might have left out that the common type of pairing usually only lasts a year."

Thyel let him go. "Is that all? Well, that's okay."

From the hooded look lurking around Fane's eyes, Tamara guessed there was more. She prodded his shoulder with a pointed finger. "And?"

"Then the dragon's left infertile and the human might die."

"What?" She turned Fane toward her in shock. An icy tremble swept through her at what they'd inadvertently done. They'd not only trapped themselves in this other world, but the only way out could mean this boy's death.

"You didn't think that was significant?" Skye asked, coming up to him, looking as upset as Tamara felt. "You said if the dragon bonding were broken, you might lose your sight or have some other injury, not that after a year you would die!"

"Fane, why didn't you mention this before?" Jarrod asked in a concerned tone.

"Rather a vital bit of detail," Thyel agreed.

"The opportunity to bond with a dragon is what I've lived for all my life." Fane squirmed out of Tamara's hold. "It's what I want to do."

"How can you choose to die in a year?" Skye asked.

"It explains why the dragon cult kept the ritual such a secret," Tamara murmured.

"We can't allow you to sacrifice yourself like that," Skye said in an adamant tone, though Tamara could see how much it hurt to say it. She was admitting they must give up their chance to find Bevan, leaving them trapped here forever.

Tamara stumbled back, seeking the support of a tree trunk. She hugged it to her back and ordered the world to stop spinning.

"I suppose the choice is his," Thyel said.

"It's not," Tamara and Skye said together and then looked at each other in surprise.

"Wait a minute," Jarrod said. "Your master bonded with a dragon and he's an old man."

Her companions crowded around Fane, looking as thoroughly confused as Tamara felt. Did the dragon-human-pairing kill the human or not?

"There are two types of pairing," Fane explained. "One that lasts a year, with dire consequences for both participants. There is a second type - a rare one. This second type can last a lifetime. This is the kind my master had with his dragon. The first is a superficial bond, while the other," he paused and a gentle smile settled on his young face, "is a natural linking. A melding of minds without any effort. The kind the villager who found the dying dragon formed."

"Have you left anything else out?" Skye asked, now all suspicion, as she grabbed his tunic. "Tell us everything. Now!"

"All right, but let me go." He waited until she did so.

"Well?" she asked.

Fane stepped closer to Jarrod, no doubt the safest to hide behind. "Only one type of bond will enable a rider and dragon to fly between realms."

The silence this time was long and pregnant.

"The natural kind," Tamara said in a dead voice.

The chances of them leaving this world plummeted as if a sinkhole opened beneath their feet. Her world shattered for the second time and her throat closed. She took a breath and then another, forcing air in and out until her foggy head could clear.

"Until the pairing process is complete," Fane's words tumbled out, his eyes pleading with Tamara to forgive him for bringing her here, "one cannot tell if it has taken a deep root or formed a superficial bond. If you want to find Prince Bevan, if you all want to return home, you have to let me try."

"You believe you can bond in this particular way, don't you?" Thyel's skepticism layered his tone. "That's why you're so eager for this adventure. Once bonded, you don't believe you'll die in a year."

"That's my hope, sir." There was quiet dignity in Fane's tone. "I come from a family where for four generations we've made natural pairings and lived to old age. That was one of the main reasons my master chose me over all the other children to train to become a dragon rider."

"You're willing to risk your life on it?" Skye asked.

"The choice is mine," Fane said with finality and continued up the path with purpose.

A glance at her niece reminded Tamara of what this meant for finding Bevan, and her own fears of never going home, never seeing the rest of her family. Of being stuck where she didn't want to be.

Nothing really mattered next to losing Bevan. He was destined to be the salvation of Ryca one day. She'd only known him for the past five years, but her blood sang with the certainty of what he would achieve. Just as her mother must have known all those long years ago, that if her powerful husband perished, her family would have little to no chance to stand against the monster that had killed him.

Little by little, the decision the queen made to freeze herself, her precious son and daughter began to seem the best choice she could have made. Would she ever have the chance to face her mother and tell her she was sorry for all the recriminations she'd poured on the queen's head since the day they were awoken?

Jarrod was suddenly next to her, his arm pulling her close, his chin brushing her forehead in sympathy.

"Skye needs me now," she whispered to him and stepped away to put an arm around her niece.

Skye looked at her in surprise, which soon turned to gratitude as tears welled in the young girl's eyes. At moments like this, Tamara was reminded of how young Skye really was. Still a child in need of her mother's comfort and terribly missing her little brother.

She hugged her niece close as they trailed after Fane.

Jarrod and Thyel followed behind in silence.

Close to sunset, Tamara decided she couldn't take one more step and stopped. "Let's camp here. I see a lake through the trees to our left. We can get fresh water and maybe fish for dinner."

"My uncle's village isn't much farther away," Fane said. Map unrolled, he squinted at it in the semi darkness.

"Fane, you've been saying that for the last three hours." Tamara sat on the ground. To be more precise, her legs gave out and the earth pulled her down. She noticed she was shivering. Probably from the continued tension she'd been under during the long walk, unable to shake her constant fear of the giant's return and afraid of the odd things she kept hearing and seeing.

At this point, she didn't care if a giant crashed through the trees, picked her up, and proclaimed a possessive, "Munno." She would take it as a sign to nap while someone else carried her around.

Thyel circled the clearing. "Tamara's right. This would make a good spot to camp. It'll be dark soon. Continuing to walk through unfamiliar territory when we can't see where to place our feet will not only get us lost, but turn deadly."

Jarrod shut his book. "Good idea." He put away his quill and shook his hand, flexing his fingers.

Hand cramping? Tamara thought sarcastically.

His quick look at her suggested he heard her quip. Could he hear her as easily as she felt his emotions? She was too exhausted to work it out. The weight of her body flopped her onto her back.

"We'll be stopping here then," Skye said and chuckled.

Eyes shut, Tamara listened to the rustle of their movements and quiet whispers.

The next time Tamara opened her eyes, it was dark. Skirts rustled beside her. Skye? "Where is everyone?"

"Fishing," Skye said. "Don't hold out hope for a tasty meal, though. I've heard a lot of shouts, but none were triumphant."

A robust fire crackled and popped not two arm-lengths away.

Tamara forced herself to sit up and toss off her chainmaille, unstrap her sword and set it aside. She should have taken off the chainmaille before sleeping. Her skin probably looked like a fish. Smothering groans as her painfully stiffened limbs protested each movement, she finally took off her boots.

"Did you magic that fire?" she asked Skye.

Her niece gave her a cautious glance. "No. Jarrod did."

Tamara nodded, wondering why Skye seemed so on guard. She was too weary to ask. She faced the flames, wrapping her arms around bent knees to keep them from flopping over.

Her niece continued to study her and then asked, "Would you have been upset if I said, Yes?"

"I would have said, Thank you."

"Truly?" Skye asked sounding pleased. A small smile appeared on her face. "I'd wondered."

"About what?"

"Jarrod said you didn't resent my magic," Skye murmured. "I guess he was right."

They had talked about her? "What else did he say?" she asked, unsure if she found the information pleasing or irritating. Why had they been talking about her?

Skye gave her another under-the-lash, sideways look. "This and that."

"Such as?"

"He seems to think you miss your father."

The answer shocked Tamara, not only because he would say such an odd thing, but because the statement rang with an uncomfortable clang of truth.

"Does he read your thoughts, too?" Tamara asked.

"Jarrod? He can read thoughts?"

Did Skye's shocked question mean Tamara was the sole recipient of his special attention? "Why would I miss my father?" She returned to their earlier, less troublesome, topic. "He could have saved himself if he wanted to. He chose to end his life."

"Tamara, how can you say that?" Skye asked. "Grandfather was murdered while he slept."

"He was more powerful than your brother, Skye. He should have seen what was going to happen and made plans to safeguard his family. He chose not to. Anyway, I don't wish to discuss my father. Or Jarrod."

They fell into an awkward silence.

Tamara's legs were pleasantly heated by the time the men returned.

"No fish," Thyel said in a disgruntled tone.

"Got too dark too fast for us to be able to see any," Fane explained. "And it's too late now to hunt for rabbits or pheasants."

They settled for what Jarrod could muster from his magical travel pack. He obligingly took out flatbread and broke it, the pieces growing with each break.

As grateful as Tamara was for the bread and his always-filled, always-cool, drinking water, she felt deprived of a proper fare. She couldn't remember the last time she'd eaten a decent meal—one with roasted meat and salty gravy. More so than that core need, what she missed desperately was a bath.

The nearby lake lapping by the shore only added to her misery. "Is it too late to wash up?"

"I wouldn't risk it," Fane said. "The lake dips dangerously by the shoreline."

"I know how to swim," Tamara said.

"Are there monsters in the lake?" Skye asked.

Tamara's heart thumped in alarm. Isa already had giants and dragons. Wasn't that enough? As filthy as she felt, she wasn't going to set a toe into waters that might have something gigantic lurking beneath the surface.

Still, she looked longingly in the direction of the water, and sighed. If dangerous creatures lurked in those depths, the lake might as well be on Ryca as ten steps away for all the use it would do her.

"No monsters," Fane said

"Monsters or not, it's too dark to swim." Jarrod said.

"Don't know how to swim, Councilor?" Tamara asked.

"I hail from a desert community." He gave her an intense look and shivers that had nothing to do with exhaustion spun up her spine. Why did he have such an effect on her! "Since my people are especially cognizant of the importance of bodies of water, we're all taught to swim at an early age."

As he spoke, Tamara saw a group of young children, all dark skinned, laughing as they rushed into a spring in the center of an oasis, splashing each other with the clear water. Along with the image a sense of peace and well-being washed over her.

She sighed. As much as she hated Jarrod invading her mind, the emotions he sent her way always filled her with peace. She unconsciously savored each moment and groaned in disappointment as the emotion washed away like a receding wave.

She wanted to lie back. No, she wanted to float on her back on that cool lake behind them and feel as clean and fresh and beautiful. Not filthy and smelly, with greasy hair plastered to her forehead and fishy pock marks on her skin.

Most unfairly, Jarrod didn't seem in the least rumpled. His black locks gleamed like silk in the firelight, as if freshly washed. She'd bet her last piece of bread he smelled nice, too.

When he glanced at her with a narrow-eyed suspicious look, she realized she was leaning toward him, nostrils flaring. Flushing, she lay back, disgruntled.

"We can wash in the lake before we set off in the morning," Skye suggested sympathetically.

Tamara stared at the night sky. Tomorrow couldn't come fast enough.

Chapter 9

UNABLE TO REST, TAMARA stood and turned to Fane. "Are the lakes on Isa dangerous or not?"

"Not this near the mountains. Want me to keep watch while you wash up?" he asked, getting to his feet. Then he flushed, probably realizing she would likely be naked.

"Why don't I join you?" Thyel's eyes brightened as he, too, came to his feet. "Then we won't have to worry about your safety."

It was Tamara's turn to flush at the suggestive look in his gaze. She'd welcomed his attentions recently. Tonight, she wasn't so sure.

Jarrod stood abruptly. "If you're set on this, I'll check the shoreline to ensure it's safe. Once you go in, we'll all keep an eye out for trouble."

His hidden command for Thyel to stay away from Tamara rang loud and clear. Jarrod headed for the shoreline, and a scowling Thyel followed him. Fane grinned, seeming to enjoy the silently sparring men as he went after them.

Tamara turned to Skye. "Will you come into the water, too? We'll be safe with those three on watch."

"Not to swim, but I might wash by the shore. I don't know how to swim. Never learned while in Nadym, and never had the opportunity to in Tibor." With a smile, Skye added, "I'll make sure you have privacy."

"Thank you." Tamara made a mental note to be sure to teach Skye how to swim once they returned home. She was done with avoiding her family.

The water appeared still and black as the night sky. No ripples disturbed its silent beauty. No breeze stirred the still air. With so many to keep watch, Tamara felt perfectly safe.

Behind nearby bushes, she shed all but her shift, which she had worn tucked beneath her tunic and trousers. Then she ran toward the water and waded in. As Fane had warned, within five steps, she was chin deep and shivering.

Skye prudently stayed kneeling by the shoreline, only splashing her face and arms and legs. The men lazed by a rocky outcrop beneath the shelter of a large willow.

Tamara dipped until she was completely submerged and then came up, gasping for air, relishing the cool clean water washing over her. The lake had doused the heat from her hot skin and soon enough, her body became accustomed to the change in heat level.

Feeling contented, Tamara swam to the center of the lake. Though she had hesitated at the idea of Thyel joining her, if Jarrod had offered to come in, she would have been thrilled. A little smile tugged at her mouth at the idea of the studious historian stripping down, exposing the hidden muscles she'd felt under his robes and plunging naked into the cold water.

She turned over to float on her back and gazed at the vast open sky where the three moons held celestial reign.

She shut her eyes and imagined Jarrod beside her, one arm extended beneath the water to slide boldly along her back. The idea of urging him to come to her rescue began to appeal.

Suppressing a mischievous grin, she opened her mouth to call out to him when a breeze wafted by, tingling her skin with its warm breath. Something obscured the moonlight shining on her face. She flashed opened her eyes.

High overhead, a dragon coasted. Its wingspan obscured one of the Three Sisters and stirred the peaceful lake with a hot draft.

Her slightest movement or sound might alert the giant beast to her presence, and to those on shore. Her blood pounded like a cresting wave and the shout in her throat died. She stilled her movements, sank as much as she could beneath the surface and held her breath.

As if sensing her below, the dragon began a lazy descent, circling the lake. As it descended, all around her, water rippled like her nerves.

In the moonlight, she caught a gleam of glinting scales.

"Tamara!" Skye shouted, a desperate warning.

It wasn't needed. Even in the dark, she knew the bronze dragon had seen her by the way it changed its flight pattern. Then it flew directly toward her.

Tamara sank completely beneath the surface.

The dragon swooped low until its talons skimmed the surface of the lake above her head but not deep enough to touch her. Then, with a bellow loud enough to wake the dead, it soared back up. The beat of its wings churned the lake into waves before it disappeared over the horizon.

Tamara surfaced, gasping for breath, her heart hammering a mad tempo. She had stared death in the face and it had gazed back.

Confused and shaken, her legs and arms felt too weak to take her to shore. She didn't even realize Jarrod was beside her, his arms tugging her to the safety of land.

She lay on the shoreline, shaking, still stunned by that incredible encounter.

"Are you hurt?" Jarrod asked, fear written clearly on his face. His searching hands skimming over her intimately brought her back to reality.

Thyel's gaze swung down from searching the sky and he grinned appreciatively, studying what parts of her the moonlight clearly revealed.

She covered herself with her arms and bent knees. In the wet shift, she might as well be naked.

Skye ran toward where Tamara had left her clothes and then returned with her aunt's tunic and trousers.

"Everyone turn around," Tamara demanded. Once they did, she pulled off her wet shift and dressed in just the tunic and trousers. "You can turn around now."

"Fane, come back to shore," Skye called out.

Only then did Tamara notice the young would-be dragon rider was standing up to his knees in the lake, staring up at the moonlit horizon.

"That was a dragon," Fane finally said as he sloshed back to shore.

"I know." Skye spoke in a matter-of-fact tone, though a wide grin seemed permanently pasted on her face.

"We'd been walking all day in dragon territory and not seen a single one," Fane said. "I'd begun to wonder if the giants had destroyed all of Isa's dragons. I was too worried to voice my fear."

"Unfounded fear," Skye said.

"Obviously I was wrong," he said.

"Obviously."

Tamara couldn't help herself. She hugged Skye. "We're going to find Bevan."

"Yes, we are," Skye said with absolute certainty.

"I felt him in my head," Fane said. "In my head! He was searching for something. Someone."

"You, perhaps?" Thyel asked, with a mocking laugh.

"No," Fane replied, sounding perfectly serious. "Not me. Someone else. Another dragon."

• • • •

AT FIRST LIGHT, HANDS shaking, heart thumping like a giant's foot stomps, Jarrod pulled Falcon's Tome toward him. The first page was blank. He'd known that from looking at it the day before. Yesterday, a good twenty pages had gone blank. Jarrod had hoped after spending a day away from whatever dark magic affected Ryca, the tome might have recovered. His fingers frantically flicked page after page - a good half of the tome was now bare, as if it had never been written upon.

He shut the book. Why had leaving Ryca not stopped this endless plundering of his people's work? His magic, which had faltered on Ryca, worked well on Isa. So, why did his people's words continue to vanish? The question bounced around in his mind without rest as his group stirred.

Though Tamara remained curled into a ball, apparently not yet willing to greet a new day, on her other side, Skye sat up and stretched. Across from them, Fane rose and glanced at Jarrod with a face still creased by sleep. Thyel, too, was awake, but chose to watch them all without comment. He had the look of a predator. Jarrod frowned, wishing for the hundredth time that this man had never come along with them.

"Is anything wrong?" Skye asked him.

Jarrod stood. "I need morning privacy," he mumbled and with Falcon's Tome hugged to his side, he went in the direction of the lake.

He must have sat, book clutched to his chest, unable to move for too long, for Skye suddenly sat beside him, her hand his arm. "Tell me what's wrong."

Despite not wanting to add to her worry about Bevan, his words tumbled out. "The Erovians were disappearing before I left. Now our work vanishes from Falcon's Tome. Skye, what if my world as I know it is not there when we return to Ryca?"

"Show me what's happening to the book," she said.

He handed the book over.

After the fifth empty page, she sat staring at the blank sheet for a moment. Then she raised her hand, palm up and a tiny Light ball formed.

"What are you doing?" Jarrod asked, more from curiosity than any real sense of hope.

"The strength of my magic is to find things. Let's see if I can discover the whereabouts of your words."

"Do you think you can?" Excitement spiked his tone.

In answer, she dropped the Light ball onto the page. It rolled in a zigzag fashion from one side of the book to the other, like a hound seeking out a scent. The pages began to flutter, turning until one with words appeared. There, the search Light's movement slowed. With infinite patience, the Light rose, fell and circled each stroke of each letter and then stopped and lay unmoving in the middle of the page.

Jarrod's hopes deflated. He opened his mouth to say, "Thanks for trying," when the little Light leaped off the page and hovered before their faces. Then it burst into a blinding spray and fell backwards, pulling Jarrod along with it.

He found himself in a land of darkness, of nothing. Complete and absolute emptiness. He couldn't see where he stood, or if he stood on anything. Or how to get back to where he'd been. He swung around, heart pounding in fear when from out of nowhere, a cacophony of voices bellowed, "OUT!"

Something picked him up and flung him violently, sending him sailing over an immense chasm. His vision cleared to show he still sat beside Skye on the grassy shore. Had he imagined that moment of being somewhere else? His body still shivered and trembled as if the source of all Darkness had swallowed him. Then spat him out.

Skye stared at him with confused eyes.

He rubbed the sides of his ears to clear the painful high-pitched ringing. "Do you hear that?"

She looked at him with grave eyes. "What?"

"A million voices ordering me to get out."

"Odd. When my Light flared, I had the impression it dove in search of your words into someplace frightening. Then it died. Before that, I received a word."

His heart leaped in anticipation. "From where? What was the word?"

"I didn't get a sense of a specific location, or of people, as you seemed to have. Just, 'Beginning.' Saying that fills me with dread, Jarrod. I don't think it's a good place."

"Wherever the record of Ryca's history has gone," he said, "frightening or not, it's my duty to retrieve it."

"But how?"

"I have to find a way. Erovians record the passage of lives in Falcon's Tome. Stories of people to preserve Ryca's past. I have to find a way to bring back the missing words or lives as we lived them may never have existed."

"How is that possible?"

"Everything, everyone is dependent on what happened in the past. The disappearance of my historians is the start of our world changing beyond recognition."

"We need Bevan's help. If anyone can discover a way to restore Falcon's Tome, he can." Skye closed the tome and handed it back to him. "This means finding my brother is more imperative now than ever."

They broke camp shortly after. Jarrod picked up his pack, his mind whirling about the destiny of Falcon's Tome. Ahead of him, Thyel took Tamara's hand. Though she soon shook off his hold, Thyel's proprietary behavior irked Jarrod. Perhaps because the problem with the tome had already vexed his humor, he had the urge to walk up to Thyel and punch him.

"Calmmmm," he murmured to himself, repeating the word until his temper settled.

Skye fell into easy step beside him.

Fane ran to catch up to them.

Around the campfire last night, they couldn't quiet the young lad from talking about the dragon encounter. Only Tamara had slept through the lively discourse, seemingly too worn out to let any noise bother her.

She had looked peaceful in sleep, her face relaxed, the frown lines gentled, her breathing soft and even. Once, late into the night, he'd heard her whimper. He'd turned sideways, bent his arm until he could rest his head on his hand and stared at her by the flickering shadows of the dying fire.

When her cries mounted he sent soothing thoughts her way, of a wispy wind brushing her golden hair, of the two of them sitting side by side on a mat under a bright blue tent gazing at a desert landscape, the sands shifting gently, the air pleasantly warm and restful. Her cries faded and her exhausted body carried her into deeper sleep.

"I've thought a great deal about that dragon last night," Fane said.

Jarrod hid a smile.

"I've come to the conclusion it's the one I'm meant to bond with. I believe it flew by us because it sensed my presence. If so, this portends well for a natural bonding."

"One that could take us off Isa and grant you long life?" Skye asked.

Thyel dropped back. "What's all the excitement?"

"Fane thinks the dragon from last night might be a natural bond for him," Skye said.

"I thought you couldn't tell that until you actually bonded." Thyel's tone and raised eyebrow suggested profound doubt.

"True," Fane said, "it's not easy to tell for sure until after the bonding. The fact I sensed his thoughts is a wonderful sign, sir. My master sensed his dragon before they met formally. His was a lifetime bond!"

The words warmed Jarrod and despite his best efforts to remain rational, hope again circled his heart like a purring sand cat.

Tamara, too, joined them, her eyes eager.

This news meant that not only would they no longer be trapped on Isa but, once they found Bevan, she could return home. To marry.

Jarrod glanced at Thyel with distaste. In all likelihood, she would choose this man to present to her mother.

He shook his head at his train of thought. He'd lost his perspective. Who Tamara married was none of his affair, other than to record the event in his tome. Yet, the thought of her and Thyel together churned the acid in his empty stomach. That reminded him they'd all left without eating.

He fished in his pack for another flatbread. "Anyone hungry?"

They stopped for a short rest and passed the food around. Jarrod ate his portion, and then opened his tome and took out his quill. His obsession to write grew with each passing moment. Perhaps he wished to counter the effect of the gradual eroding of his people's missing words. If so, this was a sad substitute, but he could not refrain from indulging in the practice.

"I don't see how you can be so sure this one dragon is the right one?" Thyel gestured to Fane with his piece of bread.

"I might be mistaken, sir," Fane said gravely, "but I sensed this dragon's thoughts without any ceremony of bonding. That is promising. I've heard tell that sometimes dragons call to a human who is its proper match, even across realms."

Tamara drew in a sharp breath.

Jarrod glanced at her. "Something the matter?"

Her eyes filled with confusion, she shook her head.

"Have you been getting such a call?" Skye asked Fane.

"No," Fane admitted, "and that could be a fanciful dragon tale the keepers pass on."

"Tell us more of this bonding process," Jarrod said.

"The ceremony is convoluted," Fane said. "The dragon's emotions – its fears, anxieties and pleasures - all become absorbed by the human. The dragon takes a drink of the human's feelings. This first step is to ensure safeguards are in place. Most of my lessons were about keeping my mind and thoughts protected, separate. Else, during the bonding, the most dominant mind could take over."

"Is that possible?" Thyel asked. "Can a man control a dragon?"

"It's forbidden," Fane replied. "There have been tales of humans and dragons effecting such a dark binding. It's always ended in disaster for both. Dragons, especially, take high offence to being constrained."

"Is it during the bonding ceremony that a human begins to sense the dragon's thoughts?" Tamara asked.

"Yes. Yet, last night, for a moment, I was up there with that dragon, searching for someone important."

"You still don't know who though, do you?" Skye asked.

"No."

"You said before that this human-dragon bonding also affected the dragons?" Jarrod asked. "In what way?"

"Something in the bonding accelerates breeding in the dragons. My master didn't understand the process, just that over the centuries, it's proven true."

"Did the bonding have an effect on dragon society as a whole?" Jarrod asked.

"The family lines of dragons that successfully bonded with humans became highly placed members of the dragon council. The one that could bond for a lifetime, that dragon's family traditionally ruled the dragons of Isa."

They set off again, listening to Fane talk of dragons and their ways. A crash through the shrubbery ahead alerted them to trouble.

A man raced toward them down their narrow path.

"Traveler, may we speak with you," Fane called out.

"Run!" he shouted and shoved his way through their group. He ran off behind them, arms flailing

"What's he running from?" Tamara asked in fear. "A giant?"

Shouts came from ahead.

"Whatever it is, it's coming our way." Jarrod shut his book. "Take cover!"

They scrambled to either side of the pathway. Men raced through the woods, shouting. Behind them, branches snapped and hoofs pounded a thunderous rhythm. Soon, a herd of sturdy looking elks tore through the path, fleeing in all directions. One charged directly at Tamara. Before Jarrod could go to her aid, Thyel pulled her out of harm's way.

Jarrod herded Fane and Skye in the opposite direction as another frightened animal charged by. A fallen branch tripped him. Tumbling off balance, Jarrod reached for the other two, hoping to whisk them all magically to safety. A hoof smashed onto his extended left arm. A sharp *crack* and a flash of pain shot up to his shoulder. He cried out.

Hands grabbed and pulled him out of the stampeding animals' path. He gritted his teeth as breath-searing throbs swept through his body in waves.

Once the panicked animals swept by, Tamara rushed over to his side.

Jarrod tenderly nursed his left arm, but even that slight movement sent a jagged spike rushing up to his shoulder and brought embarrassing tears. To avoid her stricken gaze, he glanced around at the rest of the damage the stampede had caused, and spotted his trampled book, its pages scattered.

"Falcon's Tome!" he cried out. The loss of the tome eclipsed his physical discomfort. He reached for the pages, but Tamara firmly held him in place.

"Skye, Fane, collect Jarrod's book and pages. Thyel, help me hold him still." Gingerly, she inspected his injury.

With his entire left side aching, Jarrod followed her gaze. Blood stained his white sleeve and a piece of bone protruded angrily through his dark skin.

Fane came over, clutching a few sheets to his chest to stare at Jarrod, aghast. "It's broken."

"Yes, and needs setting." Tamara met Jarrod's gaze with such tender sympathy, he almost fainted with surprise.

"Whatever frightened those villagers and animals is probably headed our way," Thyel said. "There's no time to tend to Jarrod."

"He's right," Jarrod said through gritted teeth, trying to control the pain so he could think. "Your safety comes first."

"Could you magic us elsewhere?" Fane asked.

Jarrod tried and the world went black. He regained consciousness in time to hear Tamara speak.

"Magic's out then," she said. "He can barely stay awake. The rest of you go. I'll stay with him."

"No," Jarrod and Skye spoke together.

"I'm not leaving either of you." Skye glared at her aunt.

A loud roar vibrated his eardrums. One of the elk, separated from its herd, bellowed in fear as it raced by. In its wake, a swath of fire parted the trees.

"Stay low," Thyel whispered. "Too late to go anywhere now."

The elk jumped to clear some low bushes. A green dragon, with shimmering scales, plunged down and plucked the elk in mid-leap. It then swooped up, the force of its wing beats bending nearby trees and flattening Jarrod to the ground.

The dragon's flight faltered, its startlingly iridescent wings flapping rapidly to keep it airborne. The elk still clamped in its powerful jaws, it turned and hovered, directing its disconcertingly golden gaze straight at them.

"It's seen us!" Jarrod shouted. "Run!"

• • • •

AN INTENSE HUNGER TORE through Tamara's innards. Her legs gave out and she sank to her knees.

The dragon, too, lost its balance. Still clutching its meal in its jaws, it crashed, landing in a contortion of wings and limbs and broken branches.

Falcon's Tome in her arms, Skye knelt beside Tamara and whispered, "What should we do?"

Thyel gestured to Fane. "Time you lived up to your part of this journey, boy. Go talk to it."

Fane handed the sheets he'd gathered to Skye and walked toward the dragon.

After barely two crunches, the dragon swallowed the elk and glanced again in their direction.

With her stomach rumbling and rolling, Tamara searched for Jarrod's pack. She wanted to tear into it in search of a flat bread but the pack was nowhere in sight.

Frustrated, she looked up in time to see Fane stumble back and waited for him to say, "It's hungry, so very hungry."

Instead, he appeared confused. "That's the wrong dragon. That's not the bronze from last night. I sense nothing from this green."

Stunned, Tamara stared at him. How could Fane be impervious to that intense need to eat?

The dragon let out a great roar.

Tamara looked over. *It's glaring at me!*

As if she were to blame for its lack of sustenance.

"She's obviously hungry," Tamara said. "We must find her more food."

"Her?" Skye asked in surprise.

"Hard to tell if it's male or female," Fane said. "Though the face does seem feminine, with the shorter ears and rounded forehead."

"She's probably looking at us as her next meal," Thyel said.

"Dragons don't eat humans," Fane said in protest. "At least they haven't in a long time."

"What makes you think she's hungry?" Skye asked.

"She looks weak," Tamara said. "Why else would she have tumbled down like that? If we find something to feed her, maybe she'll leave us be."

She looked around desperate to find the green dragon something to eat.

"Tamara's right," Jarrod said. "Get her more food."

"How?" Skye asked. "And what about you, Jarrod? We can't leave you here, helpless. What if she decides you'd make a tasty meal, lying here all bloody?"

"I'll stay," Thyel said. "My mother was a midwife, I know how to set his arm." Already squatted, he tore off strips of cloth from Jarrod's robe and tied it above the wound.

The bleeding did seem to slow down after that move.

"The rest of you, find that dragon some food," Thyel ordered.

Chapter 10

TAMARA WAS IMPRESSED with Thyel's take-charge attitude. He seemed confident he knew what to do about Jarrod's injury. As for the green dragon, she suspected berries and fruit would not satisfy her intense hunger.

"How do we capture an animal big enough to satisfy that dragon?" Skye asked. "The elk she gobbled up didn't seem to be enough."

"Those men who ran by us," Fane said, absently, his eyes still focused on the dragon, "they looked like hunters."

Tamara turned Fane to face them. "So?"

"They weren't carrying any weapons, but that could be because they dropped them in their fright."

"Yes! A weapon would help us bring down another elk," Tamara agreed, her mind racing at the possibilities. Her sword was good for close work, not long-distance hunting.

"Go." Jarrod's eyes squinted with great pain. "Find what will appease that beast. Quickly."

"Skye," Tamara said, "use your talent to help us locate a suitable weapon."

"Of course!" She held up her hand and released a ball of Light. It flew between the trees in the direction the hunters had come from. She set Falcon's Tome beside Jarrod and raced after her Light ball.

Tamara turned to Fane only to find the boy headed back in the dragon's direction. With a resigned sigh, her stomach rolling like an angry ocean, she ran after her niece.

"Over here," Skye called.

In a clearing about sixty yards away, her search Light hovered above a cache of fallen spears and a crossbow.

Skye chose the crossbow while Tamara picked the sturdiest of the spears. Not that she knew how to use one. Nor had Tamara ever killed anything before, and doubted Skye had either. She had an advantage over her niece. In some mysterious fashion, the dragon's hunger had become Tamara's. Finding and killing prey were now her greatest needs.

"Shall we?" Skye's eyes shone with excitement.

Tamara gave a firm nod, scanning the horizon for a target.

Her niece held up her hand and her ball of Light retuned to rest in her palm. "Find me an elk."

"That dragon seemed ravenous," Tamara warned.

"Two large elks." Skye set her Light on the hunt. Her niece's magic led them directly to their quarry.

As if someone else controlled her actions, Tamara flung her spear. The weapon flew with incredible speed and astonishing accuracy. The animal dropped to the ground.

Tamara stared at the result of her throw in shock. How could she have managed that? She'd never ever lifted a spear.

The other elk gave a startled cry and leaped for the cover of the woods.

The search ball relentlessly followed. Skye raced after it, crossbow clutched to one side and several arrows held in her spare hand.

Tamara hesitated between following her niece and dragging her kill back to the dragon.

A protesting bellow settled her quandary. She ran up and lifted the elk by its hind legs but could barely budge it.

HUNGRY!

Suddenly, Tamara could haul her kill as if it were a lightweight doe. She dragged the carcass through the brush. The hot sun beat down on the back of her neck and perspiration poured freely. She had barely made it to the edge of the clearing when the dragon lumbered over.

Tamara jumped out of the way as the beast's jaws chomped down on the elk.

"She's magnificent, isn't she?" Fane asked from the shadow of a nearby tree.

The dragon's head swiveled toward the boy and a large glinting amber eye studied him before the gaze turned to Tamara.

With a thoughtful expression, the green chewed and swallowed. As its hunger lessened, the golden glance changed from imperative to merely impatient. *MORE!*

The command slammed into Tamara's mind and she winced. Hunger lessoned, but not vanquished. A glance at Fane, who looked relaxed and awestruck, suggested he'd not heard the order.

"I have to find Skye and that other elk," she told him. "Keep an eye on the green."

She sprinted around the beast whose forelimbs were the size of massive tree trunks. They were also bloody and torn. No wonder she'd had trouble bringing down her own food. No other obvious wounds on the rest of her to indicate she'd been in a fight. Odd.

Tamara raced to the other side of the clearing, an unpleasant thought shadowing her. Could this green have been trapped somewhere? Considering her ravenous hunger, it must have been for a long while. Her sympathy stretched toward the dragon, for she wouldn't wish being imprisoned on anyone.

Cracking branches and the sounds of a struggle led her toward the woods.

Skye had captured her elk, too. It wasn't dead. It struggled, bleeding and thrashing about on the ground. A couple of crossbow bolts stuck out of its right side.

Skye stood beside her prize, crying as she tried to wind the crossbow up for another shot.

Tamara hurried to help her niece.

Snapping trunks warned of the green's approach. With one bite, she put the terrified elk out of its misery.

Tamara glanced up with vengeance in her heart that she'd chosen to help the dragon over her niece. *You'd better be satisfied now.*

The dragon licked her jaws, eyes gleaming with satisfaction.

Tamara's stomach churned, but in fear this time. She had allowed that animal to control her. She hadn't resisted her pull. In fact, the urge to oppose hadn't even occurred.

"It's over," she whispered, pulling Skye into a tight hug. The girl was shivering.

THANK YOU! The words resonated along with an intense sense of gratitude.

Tamara instinctively closed her thoughts and backed away, frightened by this beast's ability to overwhelm her with its thoughts and emotions. Her needs had not mattered; Skye's needs had been eclipsed; only the dragon's intense hunger had driven her actions.

HUNGRY LONG TIME, came a mournful thought.

Tamara gave a glare over her shoulder. How did the dragon do that? Read her as easily as Jarrod seemed to. At least he mostly pretended he couldn't do it. He never ordered her about. Only soothed her when she was troubled.

Meanwhile, she'd blindly followed the dragon's commands as if she possessed no self-will. The realization took her to the first moment she found herself trapped within the time spell. Unable to move, her mind screaming at her to flee, but her body under the complete control of her mother's spell.

She had sworn to never allow anyone to do that to her again. This dragon would not rule her now. Mentally, she slammed shut imaginary gates until she could no longer sense the beast's feelings.

It had already forced her to kill. Worse, she'd encouraged Skye to attempt the same. Look at the result!

Skye, who loved all animals, would never be the same after this experience.

Jarrod, weak and hurt, she'd left him in the uncertain care of Thyel, of all people. She'd sensed animosity between the two men.

Fane, following this dragon around like a lovesick fool, wasn't there to ensure Thyel treated Jarrod well.

"I have to check on Jarrod," she said to Skye.

Her niece nodded and together, they raced back to the men. They arrived to discover an unconscious Jarrod. His arm was strapped to a sturdy piece of wood with bandages made from strips of Jarrod's torn robe.

Thyel looked up from his work. "You were successful?"

Tamara nodded, releasing Skye to kneel by Jarrod's side. His arm looked as if it was set correctly. She breathed a sigh of relief.

Skye walked away a few paces to lean against a trunk, holding her stomach.

At Thyel's inquiring look, Tamara murmured, "She needs a little quiet. Will Jarrod be all right?"

"Yes. He lost consciousness when I set the bone. I made a paste from some herbs I recognized nearby to speed up the healing." Thyel turned to Fane, who had approached in the wake of the women. "Any luck talking to the dragon?"

The young lad shook his head. He turned to Tamara. "She seemed to be able to communicate with you though."

She almost screamed out, *Yes, I hear her!* But then she recalled Fane's earlier conversation about how only a "natural" bond could aid travel between realms. He'd said his ability to mind-touch with the bronze dragon from last night without the benefit of a bonding ceremony indicated a "natural" bond was possible. If so, that same logic applied to the green's ability to speak to Tamara. To control her actions.

At the idea of giving up her control to that dragon again, an iron fist clamped onto throat and strangled her words.

"Tamara?" Thyel looked at her with astonished eyes. "Could you really hear that dragon's thoughts?"

"No!" she croaked out. Unable to look at him or Fane, she focused on Jarrod. Gently, she touched his face. He was hot and feverish. Could he die if they didn't get off Isa?

With a touch, her sister Anna could easily heal him.

On Ryca.

A tear slid down Tamara's cheek as she realized what she must do to save Jarrod. Her lips quivered in protest.

Skye's hand came to rest on Tamara's shoulder. "Our best bet is for Fane to find and bond with the one from last night. He seemed to sense its thoughts so he's the dragon most likely to fly us out of this world."

A huge weight rolled off Tamara's shoulders. Unable to help herself, she rose and hugged her niece. "I'm glad you're feeling better."

Skye hesitated, as if shocked at Tamara's rare show of affection. Then she fiercely hugged her back.

"You two must have satisfied the green's hunger," Thyel said, "else she wouldn't be here looking at us so placidly."

Tamara broke away to turn to where he pointed. The green dragon sat hunched not ten feet away, watching them. No, not them, *her*.

"What does she want now?" Skye asked in an angry tone, unconsciously mimicking Tamara's turbulent feelings.

"I don't think she's hungry anymore." Fane walked up and tentatively extended his hand toward the green. The dragon pulled back, a haughty eye ridge rising. Once she weighed and judged the young man worthy, she lowered her snout until it brushed Fane's palm.

"She likes you," Thyel said with a note of envy. He, too, approached. The dragon retreated and stayed back. With a disappointed frown, he returned to their side. "What's our next move then?"

"I must find the bronze," Fane replied.

The green roared. The sound reverberated in Tamara's body with a sense of urgency and fear.

"I'm not killing anything else for her," Skye said. "She can hunt for her own food from now on."

Tamara, too, refused to heed the call, though she sensed hunger was no longer the problem.

The dragon's long tail swished and her ears flattened.

Tamara ignored those clear signs of the green's displeasure, deciding that if this dragon needed to communicate with them, she could talk to Fane.

Yet, questions continued to prod. Why had the green been so hungry? Who could keep a dragon trapped for so long? And why?

She groaned, not wanting to think about the dragon's problem. Yet, if the green feared something, her presence could draw that problem straight to them. Jarrod was in no shape to face any more disturbances. They needed to know what to prepare for next. To safeguard Jarrod.

Tamara slid her mental gate open a sliver. Enough to voice one question. *What's wrong?*

DANGER. MUST HIDE!

Great! She slammed closed her mental gates. If the green insisted on staying with them, they were all in trouble.

She frowned at the dragon. In the corner of her eyes, something slithered away into the branches of a nearby tree. A wisp of olive-colored fluff that winked in the wind, as if something small and swift hid in the tree's thick canopy. "What was that?"

Everyone looked over, including the dragon.

"Where?" Thyel asked.

Tamara walked over but could see nothing in the tree to account for the movement she'd seen.

"I don't see anything," Skye said from beside here. "What did you see?"

"Something green and fluffy."

"It might have been wind flicking leaves," Fane said.

"That dragon's making me jittery too," Skye added.

Tamara cringed at the sympathy in her niece's eyes and turned away. "Yes, that's probably it."

A glance at the green and the dragon's urgency to hide immediately returned. How to convince her group to move? Then her glance fell on Jarrod's resting form.

"We need to find shelter," she said. "A place where Jarod can heal while we help Fane hunt for his bronze dragon."

"Yes," Fane said. "Dragging a wounded man around would do him no good and slow us down."

"Skye, would you be able to locate a safe place for us to set up a camp?" Tamara asked.

Her niece nodded and held up her hand. A ball of Light formed.

HIDE ME! The dragon's plea was swift.

Tamara started. How had the dragon broken through her mental barriers? Still, the request resonated with such terror, Tamara clutched at Skye's arm before her niece released her Light.

"Make it a big place." She glared at the dragon over her shoulder for yet again taking mental liberties without permission. "One large enough to hold the green, in case she remains as friendly as this."

Skye smiled for the first time since the elk incident and the rigid knots of tension in Tamara's tense shoulders loosened.

"Skye," Fane looked at her hopefully, "could you locate my dragon with one of your Light balls?"

"Probably. Once we settle Jarrod, we can search together." She set her search Light aloft. The green dragon blew on it, sending the Light flying to the side. Skye laughed. With a whirl of her forefinger and a chant, she directed the Light ball to find a safe place to stay.

It bobbed and rose high up into the air. Then the Light twirled rapidly, as if in impatience.

Skye looked at the dragon speculatively. "It would be faster to follow my Light through the air than us walking. Easier on Jarrod, too. Do you think she might let us ride her?"

"Fane," Thyel said, "you're the dragon expert. See if you can convince the green to take us."

Fane looked at the dragon and formally made the request.

The dragon stared back with a blank look.

He tried hand gestures. Finally, he shrugged and turned to them. "I can't seem to make her understand."

Tamara sighed. She didn't want to further her relationship with this dragon. Jarrod's pallor beneath his dark skin suggested Skye was right, though. Carrying him would do more harm than good. The ride on the dragon would be easier, marginally, than bouncing him along their every step.

Her back still turned to the dragon, she lowered her barriers and made her request.

Would you please carry us to safety? To a place to hide?

HALLA!

Tamara cringed as the word slammed into her mind. It was the green's name.

"Are you all right?" Skye asked.

"Yes." Tamara rubbed at her temple. "Just a little headache."

HALLA!

"I know," Tamara shouted.

"Know what?" Thyel asked.

Tamara blushed at his confused look. "Sorry, I meant I know what we could try. If one of us climbs up on her, she might understand."

Thyel gave a nod. "Fane, you try. She likes you."

Halla, Tamara watched Fane approach the dragon, *would you let us ride you?*

TAMARA!

The name flashed to her in triumph, as if the dragon was proud to have plundered that bit of information.

She disliked this game. *Yes, that's my name. Will you take us to where Skye's Light ball leads?*

FLY, TAMARA, AND FRIENDS.

The dragon knelt, giving Fane easier access to her bent forelimb.

"She's going to let us ride her," Fane said in excitement. "I'll go first and then you can hand Jarrod up."

"We can use my Light to lead her to where we want to go," Skye added. "She seems to like to play with it."

Tamara bent to help Thyel pick up Jarrod.

"Be careful," Thyel warned. "Else I'll have to reset that arm and I don't think the Erovian will thank me for it."

He took Jarrod's upper body while Tamara lifted his legs. Jarrod, barely conscious, made it difficult for Thyel to climb up and still hold onto his patient, and the greater weight of their burden fell on Tamara.

Jarrod awoke with a scream.

Tamara's legs turned to mush at the pain in his voice. Thankfully, he again lost consciousness.

The dragon sent a profound wave of sympathy toward Tamara and a boost of strength straightened her legs. She was able to lift Jarrod back up. She'd taken no more than two steps when Halla's snout gave her bottom a gentle push up.

They made it to the top and Tamara sat cradling Jarrod's head against her shoulder, cushioning him as much as she could. She felt proud to be able to help the normally self-sufficient Jarrod. Gently stroking his cheek, she sent a silent, *Thank You*, to Halla.

WELCOME! the green replied sounding happy that Tamara seemed happy.

Tamara waited for everyone to settle down around her. Now she thought of it, she had been so careful to push her family away, afraid they would try to control her behavior, she couldn't recall anyone ever asking for her help. Except for Skye, and Bevan.

She had let both of them down.

FIND BEVAN?

The question startled Tamara. Then her guilt at not using this dragon to find her nephew, at wanting to wait for Fane to bond with another, seared her flesh.

"Are we ready?" Skye asked from in front of her.

"Yes," Thyel replied from behind.

Not yet, Tamara said to the dragon. *Later.* If Fane's quest to find his bronze dragon proved useless, she would have no choice but to confess to this special relationship evolving between her and green.

WHEN? Halla asked.

Tamara studiously shut her mind to the continued mental intrusion. Perhaps she should post a sign that said, "Do not enter! Private Property."

A narrow-eyed backward glare was her reward for that ungracious thought.

Skye brought her Light around and thankfully distracted the disgruntled green. The dragon rose into the air, her flapping wings creating an air current as she raised them higher than the surrounding canopy of the trees.

Tamara's stomach sank. She instinctively clamped her legs tight around the dragon's side and held tight to Jarrod. If she tipped, it would take them both over the side. She didn't like this sensation of being off the ground, unbalanced and out of control.

Thyel's arm wrapped around her middle. "I've got you," he whispered in her ear.

The thought comforted her.

Jarrod leaned into her shoulder, bringing with him the uniquely enticing blend of velum, ink and Jarrod. The aromas made her smile and hold him tighter, laying her cheek against his hot forehead.

Fane, who sat behind Skye, leaned around her, looking in every direction.

At Skye's bidding, her ball of Light flew a few feet in front of Halla. The green slashed at it with her foreleg. The Light leaped forward and whizzed away. With a challenging bellow, Halla followed, tilting dangerously.

Tamara slid to the right, the weight of Jarrod adding to the fall. *Steady!*

Thyel's hold became a vice grip, preventing any of them falling off.

The dragon straightened, and gave a sheepish look over her shoulder, before resuming her chase of Skye's Light ball.

The flight took them over a verdant forest, an open grass plain and then past black sharp-tipped mountains. As they rose higher to crest the range, the air became cooler. Tamara was glad of Thyel's hold and his warmth that shielded her back from the bite of the cool wind.

"We're almost there," Skye shouted. "There's a cave below." She pointed to a dark peak, not as tall as those that towered around it, but still higher than any mountain Tamara had ever climbed.

The Light ball swooped downward and Halla followed.

Tamara searched for the entrance among the black rocks and jagged peaks, but could see no opening. They flew lower where bushes and grasses covered shelves and dips. Still, they descended to where the mountain face was bounded by scraggly pine trees clawing up the cliff side.

The ball then disappeared into the trees.

The dragon hovered midair and then with a bellow of triumph, swooped into the trees.

Tamara covered Jarrod with her body before a branch knocked them both off.

Her companions shouted in alarm.

Having apparently seen where the Light went, Halla was determined on the chase. She ignored all calls for caution and dove for the barrier of brush. She landed in a skid onto a well-concealed ledge. Before anyone could dismount, Halla took off at a sprint into the opening.

Tamara's legs clamped down on the dragon until they finally came to a halt inside a larger inner cave.

Tamara instructed Halla to let them descend.

The green obligingly settled down on the ground.

Bringing Jarrod down safely was as painful and difficult as taking him up. Jarrod, unfortunately, came awake half way through their progress. Tamara was impressed by the colorful language streaming out of the normally composed and unflappable Chief Councilor of Erov.

Recording the history of Ryca must have taught him how to curse in several Rycan dialects. The more she discovered about Jarrod, little hints to his past and his character quirks, the more endearing he seemed. She had to smile at the irony of being attracted to a scholarly man who found her anything but studious.

"None of this is amusing, Tamara," Jarrod muttered in a curt tone.

She did her best to wipe her smile off her face.

Jarrod might disagree, but travelling by air had been the best plan. It would have taken days to get here otherwise. Next to impossible coming this high up a mountain. Halla had flown them over here in less than the time it would have taken to plan their route out. Once Jarrod was rested and his arm began to heal, he would forgive his friends for putting him through this traumatic ride.

Thyel was checking on Jarrod's arm. She had thought the two men disliked one another. Yet, Thyel had done a creditable job of binding Jarrod's broken arm and now showed inordinate care for his patient.

One of the reasons she'd wanted Thyel to come with them on this adventure had been to discover if he would be a good match as a husband. As adversity mounted, she began to doubt his sincere love for her, but since Jarrod's injury, Thyel proved to be a man she could rely on.

Was she wrong to constantly question his motives? Had she allowed her mother's distrust of Thyel to color her views of the man?

Beside Thyel, Jarrod was studying her in his quiet enigmatic way through pain-glazed eyes. Had he read her thoughts again? She shuttered the mind gates she used on Halla. Would they be any more effective against the Erovian?

Seeing him frown, she suspected she'd been successful.

Excellent!

It was completely unfair that he could read her while she couldn't pick up a single hint of what went through his convoluted brain. At least with the dragon, the exchange seemed mutual. That idea startled her and she glanced toward the green.

Halla had fallen asleep.

Chapter 11

TAMARA WAS ABLE TO easily pick up on the green's utter exhaustion, especially while she slept. The short flight must have overspent Halla's remaining energy.

Someone or something had prevented her from feeding. The dragon must not have been resting well either. Had she been too frightened to drop her guard? Did she do so now because she believed she was among friends?

A sense of satisfaction swept through her at the idea this dragon trusted her, and by extension, Skye and the others. Trusted them enough to be vulnerable in their presence.

She walked over to the green. Unable to help herself, she gently stroked the tender skin by the green's nostrils.

One golden eye opened a slit. Warm smoke puffed out and heated Tamara's arm. *ALL WELL WITH TAMARA?*

She frowned and withdrew her arm. What use were mental gates that never worked? *Go to sleep.*

Next, she went in search of Fane and Skye. They were at the edge of the ledge, speaking excitedly.

Skye turned to her. "It worked."

"What did?"

"Her magic Light," Fane said, sounding impressed. "It's discovered whereabouts of the bronze from last night. If we leave right now, we should be able to find him in no time at all."

The news thrilled Tamara. They would be able to leave Isa after all and get Jarrod real healing help.

"We should get the green to take us," Fane said. "It would be faster than walking."

"No," Tamara said.

"Why not?" Skye asked.

"The green's sleeping."

"Fane, you go wake her," Skye said.

"No!" Tamara drew the young lad back by hooking his elbow as he headed toward the entrance.

120

"Why not?" he asked.

Because Halla needs the rest. She couldn't say that. "We've all had a long day, and the sun looks to set soon. Too dangerous to travel after dark."

"But..." Fane began.

"I'm as anxious to find the other dragon, Fane. Let's do it in the morning, after we've rested. If Skye's Light found it now, it can find your dragon again then."

Fane reluctantly nodded. "All right."

"For tonight," she said, "we need food. I'm tired of eating Jarrod's flat bread."

"No more elk!" Skye warned.

"Maybe a rabbit?" Fane suggested. "I used to be good at hunting them as a child."

"I'll look for vegetables," Skye followed Fane down the mountainside.

Watching them head off, it occurred that those two were becoming fast friends. They were of a similar age, so their camaraderie shouldn't be a surprise. She could easily see why he was enchanted by her niece.

She smiled remembering Fane's awe the first time Skye used magic. In addition, the girl was brave, loyal and open to trying anything at least once. She had also entirely captured Jarrod's affections, and truth to tell, hers, too. Unlike Skye, making friends was not Tamara's strong suit.

Case in point, the ever-aloof Jarrod. She returned to check on him.

A quarter of the large cave was taken up by Halla, who was sitting up dazedly despite Tamara's order that she go to sleep. The green's tired eyes were half closed as she watched the human activity with little interest. On Tamara's entrance, Halla's gaze swung to her and never left. Eventually her weary head drooped to rest on her forelegs and her eyes closed as sleep overtook stubbornness.

Halla's continued interest in her was unsettling. How could such a strong connection have formed between them so quickly?

She approached Jarrod who looked as exhausted as Halla, only he was fully asleep. She deliberately lowered her tone while speaking, so as not to disturb either the sleeping man or dragon. "How is he?"

"Not well," Thyel said. "He lost a lot of blood. The flight reopened the wound. I've re-bandaged it."

"You've been good to him, Thyel. Thank you."

He gave her a thoughtful look. "You care for him a great deal, don't you, Tamara?"

Did she? She glanced at the restless sleeping form of the Chief Councilor of Erov. "He's my sister Saira's closest friend. Skye's, too, now."

She hadn't answered Thyel's question of how she felt about Jarrod. The answer wasn't an easy yes or no. What was the point of loving someone who barely noticed you?

As twilight descended, Jarrod's dark face was frighteningly pale. His soft curls glinted in the thin shafts of light that penetrated inside the cave and reflected off the polished stone walls. His perpetual frown was back, an indication of his deep pain.

She gestured for them to leave so their voices would not disturb the two sleepers. They walked outside and followed the sounds of trickling water to a nearby stream.

Tamara sank tiredly onto the ground. Thyel knelt beside her, closer to the stream so he could clean his hands, soiled from tending Jarrod.

The day's stresses had settled well into her tense shoulders, which now ached in protest. She doubted a night's sleep on this rocky ground would do them any good either. She rubbed at her neck. Thyel walked behind her, and after wiping his hands, kneaded the knots out of her tired neck muscles.

He had a firm touch that could be gentle when he chose. Yet, his close presence made her uncomfortable. She thanked him but twisted around so the contact would be broken.

He smiled and leaned on arms stretched backwards to support him. "Tell me how you met Jarrod."

"He helped my sister rescue my mother, brother and me from a time spell cast to protect us from Tamarisk, my uncle's sorcerer." She continued the tale in a long straight string, purposefully leaving out the convoluted loops and ties.

Thyel's gaze wandered away. Had she bored him? This was a five-year-old tale.

"Jarrod's almost a part of my family, I suppose," Tamara ended. "Perhaps you sense that connection."

Thyel gave a harsh bark of laughter, his gaze now lively. "I doubt you see him as a brother, Tamara, any more than he sees you as a sister."

A smile quirked her lips, too. "Jarrod sees me as an annoyance. He always has."

"An appealing annoyance then." Thyel leaned forward, bringing them closer. He brushed her hair behind her ear. "I don't blame him. You could distract any man from his goals."

"Do I distract you?" She tilted her head and raised an inquiring eyebrow.

His eyes were as dark as Jarrod's but more intense. "My goal is the same as yours."

"Which is?" she asked.

"To free you once and for all from your mother's control."

The answer surprised her. It shouldn't have. They'd certainly talked enough about her mother's smothering hold. Yet, hearing him voice her anger made her uncertain if she truly wanted to be free. At this moment, she would have loved to be enfolded within one of her mother's rare hugs.

She abruptly stood and together they returned to the cave. Thyel strode by her side, a handsome and solid presence.

As they entered the cave, her gaze first slid to the green dragon. Halla snored, sending a warm breeze whirling dried leaves and pine needles through the cave.

Skye and Fane followed them in, the young girl holding up a fold of her skirt filled with something green. Fane carried three dead rabbits strung up by a vine.

Tamara nodded a greeting and went on to check on Jarrod. He slept fitfully, cradling his broken arm.

With a heavy heart, she sat beside him. His skin was flushed and his forehead beaded with perspiration. Freeing herself from her mother's control seemed the least of her worries. Her past rages and defeats inconsequential.

What did she want now? The answer came easily.

Jarrod's swift recovery.

Bevan's safe return.

Returning home.

All Tamara's previous energy and actions had been aimed at outwitting her mother's perceived control. Now, her past behavior seemed a colossal waste of precious time.

In hindsight, she doubted her mother had ever wanted to control her. Perhaps all the queen wanted was what Tamara wanted now. For her family and friends to remain safe in an uncertain world. The queen's desire had sprung from a deep concern for those she loved, as Tamara's current worries bubbled up from the same place of caring. She loved Skye and Bevan. Her coming on this journey showed the depth of her feelings for her family.

As for Thyel, he was a mystery. He'd showed an unexpected kindness in taking care of Jarrod. Yet, at odd times, she sensed a hardness that was unsettling.

Her gaze returned to Jarrod. His gentle, often distracted, face was covered in lines of pain and her heart ached. She ran the back of her fingers down his smooth hot cheek. The touch of his skin sent a shiver through her that warmed and melted her resistance.

No, she answered Thyel silently; *the Chief Councilor of Erov is certainly not my brother.*

Soon the mouthwatering scent of roasting rabbit invaded every crevice of the cave and woke up the exhausted dragon. Though Halla couldn't seem to find the energy to open more than one eyelid, she managed to use her one-eyed gaze to effectively glower at Tamara from across the cave.

Tamara ignored her until the green's protesting howl deafened them. Jarrod came awake with a start.

While Thyel went to see to his patient, Skye and Fane laughed at the dragon's complaint.

With a deep sigh, Tamara asked and received permission from the others to take over the third cooked rabbit to the protesting dragon. Halla was no longer truly hungry, but the scent of roasting meat must be difficult to resist.

Tamara returned licking juices off her fingers to find Skye and Fane observing her in silence. "What?"

"You seem to sense the dragon's needs rather clearly," Fane said.

"Almost," Skye added, "as if you were in tune with her wants." Her niece raised an eyebrow as she assessed Tamara.

"What's to sense?" Tamara took a bite of her tasty dinner. "We all knew why she howled."

"Only you went to feed her," Skye said.

Tamara gave her niece a hard look and decided her best defense was to attack. "Yes, I did. Why didn't you two?"

Thyel returned then, interrupting their sputtered responses. "Jarrod's nodded off again."

"Good," Skye said. "The more he sleeps, the better."

"Tomorrow," Fane said, sounding excited, "we're going in search of the bronze!"

"Do you think the green will be agreeable to taking us?" Skye asked Tamara.

She pressed her lips closed to prevent herself answering. Skye was suspicious enough, she wasn't about to give away anything. In a way, she was grateful Jarrod remained unconscious. Else, with his ability to worm his way into her mind, the secret of her connection with Halla would be out.

As the silence drew on, Fane came to her rescue. "We'll all find out tomorrow how willing the green is."

"Will you come with us?" Skye asked Tamara.

She thought over the suggestion. It would mean she'd be riding Halla again, prolonging the contact between them. Separation might encourage the green to stop talking to her.

"I'll watch Jarrod," she said. "Thyel can come with you."

"I need to see to his wound," Thyel said.

"I can do that," Tamara said.

He shook his head. "No, better if I stay. Fane and Skye don't need me for this errand."

"Then why don't you come with us?" Skye's frowning glance swept from Tamara to Thyel and back.

Why was she so insistent? Oh, wait. Skye knew about her being found in Thyel's bed. A blush heated her cheeks. "Thyel, I'd like you to go with them, please, to make sure they don't get into trouble. I'll change Jarrod's dressing when needed." Before anyone could argue, she stood. "Now that's settled, I'm turning in."

She chose a corner of the cave near where the dragon slept. It was the warmest part of the cave. Hoping the green wouldn't stretch out and kick her into the walls, Tamara bedded down. Halla's lids slid up but the dragon didn't move.

Skye joined her.

Thyel and Fane settled on the other side of the fire pit beside Jarrod.

Tamara stretched on the hard ground on her back.

"I'm glad you're not going to be here alone with Thyel," Skye whispered.

"Why?"

"There's something about the way he looks at you. It isn't love."

She glanced at her niece with worry. Maybe sending him off in Skye's company wasn't such a good idea. "What do you suspect?"

"Grandmother doesn't like him."

"She doesn't like anyone I like."

"Not true!" Skye said swiftly. Then, "Okay, maybe true, but only because you delight in befriending people we distrust."

We? "Mother discussed my behavior with you?"

Skye looked guilty and then breathed out, "With all of us, Aunt Tamara."

Tamara sat up, leaning on one elbow, and staring in shock. "The whole family?"

"We were worried."

"For how long?"

"Always."

The answer stroked and soothed her ruffled feathers, as if all her sisters, brother, niece and nephew, and even her mother had given her a fervent, heartfelt hug. As Halla had somehow inveigled her way past Tamara's defenses to lodge within Tamara's heart, so now did her family.

She lay back, gazing at the dark ceiling and blinking back tears. All this time she'd thought herself so alone. How wrong she'd been.

Tentatively, she took Skye's hand. With that small gesture, she allowed her family to invade the emptiness of her lonely life. "Skye."

"Yes?"

"We're now friends as much as family. Call me Tamara."

· · · ·

EARLY THE NEXT MORNING, Tamara stood back and watched Fane, impatient to be off, try to wake the snoring green. No amount of poking and prodding could get her to stir. He finally gave up and went outside with Skye, planning to set off on foot once Thyel joined them.

The exhaustion Tamara sensed in Halla had obviously taken hold. At this rate, it might be days before she awoke again. When she did, she would be hungry. Tamara didn't want to broach the touchy subject with Skye around.

Following the two outside, she suggested Skye fetch Thyel. Once Skye was out of earshot, she turned to Fane. "While you're out, keep an eye for any herds grazing nearby. Maybe goats. The green will be hungry when she awakes."

"Good idea," Fane said.

Thyel joined them on the landing alone. "Skye's saying goodbye to Jarrod. He woke up briefly." He gave a nod to Fane. "You can start if you want and we'll catch up. I want to speak with Tamara alone for a moment."

The young man nodded, and grinning, headed off past the ledge, down the mountain.

Thyel pulled Tamara to him. Before she could protest, he kissed her soundly. It took her back to the moment when they'd been alone in his bedchamber as he disrobed her, one layer after another. Each piece of clothing flung away had peaked her excitement that much more. She came up for air, breathless. Thyel was an amazing kisser. When he touched her, she could never remember what bothered her about him.

"That's to remind you that the invalid I leave in your care is not the man you desire," he said, sounding a little winded himself.

She smiled in gentle understanding. This is why he didn't want to leave her behind. He was jealous. Of a mirage. "You've nothing to fear on that score, Thyel. I'm not the one whom Jarrod likes."

"So you keep saying."

"I also don't know about that." Skye came up behind them giving Thyel a cross look until he reluctantly released Tamara. "Jarrod liked you enough to give up his own problems in order to follow you to Isa."

"He'd left his second in charge to deal with the missing historians," Tamara pointed out.

"Didn't he tell you?" her niece asked with an arched brow. "He's worried the problem in Ryca will get worse in his absence. If he awakes, talk to him about that and what's happening with his tome."

"We should go." Thyel sounded impatient. "I wouldn't tax Jarrod with questions today. The more rest he gets, the better." He turned to Skye. "Shall we?"

Tamara waved them off, her thoughts turning to what might be worrying Jarrod. Once again involved in her own problems, had she failed to consider Jarrod's needs?

Determined to uncover everything that bothered him, she strode inside the cave. Then she remembered Thyel's warning to not tire his patient with questions.

With a frustrated sigh, she slumped down and gazed from Jarrod to Halla. Both were sleeping soundly.

This was going to be a long day.

His pack drew her bored glance. After Skye and Fane had quickly gathered all the scattered pages and stuffed them back into Falcon's Tome, the book was probably in sad shape. That would only add to whatever worried him.

She took the tome out of the pack and then hesitated. Jarrod didn't like anyone touching his precious book. Anyone, except Skye. It wasn't as if Tamara meant the book any harm. She only intended to order the perpetually untidy pages. With an injured arm, he would have a hard time even with such an ordinary task.

Tentatively, she opened his book.

• • • •

JARROD STIRRED, COMING slowly awake.

Thirst struck him first, with a parched and itchy throat. The burning pain in his arm caught his attention next. He resisted groaning, keeping his eyes shut tight, trying to control his reaction to the searing ache.

Sound registered next.

Loud snores.

He opened his eyes a slit and glanced to the left where the noise reverberated. A green dragon slept curled on its side, tail tucked into its body.

Then he sensed another presence.

To his right, by his feet, sat Tamara. Her legs were crossed, arms folded across her beautiful chest, glaring at him. No surprise there. Little about him endeared him to Tamara.

Her long sunshine bright hair was braided back, wisps hanging down the side of her face. An adorable frown marred her beauty, or did it enhance it? He resisted smiling, knowing she would not appreciate his amusement.

She'd shed her chainmaille and sword, wearing only her tunic and those long lovely legs displayed in trousers.

What had upset her this time? By that glare, he must have played a part in stirring her anger, even while unconscious.

Her frown seemed to increase the longer he studied her in silence. "May I have some water?" The rawness in his throat ached as his words trickled out.

A blush stole up her creamy cheeks. She reached for his pack and pulled out his water cask. She helped him sit up and held the container to his mouth.

Ignoring his burning arm, Jarrod sipped with eagerness. Then he cringed as the cool liquid washed over his dry, swollen lips making them sting. The water sliding down his raw throat tasted of fresh air and desert winds. He sighed in pleasure. He missed Erov.

After his third heady gulp, she said that was enough for now, and with utmost care laid him back. Then she adjusted a rolled cloth under his head. Kneeling close, she brushed hair off his hot forehead.

The gentle gesture touched him and spawned a yearning for more. It felt right to wake up and find her nearby, whatever her mood. As if she belonged beside him. Always.

He surreptitiously inhaled a lungful of the faint hint of lavender that lingered about her. Today, it seemed as refreshing as the cold water he'd sipped.

He glanced at her with curiosity and a touch of worry. Why all this tender attention? "Thank you."

With a firm nod, she returned to her place by his feet, stretching out her legs this time, her lips clamped as if afraid she'd say something rude if they weren't under strict control.

Just as well. He wasn't up to a shouting match.

Beside her, he finally noticed Falcon's tome. His heart beat faster with joy. It hadn't been lost! In fact, it seemed tidier than normal, and securely wrapped by a vine, lovingly tied with a bow on top. Skye must have done that. He should remember to thank her later. His taut shoulders relaxed and he shut his eyes as sweet relief washed over him like a cold bath on a hot day.

When he opened his eyes again, Tamara was still there, watching him.

Ever since he found her in Saira's room, gown half undone, looking far too desirable for a scholar's concentration, his thoughts and emotions rebelled against common sense. Enough to bring him to this point – thrust into a foreign realm, lying injured, perhaps dying, with Ryca's history vanishing with each breath he took.

"Why have you never married, Jarrod?"

The question breaking into the heavy silence surprised him. She sat there waiting as if she was serious about his answer. "Why do you ask?"

"Saira said all Erovians pair at a young age, and marry soon after they reach their majority." She picked up the tome and laid it on her lap, her fingers tracing the vine wrapped tight around it.

He couldn't take his eyes off her holding the book so tenderly. As she caressed that vine safeguarding his book, each stroke of her fingers seemed to trail over his body with infinite care.

"Is it because Saira chose Tom instead of you?"

"No. I was engaged to be married before I ever met Saira. My betrothed's name was Mayla."

"You're married?" she asked in an aghast tone.

He frowned in confusion about this entire topic of conversation. Perhaps it was his wound that throbbed agonizingly. He couldn't figure out what he could have possibly done to upset her while he slept. Or why she was interested in his sorrow-filled life.

"Mayla died before we could wed." His words came out rough but not because of his loss. He'd long since recovered from that ill-timed episode.

Though he had grave doubts he could ever extricate himself completely from the net Tamara was weaving around his heart.

Her glance returned to his book, a much less complicated subject. "In case I'm asleep when Skye comes by, will you thank her for taking care of Falcon's Tome?"

"Are you forbidden to choose another? Or do you still miss Mayla?"

Tamara seemed obsessed with his past. "Mayla murdered my father. Then tried to kill Saira. Finally, she killed herself. She was caught in one of Tamarisk's mind spells."

"Oh, I'm sorry."

"She should have turned to me when the evil impulses stole into her. She didn't."

Her fingers smoothed over her outstretched legs and Jarrod shuddered as if it were his hand caressing her leg. He clenched his right hand and when his left hand tried to match that action, his wounded arm protested in pain. A wave of heat swept over his body and he thought he might fall unconscious again.

"Not everyone finds it easy to ask for help," she said in a soft voice, her gaze fixed on his book. "It's difficult to rely on others. What if they let you down when you need them most?" That last came out in the barest of whispers.

Jarrod breathed deeply until his mind stopped spinning with pain. As the waves subsided, it slowly occurred that they were no longer speaking about poor doomed Mayla. He thanked Heaven that Tamara had stopped stroking herself. "Without the ability to trust, even erroneously, you can never find out how much someone cares for you."

Her gaze locked with his then for a breathless moment. She shifted her enigmatic attention toward the dragon. Through Tamara, he sensed the beast's deep exhaustion, and beneath that, a thread of utter terror.

He, too, looked at the green and then at Tamara in surprise. Their gazes collided for a second time.

A distinct guilty flush stained her pale cheeks.

"You can communicate with that dragon," Jarrod said.

"I didn't want to."

"It can..."

"*She* can," Tamara corrected. "Her name is Halla."

Jarrod lay there absorbing that font of information. Finally, he asked, "Why are we still here?"

Her flush deepened. "I haven't told anyone yet."

"Tamara!"

"Fane's out right now looking for his bronze dragon, the one he's convinced he's connected to. If that link doesn't exist or if they cannot find the bronze, I promise, Jarrod, I will confess all about my link to the green."

He lay still. The pain in his arm throbbed and another wave of dizziness swept over him. He waited for it to pass so he could speak clearly.

As the silence lengthened, Tamara said, "I wasn't to upset you and now I have. Do you need more water? Or do you need to rest?"

"I wish..."

"What do you wish, Jarrod?"

"Doesn't matter."

"Why do you always refuse to confide in me?"

She sounded angry again but he had no strength left for a fight. He shut his eyes, welcoming the peaceful darkness.

"You have no trouble getting close to Skye," she continued. "Yet, with me, you hardly say a word. Even when you have something important to share."

That brought his eyes wide open. "You've never been concerned about me before. Why now?"

Her fingers trailed across the top binding of Falcon's Tome, and he had the uncanny impression that she wanted to caress his face like that. His startled glance shot up to Tamara, for that hadn't been him yearning for her touch.

The evocative thought had come from *her*.

Chapter 12

TAMARA'S WISH TO TOUCH him brushed across Jarrod's mind the way another Erovian's emotion could if they focused together. How could this be? Tamara wasn't Erovian.

In all his studies of Light magic, only his people had an ability to magically share thoughts and emotions.

His mind whirled with excitement, shock, delight and finally, doubt. In his delirium, could he have imagined her mind-touch? Why would she feel such an emotion about him anyway? She was enamored with Thyel. The reminder tasted sour.

"At the castle," she murmured, "whenever you visited, you rarely spoke to me. I assumed you disliked me."

How to answer this? He had indeed avoided her. There was no lying about that. He did it because every time he was with her, he wanted to get closer. He chose a less complicated answer. "I assumed you wouldn't be interested in what interests me."

"Such as?

"Books. Study. History. Subjects that would bore you." He breathed deeply, trying to quiet his racing thoughts and passions. She couldn't have mind-touched. He had imagined the delicate brush of her feelings.

Her gaze captured again and held it as the back of her hand once again distinctly slid across his left cheek.

Yet, she hadn't moved a muscle.

Tamara could mind-touch!

The thought brought a thrill that was beyond simple pleasure. Did she realize it? No, there was no conscious acknowledgement in her gaze.

He glanced at the dragon. Could her connection with the green have opened a latent talent or spawned a new one? No, to the latter idea. For her to be able to connect with the green in the first place, this ability must have existed in her all along.

"You've gone silent again," Tamara said sounding cross.

"I was thinking about your connection to the green."

"Must we talk about that? I don't like thinking about it."

"Why?"

"I dislike someone else invading my thoughts."

He couldn't suppress a chuckle at the irony.

"What's so funny?" she asked.

"Tamara, have you not considered that your connection with the green may be your magical talent?"

"I don't have one. Everyone knows that"

"What if you do?"

"I don't. It's the green that speaks to me, who orders me around."

She didn't understand her role in communicating with the dragon. His mind spun with the possibilities. Then one especially unique idea obliterated all others. "What if this is the reason you were awake for all those years despite the time spell."

"What are you talking about? How do you know about that? Oh, of course. Even if you won't admit it, I know you've been roaming around my thoughts. You stole that secret!"

He had the grace to blush. "Not steal it exactly. You screamed it at me the first time we met at the banquet your mother threw to celebrate vanquishing Ywen and Tamarisk. That's one of the reasons I've avoided you in the past, so I would not inadvertently pick up any more of your secrets."

"Oh," Tamara said. "Well, anyway, my being awake all that time was my mother's fault. She didn't cast her time spell properly. It left me trapped but awake for an eternity."

"I'm sorry for your suffering," Jarrod said softly, gently. Was she finally ready to discuss that ordeal? She was so prickly on this subject. "Tamara, consider if the spell worked as it was meant to, but your talent to mind-speak was not affected?"

She scrambled to her feet, backing away, shaking her head. "I don't have any magical talent."

"Just a moment ago, you brushed my cheek with your hand without ever touching me. I felt it."

He sensed no denial in her now, but rather shock. Then he heard her wonder what else she might have inadvertently shared. He wanted to reassure her that it was okay. He'd only sensed the one stray touch, when images of them entwined in bed bombarded him. Their limbs entangled, bodies melded, sharing kisses and touches and bold strokes.

Despite his fever, the ache in his arm, and the dizziness that rolled in and out like ocean waves, a hot longing he'd been suppressing since he saw her in that partially undone gown, flared. He couldn't keep from joining her in that bed. Returning her kisses. Partaking with his own bold caresses.

With a startled cry, she fled from the cave.

He shut his eyes, trying to dampen his thoughts and emotions. To subdue his body that had peaked with intense desire. All the while, he wanted to shout with joy and triumph at the knowledge that Tamara desired him back.

He wished he could go after her, to comfort her, to tell her that he loved her. That it was all right to have such amorous thoughts. He welcomed them. He shut his mind down instead, to give her privacy to come to terms with what they'd shared. She did indeed possess a magical talent. What did this mean for her future?

An hour passed. Then another. Still no Tamara.

He dozed fitfully, coming awake to find himself bathed in sweat. The third time he awoke, he knew she had returned at some point, for his face felt as if it had been wiped clean with a blessedly cool, wet cloth. She was not in the cave. The green snored, undisturbed.

At his next awakening, Tamara was by his feet again, as if she'd never left. She stared at him boldly, a teasing smile playing at the corner of her delicious lips.

He raised his defenses, mistrusting that look.

"Jarrod, will you marry me?" she asked. He was still grappling for an answer when she added, "I think we could get along if we tried."

"We're not much alike," he said. *Yes, I want to marry you!* "I like quiet." *Tamara, please don't let me talk you out of this.* "I've become accustomed to solitude." *I'm a fool who's in love with you.*

She sat there, staring at him wide-eyed. Her eyes glowed with some wildly suppressed emotions. "I can hear you," she said. "Every word you're not saying."

Her slow, gut-wrenching, resistance-crumbling smile made him forget his injury and try to sit up so he could kiss her. The resultant pain had him slumping back.

"You mustn't move," she warned rushing closer.

Why does it feel as if I'm worsening instead of healing?

"What do you mean worsening?" she asked.

"I feel as if I've been ill forever."

"Only one day and one night." *Please don't die.*

"I'll be fine. It was a serious break. It will simply take time to heal. Now can we return to more important matters? Like your ability to speak to Halla?"

"You said don't let you talk me out of us getting married. Not in words perhaps, but in your thoughts, which is the same as a pledge!"

"Tamara, I want you to also hear what I say aloud. For I do not want you to mistake who I am. Before making such a vital decision, you must understand whom you wish to take as your husband."

"I do."

"Do you? Most of my time, even when working among others, I am alone." He gave a self-deprecating laugh. "As with all Erovians, the people of Ryca hardly notice my passing. It's the result of my magic working to keep me centered and focused on my work. I also treasure that sense of privacy."

She chuckled and he drank in her laughter, released so rarely in her troubled life. "What's so amusing?"

"Jarrod, do you not realize you're describing my life? I love history. I, too, always feel alone." *Except for now, with you, and Halla.* "I glide around the castle as if I don't really exist. Solitude, even when I'm with my family, clings to me like a wet gown." *I'm afraid of losing you because of my behavior.* "I sometimes lash out to make people notice me. *Because, for years, no one heard me cry.*"

"I hear you now." Jarrod held out his good hand.

• • • •

AT THE OFFERING OF his hand, all of Tamara's resistance crumbled. She scrambled over the tome and reverently kissed his palm. "Jarrod, do you truly believe this mind-speak is my talent?"

The idea was a welcome and wondrous thought, but also hard to believe.

"I can't imagine what else it could be, my love," he said.

The endearment swept through her until her nerves tingled as if she'd been struck by lightning. So many thoughts whirled. She breathed deeply.

All the blame she'd piled at the queen's feet withered and died, blowing away like ashes in the wind. Her connection to Halla now made perfect sense. Why she could hear the green's thoughts when Fane could not. Why only she seemed to be able to mind-speak with Jarrod.

"Tell me what's happened to the tome," she said, coming back to the topic that had upset her most.

"What do you mean?" he asked.

"Why is the book almost blank?"

He sat up and then cried out in pain. "All the pages?"

"Lie back. There's nothing you can do about it right now and I will not have you killing yourself after telling me you love me. Yes, I heard that too."

"Tamara, how many pages are blank?"

"So many I lost count. Why didn't you tell me something was wrong with the tome? You mentioned it to Skye. She told me to ask you about it."

"What is there to tell?" He lay back and sighed – a deep gush of air like the expulsion of all his hopes and dreams. "What does any of it matter now?" he asked in a flat voice. "I cannot control what's happening to Falcon's Tome."

Tamara's heart shuddered for his loss. "Jarrod, you have to care. Your book is cleansing itself!"

"Yes."

She picked up the tome and shook it. "But this is your life's work!"

"It's my people's work. There's worse news."

"What could be worse?"

"Those missing historians, it was their words that first disappeared. Now, with most of the book empty, by the time we return, there may be no Erovians left on Ryca."

"Bevan's not a historian."

"No, but he is growing up to be quite a powerful sorcerer," Jarrod said. "He could have stumbled across what is affecting my people and been drawn in. There's more."

"More?"

"History may be re-writing itself on Ryca."

"How is that possible?"

"When I mentioned to your mother about one of the missing historians, Daniel, she said she'd never heard of him."

About to speak, Tamara shut her mouth as she sorted through her memories. When she finally responded, her words came out in a hushed whisper. "Did I know him?"

He gave a quick decisive nod. "For years."

Her heart thudded in fear. "Oh, Jarrod, you should have said something."

He shook his head. "I didn't really know the extent of the damage. One or two of my people had not reported back as they should have and a page or two of the tome appeared empty. I came to ask for your sister's help but she had gone to seek Bevan. By the time we arrived on Isa, more words had disappeared."

"My family..." Tamara began.

"I'm sure are fine. They do not remember the Erovians who have been in their midst. It seems my people are being erased, like those pages, one by one. Likely because we are the caretakers of Ryca's history. Now I think of it, my coming with all of you may have saved my life. The reason I, too, haven't disappeared could be because I'm no longer in Ryca."

"Thank the Light for that." She stroked the book. "What does it all mean, Jarrod? Is it safe for you to return home?"

"The disappearance of my people could either be the result of what's corrupting the record of Ryca's history, or the cause behind it. I do not know which, yet."

"Why would someone attack Falcon's Tome or the Erovians? Or take Bevan?"

Jarrod shook his head. "If I knew the answer to those questions, I might be able to save my people."

"All of those things occurring at the same time seems suspicious."

"Especially since no one else from Ryca had gone missing, that I know of." Jarrod's fingers enclosed her trembling ones. "Thank you."

"For what?" Her cheeks heated in a blush at the tender look in his eyes.

"For tidying the pages of the tome. It was you that did it, wasn't it? Not Skye."

"It was a royal mess," she said in a soft mock-cross voice. "It's always a mess. I've tied it with a strong vine and you're to keep it that way from now on."

He chuckled and then shut his eyes, his face going inordinately pale.

"I've tired you," she whispered with contrition. "Thyel will be furious. All his good work gone to waste."

Jarrod didn't respond.

She sucked in her breath as fear settled in the pit of her stomach. The moment Skye returned, she would confess all and wake the green. It would be too dangerous to take Jarrod to Ryca, if all the historians were disappearing there. Since Anna, her wonderful healing sister, was bound for Melak in search of her son, that's where they should head.

Holding back tears of self-recrimination, she scrambled to her feet and hurried out to the ledge. Fear and impatience were her constant companions as she sat at the cave entrance awaiting Skye's return.

A brisk breeze teased the treetops, fluttering leaves and bent branches. Birds sang in sweet notes as they flew by. The peaceful sight did not register, any more than her recent startling discoveries about her ability to read thoughts. All were overshadowed by the dreaded possibility of Jarrod disappearing.

A backward glance into the cave showed the green dragon rolling over, hind legs stretching one moment, and tucked in the next. The sight lifted Tamara's dour spirits. Who could have kept such a powerful beast imprisoned? And why?

She absently bit her lip and tasted blood. It must not be the first time she'd chewed on herself with worry.

It was almost dusk. Surely Skye, Fane and Thyel would return soon.

A shadow passed overhead. Another dragon? She lost sight of it among the surrounding shrubbery. Tamara scrambled up and ran back into the cave.

Then something crashed through the surrounding trees and landed on the ledge.

Heart thundering, she stopped as she backed into something. Halla! She'd come to a stop before the slumbering dragon, as if she intended to defend it from attack.

Idiot.

It was a dragon outside and Fane, Skye and Thyel were riding it! Fane was up front, looking as proud as a father holding his newborn child. Behind him Skye waved to her and Thyel nodded, appearing bemused.

Definitely a bronze. Kneeling to discharge the riders, it gave her a keen look from one of its golden eyes. None of its thoughts jarred Tamara. This must be how the rest of her party viewed Halla. Gigantic and dangerous, but silent.

Fane scrambled down and gently rubbed his dragon's snout. In turn, the bronze blew a smoke ring at the young lad.

"They've been enamored with each other since the moment they met," Thyel said in a sarcastic tone, scrambling down and coming over to stand beside Tamara.

Skye ran over to hug her but Tamara was surprised to see her look worried. Why was Skye not thrilled? Finding this dragon meant they could leave Isa.

"How's our patient?" Thyel asked, distracting Tamara. "Did he awaken?"

"He's asleep. He is still too hot to the touch, Thyel."

"I'll check on him."

"What's the matter?" Tamara asked Skye.

Fane answered. "We have disturbing news."

"Not now," Skye warned.

"Why not now?" Tamara asked.

Fane and Skye shared a concerned look.

"Tell me!"

"Introductions first." Fane pointed to the bronze. "Tamara, this is Kiron. He's injured. He was in a fight recently." He paused and looked at Halla. "We think it was in defense of the green."

"Are you sure?"

"Fairly," Fane said. "I can easily communicate with Kiron. It's much easier than my master said it would be. I'm pretty sure the green inside is the one Kiron was searching for yesterday. Remember, I sensed he was on the hunt for someone."

Tamara nodded. "If he's injured, we'd better see to his wounds. Perhaps Thyel can assist as he has with Jarrod."

"No," Fane said. "I know how to care for a dragon. It was part of my training. On the way here, we stopped to pick up the herbs I needed. First, Kiron wants to meet the dragon we found to ensure she is the one he seeks."

Tamara stood aside as Fane led Kiron into the cave.

She then turned to Skye. "What did you not want him to tell me?"

Skye looked down at her feet and shuffled in place.

Tamara waited.

Finally, her niece looked up. "Kiron will not leave Isa. Not when the green is in danger. He insists he must remain here to protect her."

Instead of being disappointed, Tamara was warmed by the bronze's loyalty to Halla. The news wasn't bad at all, for they could all travel off Isa together.

"I'm sorry," Skye said. "I know how trapped you feel on this world."

"It's become easier than you realize," she murmured, surprised at the truth behind that. "I've important news, too."

A tear appeared in Skye's eye and Tamara quickly hugged her niece. "Don't cry. All is not lost. We *will* get off Isa and go in search of Bevan. I promise you."

"How?" Skye asked.

"With Halla, that's the green's name. I can speak to her."

To her surprise, Skye didn't look as shocked as she expected, as if this was something she'd suspected all along.

Before Skye could respond, deafening wails joined in counterpoint as the green finally awoke. Kiron crooned to Halla, whose response was just as affectionate. The joy in both was unmistakable.

Tamara was inundated with images. She saw the bronze come to the green's rescue and the fear Halla felt as a fight ensued. The pictures fluttered through her mind like leaves blowing in the fall wind, a wind that picked up in speed and strength.

She clutched at Skye, as her legs shaking.

"Tamara, what's the matter?"

She shook her head. "It's so overwhelming, this sharing of thoughts." The fear of her mother forcing her to marry Gideon was mirrored a hundredfold in Halla's terror of a black dragon threatening to force-mate with her.

"Halla is a queen, imbued with the royal blood of the ruling dragons of Isa," she said, words pouring out. "Another dragon wants to rule Isa. Tried to take her by force. When she refused, he imprisoned her. He was starving her to force her submission."

"Poor Halla," Skye whispered. "No wonder she was so hungry when we found her."

"Explains why the bronze refuses to leave her," Tamara said in a fierce voice. "Neither would I. Halla worries he's not strong enough to face that black a second time."

"Then we must leave Isa before he finds us," Skye said.

Waves of Halla's fear, both for herself and for the bronze, enveloped Tamara's mind and Skye's words faded.

"Tamara, are you all right?" her niece asked.

She sounded worried but the dragon's terror bombarded Tamara until she gave in and gave up the battle to retain clarity. She vaguely heard Skye cry out as the world went dark. Someone shouted for help and arms supported Tamara as she slumped to the ground.

• • • •

TAMARA AWOKE TO FIND the cave silent.

Light spilled in from outside suggesting another day dawned.

Her first thoughts were about Jarrod. She went over and laid a hand on his forehead – two days on and still burning to the touch. In the dawn's light, his injured arm looked like it had begun to fester, oozing and wetting the bandages, the puffy skin around the wound glistening.

Thyel and Skye were missing but Fane was tending to the bronze.

On reaching his side, she asked after Kiron.

"His wounds look to be improving," Fane said, sounding relieved. "I applied the same herbs to Halla's wounds, too. Those seem better as well."

"Jarrod gets worse. Could your herbs help him?"

"I've not much left but I know where I can find more. Take and use what remains in the bag."

"Thank you, Fane!" Thrilled to have something constructive to do, she ran back to clean and re-dress Jarrod's arm.

Thyel returned as she finished. He left Skye to put away the fruits and berries and hurried over. "What are you doing?"

At his anxious tone, Tamara finished tying the knot on the last strip of clean cloth and turned to respond. "I've re-dressed his wound with Fane's herbs."

He gave her a worried look and held up his medicinal pouch. "I need to add more of mine to properly dress the wound. I'll re-bandage it."

"No, let's give Fane's herbs a chance to work first."

Thyel looked ready to argue but then he shrugged. "All right. I need more anyway. I'll hunt for some now."

"Wait for me," Fane called out. "I gave my last bit to Tamara and need to replenish my supplies."

Half unconscious, Jarrod was heavy so she called Skye over. Together, they helped him sit up so he could drink some water. He gulped the liquid and then slumped back, asleep.

"I'm worried about him," Tamara said.

"His arm isn't as hot." Skye stroked the back of his swollen hand. "Perhaps the medicine is finally taking effect."

"I hope so."

"Rest and time will be the best cure. Tamara, may we go outside to talk? We must decide what to do next."

She nodded and followed her niece to the flat landing that overlooked the lush valley below.

"How are you feeling?" Skye asked.

"Better. I didn't realize I'd slept so long. I'm sorry. I'd hoped we could leave last night."

"You did worry me when you went unconscious. You obviously needed the rest. This is amazing news, Tamara, that you can speak with the green."

She gave her niece a sheepish look. "There's more I haven't told you yet."

"What else?"

"The green isn't the only one with whom I can mind-speak."

"What do you mean?"

"Let me show you." Tamara closed her eyes. She envisioned Skye and Bevan together, as she'd seen them the last time, playfully fighting as brothers and sisters were wont to do. When she opened her eyes, Skye stared at her in shock.

"You sent me that memory?"

Tamara nodded. "Jarrod says it's my talent, this ability to speak without words. It's how his people communicate. There's more to it than just sharing memories."

"What else?'

"I'm sorry for not confessing I could talk to the green." Then she projected, in mind-talk, *I was afraid of being controlled by her.*

"Oh, sweet Light." Skye staggered back. "I heard that!"

"It seems odd to me too," Tamara said, "to be able to speak without moving my lips. Enough of that for now. I'm more interested in discussing when we're to leave Isa."

"Sooner the better. Fane says an all-out war rages among the strongest young male dragons."

"Why?"

"Rivalry."

"Over what?"

"The right to mate Halla."

Tamara's stomach turned to lead at the thought. She glanced back toward the cave. From what she had gleaned of Halla's character, she knew the independent and fierce Halla would never give herself up as a "prize" to any dragon.

Her fists clenched and she found herself standing, arms raised, feet apart, in a defensive stance with her back to Halla. The posture reminded her of the many nightmares she had awakened from on Ryca and found herself in the middle of her bedroom in a fighter's stance, fists clenched.

Was this what her dreams had foretold? Slowly, she lowered her arms, trying to release her tension.

"Fane says she's the last of the reigning dragon family on Isa," Skye said quietly, watching Tamara, curiosity clearly written on her face. "As such, mating with her would give any mature dragon the right to rule the land."

"What's set off the rivalry? Why now?"

"She reached maturity. She'd been under the council's protection until then. Kiron began to court her once she was given more freedom. There was much dispute about his right to do so. While the dragon council argued the matter, a black named Denton lured and then trapped Halla in a hidden cave in order to force her to submit to him."

"She would die first," Tamara said with certainty.

"Kiron told Fane that."

"It's how I would react." Had reacted not so long ago. Had she really contemplated killing herself? Yes, and she might have, if Skye hadn't caught up to her that night, and never learned how Jarrod really felt about her. Or how important her family was to her happiness. It would have been a life wasted due entirely to shortsightedness.

She raised her head with fierce determination. Halla would not submit to anyone today. Or on any other day. Not if Tamara had anything to do about it.

Chapter 13

TAMARA SQUATTED TO absently play with a blade of grass from the edge of the clearing.

Skye, too, knelt, matching her pose. "I've wanted to say for a while that the ultimatum Grandmother Mamosia imposed on you was most unfair. I told her so."

Tamara turned to her in surprise. "You did?"

Skye nodded. "I warned her that you would react badly."

"You know me well."

"You are part of my family. Of course, I know you. You simply did not want to know us."

The arrow hit its target and Tamara cringed.

"Not that I blame you," Skye said quickly. "If I had been trapped awake in a time spell, it would have affected how I reacted, too."

Her niece's words shocked her. "How do you know about that?" First Jarrod, now Skye?

"Jarrod hinted at it when we were looking for the Quinlin stone, and then I put two and two together." Skye spoke slowly, as if exploring a dangerous conversational terrain. "I don't think he meant to, it slipped out."

Tamara looked over the cliff. "I don't want to talk about that time."

"It might help," Skye said gently. "Not talking hasn't helped, has it?"

She sent her niece a surprised look. Normally, her family avoided talk of "the event" as much as she did. Skye was right, though. Her silence hadn't helped. It had left her even more isolated and alone. As if she were still trapped. Perhaps this discovery of her ability to mind-speak was a signal to abandon her old unhelpful strategy.

"Since awakening," Tamara said, as if her words slipped through a crack in a heavy door. "I frequented the castle parapets."

"Why?" Skye sounded curious, interested. "Did you feel a sense of freedom, with the open sky above?"

"I often entertained the urge to jump."

"No!"

"Are you sure you want to hear more?" Tamara asked.

"Last night you said we were more than family. We were now friends. If that's so, I want to hear everything, Tamara. True friends are honest with each other."

Tamara nodded once, closely observing Skye's serious face. This young girl knew more about what friendship entailed than her. She would not underestimate Skye again. "I sought complete freedom, a sense of autonomy before the earth claimed my body."

"Why didn't you share how you felt? Grandmother would have wanted to know. To help you."

Tamara gave a harsh laugh. "Mother would have locked me up for my own safety."

At Skye's silence, she knew she'd guessed correctly. "The night I discovered Bevan had disappeared because I didn't listen to his pleading for help was the worst night of my life. I wanted to search for him, but Mother wouldn't let me. Then she incarcerated Thyel and said if I didn't pick another, I had best settle to marrying Gideon. When you interrupted me, insisting that I help, I'd been wondering how to get up to the parapets. To go as high up as I could."

"Oh no!" Skye covered her mouth.

Tamara gave an ironic laugh. "In trying to save Bevan that night, you saved me."

Halla stuck her head out the cave opening and grunted. The dragon's yellow eyes stared straight into Tamara's soul. *WE JUMP TOGETHER?*

"No!" she responded in shock.

A shadow fell over the cave entrance. All three of them looked up in time to see a dark silhouette of a dragon halt mid-air, wings flapping to stay in place. Spotting them below, it gave a challenging bellow and flew straight at them.

The fast-approaching black listed as it flew, favoring his right side. In the rescue of Halla, had Kiron not been the only one wounded? Despite the injury, the black's fiercely determined flight made Tamara quake.

Halla screamed and disappeared inside the cave.

Skye shouted in alarm. Tamara grabbed her niece's arm and together they sprinted inside. Her fear didn't subside as she and Skye raced through the entrance.

They came to an abrupt halt as Kiron reared. Fane tried to wave him down but the bronze stepped right over him. Skye and Tamara scrambled to get out of the way as the bronze dragon charged outside.

Fane sprinted after the bronze, shouting. "We have to stop him! He isn't ready for another fight."

Thyel was at Fane's heels. "All of you stay out of sight."

If by "all of you," he meant Halla, too, that wouldn't be a problem. The terrified green had wiggled her way into a side cave, leaving only the tip of her tail visible.

The green's fear palpated in the air, barreling into Tamara's mind and crushing the fragile mental defenses she had built. She gripped her pounding head, trying to shut out the dragon's emotions.

Jarrod tried to sit up, but the effort was too much and he slumped back.

Skye headed for the entrance again to see what was happening out there. Tamara forcefully pulled her back and, cautiously, inched forward herself.

On the ledge, Fane shouted into the air, but she doubted the two dragons hurtling around each other heard him. Thyel, hands on hips, watched the acrobatics as if fascinated.

Far above, Kiron and the black circled in mid-air, slashing out with their powerful hind legs and blowing fire.

Suddenly, Kiron charged. The black fell back and gave a shout. In answer, a flight of dragons rose over a nearby mountain range and flew toward the fighters.

"Behind you!" Fane yelled.

"The black's brought friends," Thyel said.

Halla backed out of the side cave. Shoving aside Tamara and Skye, she looked outside. Tamara guessed that despite her terror, the green dragon planned to go to her friend's assistance. The thought astonished her. Halla was willing to risk her hard-won freedom to help Kiron. Just as he'd shown himself willing to die for her.

Halla squatted to give herself leverage to take off.

Without hesitation, Tamara leaped onto the dragon's hind leg and swiftly climbed to sit between her shoulders.

"What are you doing?" Skye shouted.

"Come down." Jarrod staggered toward Halla, too late.

They were airborne.

Tamara hung on to her mount's neck as they rose. With a furious screech, and ignoring Tamara's warning, the green charged toward the mob attacking Kiron.

The listing black noticed their advance. Leaving his friends to finish off the bronze, he lazily swung toward Halla, bellowing a challenge. He swooped along behind her, a wicked determined light in his eyes. He was planning to forcefully mate Halla, right there in the middle of the fight.

Tamara's fury matched Halla's and together they turned to face the black. Halla spewed fire.

DENTON, she said, identifying the wicked black.

Denton swung to the side, startled, and a little unsteady. Backing off, he called to his friends. Two left the fight with Kiron to come to his aid. Corralling Halla on either side, they kept her occupied while Denton again approached from the rear.

He grabbed Halla's hind end with his forelegs, drawing her closer.

Halla's fear vibrated in Tamara. She drew her sword and stood up. The black opened his mouth as if to spew fire at her and Tamara flung her sword straight into his open gullet. Denton reared back and then spat the sword out.

Swearing, Tamara sat back down and shaking off Halla's terror, ordered, "Dive!"

The green remained frozen in place, too panicked to move. The dragon's scattered thoughts were widely flavored with fear.

Tamara shouted, *Shut your wings! Now!*

Halla instinctively obeyed. They dropped like a boulder with the wounded Denton desperately holding himself up as well as Halla.

In moments, he let go and flapped away, listing precariously as Tamara and Halla plummeted. As Denton's friends came to his aid, Tamara said, *Fly!*

Halla responded. With a triumphant shout, and strong sweep of her wings, she soon gained height. Tamara thought she intended to help Kiron again, but instead, Halla headed for Denton. This time her fire caught a portion of his unprotected, already injured underside.

Denton screamed in agony, and would have fallen if not for the two dragons beside him. They carried his entire weight all the way down until he could land safely.

With a swirl in the air that almost knocked Tamara off, Halla finally turned her attention to Kiron. The three dragons that had remained to harass him caught sight of the furious green. They broke rank, flying swiftly back to the cover of a nearby mountain range.

Halla crooned to the bronze, who had new tears and cuts. She led him toward their cave and he followed. She cooed softly all the way, giving him encouraging calls when he faltered.

Tamara held on as waves of warmth and caring emanated from Halla toward Kiron. Unrestrained joy at his presence was mixed with a belly load of concern for his welfare. The green had shed all her fear for her own safety

Despite the impact of Halla's emotional whirls, one startling concept became crystal clear. This intense caring, this willingness to chance everything to save each other, that was what love was all about.

They landed on the cave's outer ledge. Jarrod stood leaning against the opening. His deeply concerned gaze expressed a passion parallel to Halla's that bloomed inside Tamara.

Halla's attention switched from Kiron to Jarrod. She carefully studied him, then, unexpectedly, her long tongue snaked out to lick him, sending the Chief Councilor tumbling backwards.

Skye caught him, her surprised glance swinging from Halla to Tamara. A knowing look came over her niece's face as she accurately interpreted Halla's affectionate gesture as a reflection of Tamara's feelings for Jarrod.

Was she to have no privacy ever? The green could read her thoughts. Jarrod strode in and out of her mind as if no wall existed between them. Now Skye gleaned her deepest feelings as if they were written in the air. What was the point of being a separate independent female when no one respected her boundaries?

Thyel helped her dismount. "That was foolish of you. Why did you jump up on the green?"

"We don't have time for that now," Fane said from beside Kiron. They entered the cave where the bronze lay on his side panting while Halla hovered nearby.

"You're right," Thyel agreed. "That black may not remain down long, and the bronze is in no shape for another fight. Not when he's so obviously outnumbered. Best if we're gone before the black recovers."

"I doubt Kiron is in any shape to fly." Tamara looked with concern at the bronze. "The only good news is, Halla hurt Denton, the black dragon, badly with her last blast of fire. It should give us time to regroup."

"I wouldn't count on it," Skye said from the entrance. "Leaving is no longer an option. Look what's waiting for us out here."

Tamara hurried to her. Outside, scores of dragons were perched on the branches of every giant tree or crag in the valley. Her heart did a somersault in fear and wonder.

"What do we do now?" Fane asked with a tremor.

"Are they all on the black's side?" Tamara asked.

"Who knows?" Thyel said. "None look like they're on our side."

NO ONE'S SIDE, Halla said.

Tamara turned to the green in surprise.

DRAGON COUNCIL. THEY WAIT.

For what?

TO APPOINT THE NEXT DRAGON KING.

The answer sat as heavily on Tamara as it must on Halla. She looked at the green with deep sympathy.

Why can you not choose your own mate? she asked. It was not lost on her that she'd posed a similar query to her mother not so long ago.

MATE MUST PROVE WORTHY.

How? Tamara asked with a disapproving frown. *By forcing himself on you? How is that worthy?*

SHOW STRENGTH, CUNNING, DRAGON SPIRIT.

I thought it was the flight between realms that gave a dragon the ability to rule Isa. She paused as the disturbing conclusion to that thought reared its ugly head. *Kiron could show worthiness if he could transport Fane to another realm.*

KIRON NOT LEAVE HALLA. The green's words had a quiet certainty that pulled at Tamara's heart.

She didn't need prompting to understand the rest. The conclusion rudely pushed itself into the forefront. If Tamara were willing to allow Halla complete access to her mind, all of them could travel across realms together.

"We must leave Isa," Skye said with a hard, uncompromising glare at Tamara.

"He won't leave Halla," Fane warned.

Jarrod, lying slumped on the floor, glanced at Tamara with tender compassion.

"In your worry about Kiron," Skye said to Fane, "you might have missed Tamara's ride on Halla."

Fane looked from her to Tamara. "You mean…"

"She can talk to the green," Skye said with finality.

"Ah," Thyel said. "That's why you jumped on her. I wondered."

"Why didn't you say so before?" Fane sounded taken aback.

"Because she doesn't want to give control over to the dragon," Skye said

Tamara suppressed her annoyance. She'd allowed Skye to get close but did that mean everyone came in with her? This friendship business was tricky.

"You have it wrong," Fane said, surprising her. "Thyel posed the same question while we were out. Connecting with a dragon has nothing to do with control. You can't rule a dragon. They are proud creatures who won't let anyone dominate them. Which is why this war is happening. Denton wants to impose his will on Halla. Kiron says she would die first."

"I know," Tamara finally admitted publicly that she did indeed have an intimate link with the green.

Thyel put his arm around her shoulder. "You've already ridden her. It didn't frighten you. Perhaps we are not lost after all."

"Our contact was minimal." Tamara glanced at Fane, heat churning in the pit of her stomach at the type of contact it would take to travel across realms. "It would need more to leave Isa, wouldn't it?"

Fane nodded. "The binding must be complete. There can be no separation or you might lose your way during the journey. My master once told me of a rider who panicked mid-flight and was never heard of again. He believed the rider became distracted as…"

"Fane!" Skye interrupted. "This is not the time."

Too late. The threat sank in. Being trapped on Isa was bad enough, but caught between places, in the midst of nothing? Forever?

The familiar strains of her immobilizing fears returned. Her hands grew clammy, the room shrank and her heart raced until she feared she would die. She backed away, needing space, time for her body to run through this familiar terror ritual.

In a far dark corner of the cave, she slid to the floor, covered her face and willed her legs to stop quivering. Her mind would not still its silent screams. Echoes of her cries while imprisoned by her mother's spell returned with a vengeance.

From the corner of her eye, she noted Skye stop Thyel from approaching her. He nodded and wandered away.

Fane retreated to Kiron's side to tend his new wounds.

Skye quietly took some of Kiron's medicine and began to re-dress Jarrod's arm.

Tamara was grateful for their consideration. She needed time for this sense of utter panic to recede. She hated being like this – out of control, vulnerable, helpless.

You're not helpless. The thought was a whisper filled with compassion. Jarrod.

She glanced at him.

His brown gaze was filled with infinite understanding. *You're not alone, Tamara. You will never be alone again. Not as long as I breathe.*

I'm going to die.

You're not going to die. I won't let you, Jarrod said.

You're going to die.

He chuckled. *I'm not going to die either.*

You don't know that. You can't promise me that.

Can you hear your heartbeat? He asked, changing the subject.

It pounds, she whispered

Listen to mine.

Thump. Thump. Thump. Steady, like the man.

Now listen to yours, Jarrod said.

Thump-thump-thump. Rapid. Like a frightened deer.

Yet, there's nothing to be frightened of.

His reasonableness was a counterpoint to her racing pulse. There was nothing to fear.

Thump. Thump. Thump. Her heart was beating slower now. Matching Jarrod's voice. Her palms cooled. She was no longer dizzy. *How did you do that?*

I didn't do anything, Jarrod replied. *You are in control of your body. You always have been.*

It doesn't listen when I'm frightened.

It always listens. You have to tell it the right things.

Such as? she asked.

That everything will be all right. That you are safe.

She considered that advice in silence. Then softly she told herself I'm all right. *Thump…Thump…Thump.* Her pulse was slowing. She was amazed at the immediate response. Her gaze flew to his. *My heart listened!*

He chuckled again. *Yes, it did.*

Time ticked by as she commanded her breathing to settle and her muscles to stop twitching.

She closed her eyes, tears of happiness welling. In the middle of utter disaster, Jarrod had taught her how to gain the greatest control of all. Of herself.

Suddenly, she tensed. Something was amiss. *Jarrod!*

He looked at her, frowning.

What's happening? she asked.

I don't know. Something isn't right.

Kiron turned to the entryway, but his left side twitched with the effort.

A silent scream shook Tamara. She shuddered. Were the dragons attacking again? No, Fane and Skye were chatting, glancing outside and did not seem concerned.

Kiron sat up as if unsure what the problem was.

He can't hear that scream. Only she sensed the silent call for help. Halla's cry.

Someone was forcing her to endure a violation, in silence. Denton? Had he somehow gained entry into the side cave?

The cry came again.

Halla! Tamara scrambled to her feet.

"Thyel," Jarrod said aloud. "Where is Thyel?"

Skye turned back. "Why? What's the matter?"

Tamara stumbled toward the side cave where she knew Halla had been hiding "Someone's hurting Halla."

"Denton's still out there," Fane said. "I can see him."

Jarrod stirred from his resting place. "It's Thyel."

Tamara raced to the side cave with Fane and Skye at her heels. Inside, Thyel stood high up on Halla's back. A black cord was wrapped around the dragon's neck.

"Stop!" Fane shouted. "You mustn't try to control a dragon."

"I almost have her," Thyel called down to them. "Another moment and she'll obey me and we can leave."

Halla writhed in pain, her eyes rolling in fear.

Tamara sensed the grip on the green's mind – a noose of fire searing Halla's will whenever she exercised a thought.

Tamara's fury exploded. She scrambled up Halla's leg and charged at Thyel. She pushed him off and then grabbed the cord and pulled it off the dragon's neck. The cord vibrated in her grip like a squirming eel. With profound distaste, she flung it away.

The dragon reared. Tamara tumbled to the floor. The green backed away. Trying to stay away from Thyel, she smashed into the top of the cave and sent rubble tumbling.

Halla would have roasted Thyel if Tamara hadn't been lying near him.

Do it, she urged the dragon.

NOT HURT TAMARA. The green retreated further into the other cave.

"Why did you do that?" Thyel asked, rising to his feet and dusting himself off. "I almost had her."

Tamara rose and swung her closed fist straight at his jaw. It connected with a satisfying wallop.

Thyel staggered. Eyes wide in shock, he backed away from a fuming Tamara who was ready to strike again.

"You could have killed her." Fane came up to them. "That wouldn't have got us anywhere."

"I had her, I tell you," Thyel muttered looking resentfully at Tamara while nursing his jaw. "I was trying to save you the trouble of surrendering your will to her."

"What was that cord?" Tamara asked.

"It's the same one the King's Horsemen once used on me," Skye said, shuddering. "It absorbs and subverts Light."

Shock and revulsion coursed over Tamara like a wave of ants. "It can't be, Skye. Saira destroyed all of those cords. Besides, I touched it and wasn't affected." Then her understanding dawned. Of course. Her lack of magical ability meant the cord had no effect on her other than a bit of tingling. Her mind-talk mustn't be magical at all. She should have known better than to believe she had any ability to wield Light.

"Fane, get that cord." She couldn't bring herself to touch it again. While he went to do that, she turned back to Thyel. "How did you come by that?"

Her erstwhile lover shrugged nonchalantly. "Those of us with no ability to wield Light must find other ways to control those who can. You must understand that?"

"You sound like my twisted uncle." She whispered. Memories of that madman raving about his lack of ability returned as clear as if he spoke to her now.

Thoroughly disgusted, Tamara ordered Fane to get rid of the cord so no one could ever use it again – not on Halla, or Kiron and certainly not on Skye or Jarrod.

Fane did as she bid, taking it outside. When he returned from the entryway, he said, "Denton and his friends are getting restless." In his words she heard, *It won't be long before they attack.*

No more time to waste. Tamara's heart fluttered at what she was about to commit. On reaching Fane, she said quietly, "Time for us to leave."

Halla, who'd been quiet until now, let out a howl of joy.

Joy was the last thing Tamara felt. *Fear, yes. Panic, certainly. Terror, a close third. Definitely no joy.*

She scowled at the green. *After we arrive in Melak, no more reading my thoughts. No more mind melding. No more eavesdropping on my conversations.*

Are you speaking to me? Jarrod whispered in her mind.

Halla chuckled.

Tamara groaned at his mischievous look.

"It will be all right." Fane gave her a soothing pat on her shoulder.

Little you know. All he had to worry about was one dragon invading his thoughts.

"We'll need to be quick if we're to escape," Fane said, in a worried voice, "but I'm unsure how well Kiron can fly."

"Halla and I will lead." Tamara put a lid on the worry sputtering in her chest, which proved as effective as covering a boiling cauldron with a sheaf of paper. "Let's tie the two dragons together, so if Kiron flags, Halla can lend him support. That might also keep us from getting separated while travelling across worlds."

"Who goes with which dragon?" Thyel asked.

Halla's glare and the smoke puffing out of her nostrils, dared him to try mounting her again.

Tamara gave him a sour look, sorely tempted to leave him behind.

Skye leaned in to whisper, "With dragons outside, it might amount to murder if we leave him here. He was trying to help you."

Remembering Skye's horror at killing her elk decided the matter. "Thyel can ride with Fane."

"For your sake, I hope Kiron has no objections," Fane said to him in a grim tone. "Or you will find yourself a permanent resident of Isa."

"Before you ask, I'm with you," Skye said to Tamara. "Jarrod should be between us so we can support him."

"Agreed," Jarrod said readily. "Carrying three would tax Kiron."

"Of course, you're only thinking of Kiron." Skye sent him a teasing smile and snagged Falcon's Tome and his pack.

Thyel lingered by the ledge, glancing at the circling dragons above.

"We'll need a long, strong, vine to connect the dragons together," Tamara said to Fane as she and Skye helped Jarrod to mount Halla.

"I'll fetch us one," Thyel said and headed off. "Give me something useful to do."

Fane dressed Kiron's wounds one last time while he launched into an intricate explanation about binding with a dragon.

Tamara listened with care, shivering at the idea of dropping all barriers between her and Halla.

"You have more blocks than you think," Fane went on. "As one lowers, another will assert itself. When the final wall drops, you and Halla will become one being, with two bodies. You can move each other's limb separately or together."

Her stomach flip-flopped at the thought.

WE BECOME ONE, Halla said, her enthusiasm bleeding into Tamara. *YOUR FEARS, MY FEARS. MY JOY, YOUR JOY.*

Easier said than done. She was sure that instead of lowering any of her barriers, on the climb up with Jarrod, she had erected at least ten more.

Once Jarrod was settled, Tamara said, "I'll go back down and check on how Thyel's doing."

"No need," Fane called up leading Kiron forward. "He's returning with his find."

"Ready?" Thyel called up and swung one end of a vine to Tamara.

When he tried to tie it in place, Halla growled. Fane hurried to take over that task. Kiron, too, protested when Thyel came near him with the long vine. Fane finished the task of stringing the two dragons together. Then, while he looped the excess vine on the ground between the dragons, he spoke soothingly to the bronze. While Kiron was thus distracted, Thyel swiftly scaled up to sit on the bronze's back.

All too soon they were ready to take off.

Chapter 14

"DURING THE JOURNEY, you must clearly picture Melak," Fane called out to her from the bronze.

Tamara had been so involved with her personal turmoil, she'd missed Fane evolving from the fervent young apprentice she met a few days ago into this confident young dragon rider.

"See its general location in your mind, and Halla will follow that lead," he said.

"I don't know what Melak is like or where it's located." Tamara released Jarrod so he could lean back into Skye's waiting arms.

Her niece shifted, one hand wrapping around Jarrod's middle, while the other gripped the back of Tamara's chainmaille, until he was firmly sandwiched between them.

Jarrod seemed better. Fane's medicine was helping more than Thyel's had. Another strike against him. His intentions may have been good, but he had failed abysmally during execution.

"Do you remember the map in the tower room?" Fane asked. "The one that showed where Melak was located in relation to the rest of Ryca?"

"Yes." Tamara pictured it in her mind. "But what's Melak really like?"

"My master visited there once and described it as a place of high mountains and deep valleys."

Fane described the particular area over which his master had flown. He reviewed it in minute detail, from the glint of the orange sun to the color of the lakes and the fish leaping out of the water, until she felt as if she were there.

"Mind you," Fane concluded, "my master only saw all this by flying overhead. He never landed on Melak."

"Why not?" Tamara asked. "After going all that way, why didn't your master land?"

"Little is known of Melak," Fane said. "One rumor has fairies living there. Another that magic cannot function in the land. No one knows for certain. It would have been too much of a risk for my master to land."

"Yet, we plan to," she said.

"To rescue the prince," Fane agreed. "Worthy of the risk. My master traveled out of curiosity. He described the place as green and gray."

Bevan's description of tall, pale skinned warriors from Melak made her tremble at what she and her friends might encounter there. *If* they reached there safely. *If* they didn't get killed leaving this cave. *If* Tamara was successful in lowering all of her barriers in order to bind seamlessly with Halla. A great many ifs.

They had to at least try. Once they arrived on Melak, Skye could use her talent for finding things to locate her brother. Assuming wielding Light was possible on that parallel realm.

Jarrod's good arm wrapped around Tamara's waist while his legs stretched out on either side of hers. She sighed into his comforting hold, cherishing the feel of his face as it rested on her right shoulder. She was careful not to lean back though, lest she inadvertently hurt his left arm.

"Ready?" she asked her two companions.

"I will not lose you," he whispered.

Tears swelled in her throat, choking her at his promise. For with those words, he swore that even if she became trapped during this ride, she would not be alone. A wellspring of happiness sprang up and washed away the last of her fears.

"Ready," Fane called to them.

"Or not," Tamara muttered, "here we go."

Hands splayed on either side of Halla's scaly neck, Tamara shifted her bottom one last time so she fit the dips and rise of scales along the dragon's shoulders.

The two dragons ambled onto the wide ledge, and Tamara balanced, getting ready for the ride to come.

Overhead, the black hooted a challenge. He and his friends circled, calling to each other. The black still listed, suggesting the noise and dramatic flight was all for show. It would be his strong and healthy friends that were tasked with bringing Halla to heel and disposing of the bronze.

She took a deep breath, opening herself up for the full mental contact with Halla. When it came, the instant intimacy of the binding stunned her. She'd expected one barrier after another to give way, as Fane described. Instead, like a curtain rising, all the barriers lifted in unison.

Halla and Tamara became one in an instant. They flexed their wings together and tucked them back in.

Halla gave Tamara a wicked backward glance and then they took off, jumping off the cliff face and diving straight down. Kiron had no choice but to follow her lead. Without being told, Tamara knew what Halla was about.

Jarrod wrapped his good arm fiercely around Tamara's waist.

Skye screamed.

Tamara could only laugh as the ground rushed up to meet them. Knowing this was Tamara's reoccurring fear, Halla led her straight into it.

Jump together, indeed.

The sense of freedom she always dreamed such a leap would give her smacked her across her face in the form of a wild wind. Tamara reveled in the fall, the sheer joy of knowing full well that Halla would never let them touch the ground.

At the last moment, the green opened her wings and swerved up, with Kiron right beside her.

Tamara howled in triumph as they became fully airborne.

The black's contingent of dragons, at first lagging behind in obvious surprise by the green and bronze's unexpected dive, soon gave chase, to the roaring cheer of onlookers.

Tamara glanced back. Could Halla and Kiron out-fly the pack? Out of the corner of her eye, she spotted something to the left.

In one of the trees behind a large gray dragon, was a little green creature. It looked furious, shaking its tiny fist at Tamara.

The gray dragon, noticing Tamara's intent stare, looked behind at what had caught her attention. The tiny green creature vanished.

"That lead dragon is almost within reach of us," Skye shouted.

Tamara was shocked to find a brown-black dragon closing in. Carrying the heaviest load, Halla had begun to lag.

WHERE? the green asked, desperation and fear embedded in that one word.

Kiron flew parallel to them. Fane inclined his head to indicate he would implant the information he had about Melak to Kiron at the same moment Tamara did with Halla.

Leaning forward, she gently stroked the side of Halla's scaly neck and recalled her arrival at the tower room. She pictured Fane proudly pointing at the ancient, yellowed and crinkly map. This time, Halla followed her into there to look at the drawing. They studied the layout with care, seeking out where Melak resided in respect to Isa and the other worlds.

Tamara then played back the descriptions Fane mentioned about the fairy world. The high mountains, flowing rivers and ancient oaks and hawthorns.

A startling howl from behind alerted Tamara to the dragons on their trail. A glance back showed their pursuers looking confident. Holding back their fire, their eyes gleamed with the taste of victory.

One, then two and three and four lined up. *Gathering for the kill?* One reached out and swiped at Halla's tail. The green howled and sped forward.

The pack surged after her.

Expecting to be brought down, Tamara was shaken as the world shifted.

The line of dragons passed harmlessly through them. For a moment, she felt their essence and heard their howl of surprise and frustration, and then a resounding simultaneous roar of awe from the onlookers.

In a blink, they'd left Isa.

Specks of light sparkled around Tamara, whizzing by faster than Skye's magic Lights, buzzing with whispered words that Tamara couldn't quite make out.

She was suddenly alone. Her pulse racing, Tamara cried, *Not again.*

NOT ALONE, came an instant response. *NEVER ALONE AGAIN.*

Halla! Tamara looked around, searching. *Where are you?*

HERE, came the green's gentle reply. *TAMARA SAFE. HALLA ALWAYS WITH HER.*

Where are we?

BETWEEN PLACES. MY MOTHER SPOKE OF THIS. The dragon flashed a picture of Melak as Fane had described to Tamara. *WE GO THERE. WE FLY BETWEEN WORLDS.*

Tamara soaked up the warmth of Halla's presence, willing herself to breath, to calm down. Her racing pulse refused to listen, convinced the time spell was happening all over again.

An arm circling her waist squeezed. She sighed in relief, patting the hand to show she understood. She still rode on the green, and Jarrod held her tight.

Never alone again, he whispered, mimicking the dragon's words.

Tears wet Tamara's cheeks. If Jarrod was with her, Skye must be safely tucked in behind him. She wasn't alone. Remembering his teaching, she dampened her fears, focused on her thundering heart, and chanted, *You're safe.*

Slowly, her heartbeat changed – a terrified gallop dropped to a nervous canter and finally settled into a dignified trot. Her breathing quieted. In the stillness, came whispers, like the scurrying of mice down a dark corridor.

What are those whispers? She asked Halla.

I HEAR ONLY YOU.

Tamara blinked, surprised. Was she hearing things? The rapid movement of stars made her dizzy, uncertain. She touched Jarrod's arm, relishing his solid presence. He was real. Halla was real. Concentrate on that.

The world of Melak remained firm in Halla's mind and Tamara closed her eyes, shutting out the flashing stars. She clung to Halla and Jarrod as the only constants in a world gone wild. The whispers persisted, sounding louder, insistent, buzzing. She opened her eyes.

To her right, a lion lounged among the speeding stars, watching their passage with regal contemplation. Then it sat up, as if startled, and spoke. *Tamara?*

She recognized that voice, the familiar tone of censure. Her name had been spoken just so, in another lifetime; when she'd done something bad, when she'd misbehaved, when she'd displeased the king.

Father? The thought rocked her. He was dead. He couldn't be here in the midst of this confusion.

While trapped in the time spell, sometimes having lost track of reality, she'd imagine seeing beings that weren't there. Then Tamarisk would stride into the room, bringing the real world into focus. Was that what was happening? Was she losing track of what was real?

She closed her eyes and focused on the image of Melak that Halla projected like a beacon. Then, unable to resist, she peeked over her shoulder, to prove she was okay, that she wasn't imagining things.

The lion stared back, looking as shocked to see her, as she was to see it.

Tamara's heart pounded as panic galloped toward her. Halla flew as if the black's friends were once more nipping at her behind.

Did you see him, too? Tamara whispered, trying to calm her heartbeat, to reassure her body that she wasn't going mad. Hard to do when her mind was in total agreement with her racing pulse.

The dragon flashed her an image of Melak. Tamara's mind flew instead to Ashari. The world of souls. That was where her father should be. Were they traveling near Ashari? If so, that lion could indeed be the doomed King of Ryca.

Father. A flutter of desire to acknowledge him, to know he was here with her, was intense.

The last time she'd seen him was the day he died.

He'd stood tall and commanding on the balcony, looking at his people gathering from far and wide for a blessing her mother was to perform. A ceremony he'd said was needed, for Ryca quivered on the edge of disaster.

"How can land quiver?" Tamara had asked.

"All is not right with our world, Tam. It shakes and shivers and I don't know how to heal it."

"You can do anything, Papa," Tamara had replied with the confidence of a thirteen-year-old.

He'd given her a kiss on the top of her head. "How could I not, when you expect me to do no less?" He'd said with deep indulgence, but also a promise, or so she'd thought. Then he'd allowed his brother to knife him. Leaving her and her family to fend for themselves in a world turned terrifying.

Had he missed her as much as she'd missed him? His appearance switched from the father of Tamara's youth to that of a wise old man. He wore a white robe cinched at the waist and stood on an open field of green, the sky a blinding blue. He frowned, his fists resting on hips, much like he would whenever her mother brought her to him to be punished for being disobedient.

Only, he never ever punished her. Once her mother left the room, her father would throw her into the air and tell her to not do that again or next time he wouldn't catch her when she came down. The idle threat always sent Tamara into a fit of giggles.

What are you doing here? He sounded angry, not indulgent or playful.

Tamara frowned, and suddenly, Halla, too, was with her, staring with surprise at her father.

The world turned upside down and they fell.

Skye screamed. Jarrod's grip across Tamara's abdomen tightened into a band of steel.

Fane shouted across the roaring wind and spinning lights. "What's happening?"

They fell out of the between places. Halla flapped her wings to keep airborne. Kiron popped out of thin air beside them. The vine that tied the two dragons jerked him along with Halla until he, too, flapped frantically to stay airborne.

The dragons gained balance and once again flew side by side. Below, verdant fields greeted them instead of ancient ash or hawthorn or oak. The few trees that were present appeared young and vibrant, as if spring had just arrived.

"Where is this place?" Skye shouted.

"Not Melak." Guilt reared in Tamara at bringing about this disaster. She'd allowed herself to be distracted and Halla had picked up on it.

Kiron listed, hardly able to stay in the air.

Fane indicated with an arm motion for them to descend. "The bronze needs rest."

Tamara nodded and urged Halla to land by a copse of trees. The two dragons flew over a little lake in a clearing near a wood and landed.

Tamara slid from Halla's back to the ground with a thump that wobbled her legs. She slumped onto her behind. All was silent and peaceful. This place embodied a sense of calm.

Skye dropped down beside her.

Jarrod descended, too, much slower, and offered Tamara his good arm. She couldn't believe he had the energy to not only stand, but offer help. She made a show of leaning on him but forced herself to stand on her own.

Halla rushed toward Kiron, her concern obvious.

"What happened?" Skye asked, getting up.

"My fault," Tamara said in contrition. "I saw a lion and then thought I heard it whisper my name."

"Kiron says this is Ashari." Fane joined them, looping the vine that had tethered the dragons. "This is the land of the dead."

Tamara gave him a sheepish look, her worst fears confirmed. "I'm truly sorry. This is my doing. I heard my father calling my name."

"The king?" Thyel asked, approaching and looking around. "Where?"

"Grandfather?" Skye said. "Do you think he's here?"

The land around them appeared empty, deserted. Had she imagined him?

"After he died, this is where his soul would have come to rest," Fane said.

"I saw no trails or villages while up in the air," Thyel said. "Simply clean untouched land and a blindingly blue sky and nary a cloud."

"Look," Tamara pointed up. Far to their right, the three sister moons could be seen. "Those are from Ryca."

"Not surprising since all the worlds are interconnected," Fane replied. "My master said they sit one on top of another but in different realms, different realities."

It was possible her father spoke to her then. The thought at once thrilled, terrified and angered her. All these years he'd been resting here comfortably, at peace. Now the shock of seeing him was over, she wasn't sure she wanted to meet him again, even if she could.

"Shouldn't we make plans to resume our journey?" Thyel sounded edgy.

Tamara was of a like mind. How could she have been so foolish as to let the king's voice distract her? She should have shut her ears. The sooner they left this place, the better. She had no wish to meet her father. Why was Thyel anxious to leave?

"Not yet." Skye pointed to Jarrod, who looked pale beneath his dark skin. His lips looked parched and dry and beads of sweat had formed on his wide dark forehead.

"I'll be fine," he replied.

"Kiron is weak too," Fane said. "Best if we rest a while and re-dress everyone's wounds before resuming our journey."

"Let's make camp over there." Skye indicated the oasis of trees nearby. "We can take shelter under the canopy if it storms." She looked up at the cloudless blue sky and smiled. "Maybe not storm but it might give us protection from the wind and shade from the sun."

Tamara draped Jarrod's good arm over her shoulder for support. As they walked, he leaned on her as lightly as she'd pretended to lean on him. He gave her a warm look though, thanking her with his somber gaze. Skye, with his tome slung over her shoulder, kept pace beside them.

Thyel seemed positively jumpy as they entered the treed area.

"What's the matter?" she asked.

"I don't like it here. I'm going to scout around."

His tension must be catching. Her knotted shoulders only relaxed after she lost sight of him. They were going to be here awhile and already her stomach growled at the lack of food. They hadn't eaten before leaving Isa. She hoped they could find something other than Jarrod's flatbread to eat.

While Skye gathered wood for a fire and Fane strode toward Kiron, Tamara settled beside Jarrod. She unwound his bandage to apply a fresh paste.

"I am grateful for your tending," he said.

She glanced up, surprised to hear his deep thoughtful voice. Resting with his back to a tree, she had assumed he'd fallen asleep.

"You're most welcome, Chief Councilor," she said with a smile. "Though Skye's touch is likely gentler."

"It is."

She sent him a dagger glance, her humor gone.

He chuckled and then whispered, "It isn't as pleasing."

His words were a caress.

Hands shaking, she retied the knot and he winced. "Sorry," she muttered.

This time he did raise his hand and brushed her cheek. "Do not feel badly about this interruption to our travels. We will reach Melak soon enough."

"Are you reading my thoughts again?"

"I don't need to. You berate yourself for every perceived fault. No one is perfect, Tamara, not even your father."

• • • •

JARROD WATCHED HER stroll toward the lake, disappointed that he'd upset her. He fingered the chainmaille and empty sword sheath she'd shed beside him.

Skye returned with an armful of branches. She dropped them on the ground and dug a little hole to use for the base of a fire. She glanced from him to her aunt. "Problem?"

He shook his head. Skye twirled the sticks to ignite sparks. Finally, she gave up and held up her hand. One of her magic Lights appeared. With a mischievous wink at him, she flung it into the wood. "Find me the fire."

The Light ball crashed into the wood but no flames erupted. With a sigh, Skye sat back.

"No luck?" Jarrod asked in sympathy.

"I've been trying to find out what else I can do with my Lights," she said. "But all they do is find things, not create things that aren't there."

"Unfortunate." He was suddenly exhausted. The journey had taxed him. How fragile his strength was, one moment solid, the next melting like snow in sunlight.

"Do you think Grandfather is truly here?" Skye asked.

"If he is, he isn't making any great effort to find us."

"Just as well," Skye looked to where Tamara had waded into the lake until she was knee deep. "He would receive a sad welcome from my aunt."

Jarrod nodded. "She has nursed a grudge against King Keegan for a long while."

"But it's not his fault he was killed," Skye said.

"In Tamara's mind, he should have foreseen the threat and safeguarded his family."

"It's the fault of the time spell. That's why she was trapped for such a long time. That was forged by my grandmother, not her husband."

"Perhaps it is easier to hate someone who's no longer present," Jarrod murmured.

"Tamara's resentment seems to extend equally to both of them. In all the years I've known her, she and Grandmother have hardly said more than a dozen words to each other.

"For all that," Jarrod said, "she loves her mother."

"How can you be so sure?" Skye gave him a look of curiosity and, was that hope? She was a sweet girl who hated family dissensions.

Jarrod shrugged, as much as his bad arm allowed. "She cares about her mother's opinion of her, and is hurt when she disappoints her. Most of all, she's protective and doesn't want her mother hurt more than she has already been."

"Are these things written in your tome or are they mere observations on your part?"

His gaze swung to Tamara's curvaceous silhouette. Her trousers hiked up, she was bent over, silently waiting for her dinner to swim by. She looked more beautiful than any woman of his acquaintance.

Halla leaned over her shoulder and a flurry of fish disturbed the surface as Tamara's dinner escaped. She turned to the dragon and an argument ensued, involving much hand gesturing urging the dragon to retreat.

Jarrod's humor peaked as he imagined what that conversation entailed. He glanced back, and found Skye watching him as intently as he'd been observing Tamara.

"I've been wounded," he reminded her. "That leaves much time for contemplation."

"About all of us, or just my aunt?"

He ignored the cheeky comment.

Skye sat companionably beside him, having given up starting a fire. "I've an idea."

"About?" he asked with suspicion.

She held out her hand and one of her Light balls appeared. She sent it speeding toward the dragon on the shore. The ball of Light came to rest on the tip of Halla's nose. The dragon flailed at it and created such a ruckus that Tamara again scolded the green for disturbing the fish.

Halla went back to sulking.

Skye leaned past Jarrod and whistled. Halla looked over to her. Skye beckoned the green over, using the bouncing Light ball for emphasis.

Halla ambled over.

Skye, with much hand waving, indicated what was required to set the sticks on fire.

Halla obligingly blew a flame at the sticks. The stack of wood caught fire and the dragon returned to the lake to sit on the edge and despondently watch Tamara fish.

With a howl of triumph, Tamara captured a large fish and tossed it toward shore. The dragon leaned over and expertly caught it between her teeth, swallowing it whole.

Skye chuckled as another argument ensued between dragon and mistress, resulting in Halla stalking off to find her own dinner elsewhere.

"Get something for Kiron," Tamara shouted.

The backward surly roar from Halla suggested she hadn't needed that reminder. The green took off into the air.

"Maybe now we'll get some fish for dinner," Jarrod said, unable to smother his bubbling humor.

"I never doubted it," Skye replied, feeding her fire with bits of branches. "That's the one thing I've always admired about my aunt. Once she sets her mind to a goal, she always achieves it. Which is why, when Bevan went missing, she was the one I turned to. Despite the fact that she rarely, if ever, gave me the time of day, I knew if she agreed to help me, I would find Bevan."

"You will." Jarrod patted Skye's shoulder. "This I've no doubts about."

"But you have about recovering those lost historians?" Skye asked.

"The prospect is not encouraging. I've no idea why the words in Falcon's Tome are disappearing. Or why my people are vanishing. Or why the people in Ryca have forgotten the Erovians they've worked with." Until he found answers to those questions, he couldn't bring himself to accept Tamara's generous offer to marry her.

What if one day he vanished, leaving her as her father had? He couldn't do that to her.

He glanced at Falcon's Tome lying beside him. Gently, he traced the engraving that outlined a time from long ago when the world was first made. It showed a figure emerging out of darkness. The great Falcon himself.

"My biggest fear is that one morning I shall wake up and this book will be gone."

Skye looked at him with worry. "One of my biggest fears is to wake up one morning and find you gone."

Unable to hold her worried gaze, he turned his attention to Tamara. She was wading further along the lake's edge until she became lost to view behind some trees. Had his disappearing like the other Erovians ever crossed Tamara's mind?

Chapter 15

TAMARA CONTINUED FISHING as her temper simmered. Skye and Jarrod were conversing by the clearing. They didn't argue, they weren't at odds with each other, they laughed and joked and chatted as if they were the best of friends.

Their ease in each other's company echoed the sense of peace this world exuded, but their camaraderie generated a tang of bitterness at the back of Tamara's throat.

On the pretext of finding a better spot to fish she strode toward a line of willows that drooped over the water. The trees shaded part of the lake and effectively hid Jarrod and Skye from view. The shade also made it easier to see underwater as the sun's reflection changed from mirror to window. Peace returned to keep her company.

Tamara was so intent on her prey, she wasn't sure when a sense of being watched first stole over her. She straightened and swung around to pinpoint the source. There, among the trees, a lion lazed, gazing at her.

Instinct urged her to kneel before her king. She blinked, finding herself submerged in the cold lake, kneeling, with water tickling her chin. The lion was gone.

Had it even been there?

She stood, scolding herself for being a fool. She returned to her fishing, the sun warmed and dried the top half of her. It was hard to concentrate, though, when she kept checking over her shoulder. Her neck crimped. Suddenly, she felt alone and vulnerable.

Since this journey began, Halla became part of her soul. Skye and Jarrod, and even Fane, had taken residence within her heart. Despite all that, she still felt isolated. As if it would be a waste of time to turn to anyone else for help.

"Why is that?" her father asked.

Tamara whirled around, her tunic's hem splashing the surface. On the shore, robed in white, dark beard sprinkled in silver and trimmed close to his chiseled face, her father appeared as sharply clear as when she last saw him. The day he died and her family's nightmare began.

Her emotions heaved like a storm-tossed ship, shunted between joy and despair. He had left her. There could be no forgiving that. Yet, she had missed him every day since. He had been her anchor. The reason to wake up every morning so she could look at her world from the safety of her father's side. A child's foolish fantasy.

She set her jaw and turned her back. She'd estimated that she needed at least five large fish for a good satisfying meal, and probably an extra one for each of the men. Jarrod, though weak, was slowly regaining his strength. The fish swimming by her feet did not seem as plump as the one Halla had swallowed.

"Will you not speak to me?" her father asked.

"You're not alive," Tamara said. "You're dead. There is no one there to address."

She set her hands in the cool water, a foot apart and held still, waiting for a fish to swim through. By looking at her hands underwater, she could avoid looking at the reflection on the surface, of his face right beside hers. Not a splash had indicated he drew closer, yet there he was, mimicking her fishing stance.

She straightened. "Go away."

"After you've come so far to see me?" His lips twitched with humor, eyes smiling with an achingly familiar warmth.

She returned to her task. "Don't fool yourself, Father. Our stop here was a mistake. As soon as Kiron is rested, we'll be back on our journey."

He scooped a fish and flung it to shore. In quick succession, three more were sent flying over his shoulder. She set her teeth together, grinding them with frustration. Not one fish came near her hands while they swarmed around him.

She stood, glaring. "You're using magic!"

"I'm teaching you how to fish. Did you miss me, my darling Tam?"

Tears welled at his personal nickname for her and she swung away so he wouldn't notice. She moved further along and bent to her task. A fish swam by and she dived for it. The scaly slippery thing slithered past her hands and got away. She muttered in frustration and looked for another.

"Gently," he said from right beside her. "Invite it into your hands."

No movement of water or splashing, yet he was beside her again. "Stop using magic around me."

"Why? Because you don't believe you have any? What happened to the little girl who patiently waited for the Light to blossom within her?"

"She grew up to realize even her father lies."

"Did I?" His eyebrow rose in gentle inquiry. "Lie to you?"

"Yes! Everything you ever told me was a lie. How can you stand here in this spiritual realm and pretend innocence? Is there no reckoning after death? If not, all my fantasies of you roasting in the pits of hell have been a waste of time."

He nodded toward the shore. "There's nine fish on the shore. More than enough to feed your hungry horde. Let's continue this discussion beside them."

"There's nothing to discuss." Tamara strode deeper into the lake, wading until she was chest deep. "Go away."

"If we only have one afternoon to us, Tam, are there no concerns you wish clarified before you leave?"

"There's nothing you have to tell me that I wish to listen to anymore," she said over her shoulder. She looked forward and he stood before her. "I said stop that!"

"Good point. Let's talk about magic first. Are you not pleased with your talent? Is it not the best gift of all? I urged you to be patient, that your Light would show itself when you most needed it."

"I thought I needed it most when I was trapped," she whispered. "It never came. I have no magical talent, Father. I never will. Jarrod's wrong. Opening my mind to invaders is not a talent, it's merely a sad lack of defense."

He brushed her cheek gently with the back of his dry hand. "I'm sorry for that lost time. I wish I could have been there to comfort you. I watched you every day and cried with you for your pain. You must understand, your mother did what she did to keep you safe, and it worked. If not for that spell, Tamarisk would have used all of you in unspeakable ways. Though you may have cursed every day you were trapped, I thanked the Light for every moment you were protected by that spell."

"Why?" she asked, swallowing the tears in her throat. "Why did you leave us?"

"I never expected my brother would attack me."

"That's a lie."

He smiled. "How could you possible know me so well?"

"You were my hero." She said that simply, for that's exactly what he'd been.

"And you were my inspiration." He tipped her chin up. "I'm sorry I disappointed you."

"Why did you?"

He sighed and stepped away. He waded back to the shoreline and she automatically kept pace. "I saw the influence Tamarisk had on my brother. More, I foresaw Tamarisk's grand plan."

Tamarisk, the sorcerer who had been her uncle's friend. Until he turned on them. When they were under the time spell, he came every night to torment her mother and instead, terrified Tamara by spinning mad tales about him becoming part of the royal family, of raising Tamara and Garren as his own children.

Sometimes, when she felt really low and particularly angry with her father, Tamara fantasized about that being true. Guilt scorched her cheeks at having been so weak and needy that she would have willingly turned to her enemy for comfort. She glanced away to hide her shame.

Her father pulled her close, kissing the top of her head. "I never stopped loving you, Tam," he whispered. "I never will. As for Tamarisk, his plans were grander than to be the only man wielding power. He wanted to change Ryca itself. To destroy its foundation. To extinguish the Light from which magic stems. I had to stop him."

"By dying?" She was unable to keep her lingering bitterness out of that question.

"I wove a secret spell of my own. To protect Ryca, our people and the Light from being harmed. Tamarisk knew I was up to something and that the work drained my magic and my strength. When I was at my weakest, he enticed my brother to strike."

Tamara spoke slowly, trying to understand what her father told her. "You were attempting to save us all?"

"Do not paint me a hero again. I wasn't there for your mother when she needed me. Or for my children. Or all those magical guild members who suffered horribly under Tamarisk's hand. I am to blame for that. I was their king. It was my duty to protect them."

"You were protecting our entire world?" Tamara asked in a small voice, as the enormity of her father's actions sank in.

"And I failed."

"Did you?"

Father and daughter stared at each other.

"Didn't I?" he asked with a frown.

"Tamarisk drained the powers of all those guild members for years and still he could not wield a tenth of the magic you could with a flick of your finger. Saira, with Anna's help, brought him to his knees."

A slow smile spread across her father's face. "I did stop him."

"You crippled him," she corrected. "Saira stopped him. She wouldn't have been able to do that if you hadn't bound the Light from his use. He was left to rely solely on Darkness. You taught me that the power of the Dark to Light is like a candle flame to sunlight."

He nodded, and a weight seemed to release from his stiff shoulders. "Then the sacrifice was worth it."

"Yes." A similar weight dissipated from the stranglehold it had held on her heart. "Yes, it was." Impulsively, she hugged him, only to have her arms go right through. She stumbled forward. "Sorry." She stepped back with an embarrassed smile. "I forgot. You're not real."

"As real as you. I need warning to prepare first."

A light breezy touch brushed her cheek. "Now, will you introduce me to your friends? And Skye. I desperately want to meet my granddaughter."

Tamara returned to camp with her father at her side. Skye looked up first, shock registering on her gentle face as recognition came in a swoop.

Beside her, Fane, who had been squatting by the fire, vainly encouraging green wood to burn robustly, gaped at the new arrival, then gave a deep bow to the king.

Keegan gestured to the youth. "Rise, boy."

Jarrod, who rested by the tree, scrambled to stand as well.

"I thought she would refuse to speak and we'd never have the chance to meet," Skye blurted and then slapped her hand over her mouth.

Her grandfather grinned. "In convincing your aunt to forgive me, have I earned a hug from my beautiful granddaughter?"

"Oh, yes, sir." She ran and hugged him fiercely.

Tamara watched with envy, for Skye's arms did not go through.

"The queen will be so pleased," Skye said and released him. "Will you come back with us?"

He shook his head, eyes downcast. "I exist only in spirit form and am confined evermore to Ashari." He sounded broken. Tamara had thought he was at peace here. She'd obviously been mistaken. About so many things.

Jarrod held out his good arm.

Keegan shook it. "Thank you for taking care of Saira during her time of trial, Lord Jarrod. I worried she would never find your city."

"We worried, too, my liege," Jarrod said. "And please, call me Jarrod. It was a blessed day when your daughter found our wandering city."

"Or your city found her," Keegan said with a grin.

Jarrod nodded. "The Light works in inexplicable ways."

Keegan pointed to Jarrod's injury. "What happened to your arm?"

"A break, shortly after we arrived on Isa. It hasn't healed as fast as I hoped."

The king laid his hand on the bandage, a frown on his brow. "No wonder. The wound's been poisoned."

"What? How can you tell?" Tamara inched closer to look at Jarrod's arm. Then rolled her eyes at her father's bland look. "Of course, you use magic as casually as you breathe."

"How was it poisoned?" Skye asked.

"We've been applying herbs to heal it, sir," Fane said. "I used the same herbs on Kiron and he was healing."

"The exact same herbs?" Keegan asked.

All remained silent. Tamara voiced their suspicion first. "Thyel!"

"I've been concerned about Thyel's poultices too," Fane said, sounding sheepish. "I didn't want to say anything since he was your friend."

She'd been the one to insist he come along. "What does hurting Jarrod gain him?"

"He might have been jealous," Skye said gently. "Saw him as a rival for your affection."

"The whys and hows can wait." Keegan reached for Jarrod's left arm. "For now, if you will permit me, Jarrod, it's time this arm was whole again."

"You can do that?" Jarrod asked. "Even here?"

Keegan smiled as he worked on Jarrod's injury. "The loss of flesh has allowed my spirit to delve deeper into the workings of Light, not lessened my ability." A blue glow formed over Jarrod's left arm and then sank into his flesh.

Jarrod sucked in his breath. A moment later he let out a laugh. With his right hand, he fumbled to untie the bandage.

Tamara stepped up to assist and their fingers got in each other's way. "Let me help."

Jarrod huffed with impatience but moved aside. Freed of its binding, his arm appeared smooth. Jarrod gave a shout of delight.

"There's not a mark on it." Fane sounded impressed.

A sympathetic glow warmed Tamara and she tentatively stroked his newly healed arm. It was strong and gentle, capable and adept. Just like the man. "It's beautiful."

Jarrod pulled her to him and gave her a fierce hug. The gesture felt like a fervent thank you. She was about to say no thanks were necessary, at least not to her, when he kissed her.

Tamara reeled at the unexpectedly tender touch. She had dreamed of Jarrod kissing her but the action surpassed her wildest imagining. Her senses reeled as if she'd been swept into Heaven.

Their kiss slowed and changed, evolving into a tender, loving declaration. This touch hinted at a future. Of a type of togetherness Tamara had never experienced but wanted to cherish with all of her heart.

Jarrod suddenly pulled back, looking as stunned by the kiss as she was. She blushed steaming hot, feeling shattered that they had to stop, that they were in public, that he might never kiss her like that again. For she remembered Jarrod had not accepted her proposal with spoken words.

His gaze flickered in every direction, as if he couldn't believe he'd kissed the king's daughter in front of the king.

Her father's gaze, rife with speculation, first settled on her and then swept toward Jarrod. Skye's eyes sparkled with a knowing, accepting humor.

Who knew what Fane was thinking? He seemed distracted, looking from Jarrod and back toward Kiron.

"My arm is better than ever." Jarrod flexed his fingers and then his arm, obviously unwilling to acknowledge the impact his kiss had on her, their audience or on himself.

"Glad I could help," Keegan murmured.

"Sir," Fane said tentatively. "Would you do the same for my dragon? He was hurt badly in a fight."

"The gentle Kiron," Keegan said. "Of course. Lead me to him."

The moment her father was out of hearing, Skye turned to Tamara. "Well?"

"Well, what?" Did her niece want an explanation for that kiss? She wouldn't be the only one.

"Don't play innocent," Skye said. "What happened to your grudge against Grandfather?"

Not the kiss, then. Her gaze flicked to Jarrod.

He, too, waited, curiosity plain on his face.

Tamara relented and thought back to her conversation with her father; her anger, bitterness, followed by awe at learning what he had been trying to accomplish with his last magical act.

Jarrod touched her hand, indicating he'd picked up on her thoughts. This time, she was happy with their extraordinary connection. If her father and Jarrod were to be believed, her ability to mind-talk was a reflection of her magical ability.

Something she and Jarrod had in common. The idea pleased her. Never in her wildest dreams would she have seen herself as having anything in common with the studious, serious, scholarly Jarrod. His kiss confirmed that more than reading and writing drove Jarrod's passions. He'd moved from thought to action. She wanted his words, too. She wanted all of him.

"Tamara?" Skye persisted.

She flashed her niece a rueful smile. "I blamed my father for dying." She held up a hand. "I know. Unfair, illogical even, but he was the strongest sorcerer on Ryca, Skye. Yet, his magic-lacking brother murdered him. I assumed Father must have been careless or wanted to die. How else could he have been taken unaware by his brother?"

"Oh." Skye sounding stunned. "I never saw it that way. You're right. Ywen should never have been able to kill him. Even with Tamarisk's help, Grandfather was too powerful. Then how did..."

"His magical guard was weakened."

"Why?"

"He'd been weaving a spell to protect the Light, the magic of Ryca. It sapped his strength, making him vulnerable." With humble contrition, she added, "He risked it to save our world, Skye, and I've been blaming him for abandoning me."

Skye gave an exclamation of wonder. Then she took hold of Tamara's hands. "It's not your fault. If I'd been trapped for years like a butterfly pinned to a board, alive and aware of my surroundings, unable to move, cry or die, I would have blamed him and everyone else too. I didn't understand before. No one in our family did or we would not have allowed you to push us away." She wrapped her arms tightly around Tamara as if she never intended to let go.

Tamara hugged her back. She was starting to like these unexpected embraces.

Jarrod was frowning, staring after the king.

Tamara released Skye, sensing his worry. "What's the matter?"

He absently rubbed his recently healed left arm. "Do you think he might know what's altering Ryca's history?"

"I hadn't thought of that. If you explained what's been happening I'm sure he'd be able to help us decipher what's distorting Ryca. He'd want to know about it, anyway."

Jarrod grabbed Falcon's Tome.

"Father!" Tamara ran to catch up with Keegan.

He turned from attending to Kiron's injuries. The dragon flexed his wings, stretched his neck and let out a triumphant bellow.

Far off in the distance, Halla replied.

Tamara sent a mental note to the green that she was no longer angry and was sorry for having been in a bad temper.

A warm mental hug answered her and she sensed Halla winging her way back.

"Something else requires my attention?" Keegan asked.

"Jarrod has a question," Skye said.

"Sir, my people have been disappearing." Jarrod opened Falcon's Tome. "Many of the pages are blank. Something is erasing our historical records and as that occurs, those who penned the work have vanished."

"Odd," Keegan said. "Has anyone witnessed these disappearances? There might be a clue there about how this villainy is being carried out."

Jarrod shook his head. "It's worse than historians being snatched, sir. When I last spoke with Queen Mamosia, she said she didn't remember one of the historians who had worked with her for years. Which makes me suspect that not only are words being erased, and the historians vanishing, but history itself is being re-written."

"May I see the tome?"

Jarrod handed over the book. The king ran his hand along the face of each page, frowning as the number of blank pages mounted. He shut the book with an angry snap. "Someone's distorting my spell."

Tamara exchanged worried glances with Skye and Jarrod.

"The one you built to protect Ryca's Light magic?" Skye finally asked.

He nodded. "No one knew of that spell except for myself and possibly Tamarisk. He didn't have the talent or skill to alter it."

"And he is dead," Tamara said.

Worry was clearly written on Keegan's face as he handed the book back to Jarrod. Tamara then guessed what bothered him.

"He's here, isn't he?" she whispered, as if a skeleton had risen up and grabbed her ankle. "Tamarisk? He's on Ashari."

"Upon their deaths, condemned souls are drawn to the dark side of Ashari," the king said.

"Then how could he affect Ryca now?" Jarrod asked.

"He can't. No more than I could effect changes there. If he kept his madness at bay, he could have contacted his kin. As I did, at times, with Saira. Family members are easiest to reach. When she needed to be warned, or urged to follow her quest, I tried to reach her. The contact is delicate. Most people don't even sense our touch. Even Saira did not know when I gave her this idea or that, from time to time."

Tamara frowned. *He'd contacted Saira?* Then the reason came. While Tamara had been safe, for most of her life, Saira had been crippled, hunted by Uncle Ywen and a demented sorcerer across Ryca.

In comparison, Tamara's troubles shrank to miniscule proportion. What had been Saira's reward for rescuing her mother, sister and brother? Tamara had rejected and resented her for having been free while she was trapped. She squirmed at her ungrateful, petty behavior.

On her return to Ryca, she would give her sister a huge apology for years of surly responses and ingratitude. She had much to make up for with all of her family.

"Tamarisk had no family," Jarrod was saying. "I've read his history, from birth to death. There is no hint of a child, brother, sister, aunt or uncle. His parents died when he was barely six. He was brought up by a neighboring couple, who took pity on him." He grimaced as he added, "Tamarisk killed his adoptive parents once he was old enough to want more freedom than they allowed."

"I didn't know that," Skye said.

"Could he have had a child even though it's not recorded?" Tamara asked.

"No. Our seers predicted he would be instrumental in Ryca's undoing so my father kept a close eye on Tamarisk."

"As a young man, his movements would have been easy to follow," Keegan said, "but as an adult, while on guard, he could have cast a spell to hide the truth."

"If he had a child, we would have known about it," Jarrod tapped his book with certainty.

"How else could Tamarisk tamper with my father's spell?" Tamara asked.

"Let me see that book again," Keegan said. "The man lusted after my wife. He would have hidden any child by another woman. Even considered the baby not his, seeing it as less than perfect if born of any woman other than Mamosia. Here it is."

Jarrod leaned over to read. "*Son of Drummond and Raina*...but that is Thyel's parentage."

"Thyel?" Tamara asked, as dread returned.

"Drummond is Tamarisk's adoptive mother's family name," Keegan said. "Tamarisk had the legal right to choose it for himself, if he so wished. He didn't."

Jarrod took the tome back. "The truth was recorded here but in a twisted fashion."

"As you say, Falcon's Tome always records the truth," Keegan agreed. "How one interprets it, is up to the reader."

"My father must have known," Jarrod said. "I wonder why he never mentioned it?"

"Perhaps he died before he could," Tamara suggested gently. According to Saira, Jarrod's father had been killed while Jarrod was away.

"Thyel?" Skye shook her head. "Now it makes sense why he would poison Jarrod. He might have discerned Thyel's birth history from Falcon's Tome."

"As could Father," Tamara added.

"He was nervous when you said you'd seen Grandfather," Skye agreed.

Tamara had been played for a fool. She'd promised never to trust anyone again, and while rejecting her family, she ended up trusting an enemy. She wanted to crawl away in shame, but she was done with hiding.

"Where could he have gone?" Skye checked toward the horizon with concern. "I doubt he's really scouting the land."

For miles around them, the land appeared peaceful and serene. Tamara wondered if any of it was real.

Keegan closed his eyes and appeared still, as if listening to a silent message. He opened his eyes and a frown marred his forehead. "He's not on the part of Ashari I can sense. He must have gone to the dark side."

"To see Tamarisk?" Tamara asked, knowing the answer.

Her father nodded. "I wish him well with that quest. The dark side of Ashari isn't a place I would wish on my worst enemy."

Perhaps Thyel would find his just reward yet. She fervently hoped so.

"What about Bevan?" Skye said. "Could my brother's disappearance have had anything to do with the distortion of Grandfather's spell?"

"He's missing, too?" Keegan asked.

"Yes, sir," Jarrod said. "Although he isn't a historian, Prince Bevan went missing at about the same time as my people. I wondered if there might be a connection."

"He's a powerful young boy," Tamara said. "I wouldn't be surprised if he found your spell and noticed something was wrong."

"Making him too dangerous to leave unharmed," Jarrod added in a somber tone.

Chapter 16

"TAMARA," SKYE SAID, "Bevan told me he planned to speak with you that morning. Did he mention anything about Grandfather's spell?"

She shook her head. The conversation with her nephew was still unclear. How could she have been so distracted as to not listen to what he'd said?

Her father stepped closer and touched her forehead.

"What are you doing?" she asked.

"Helping you remember," he murmured.

Light sparked inside her eyes. Warmth spread from his fingers and the Light formed little balls that raced up and down at the edge of her vision. Then the Light balls rolled away.

Tamara was in the castle's breakfast parlor speaking with Thyel. The excitement of what they planned for that night tingled along her spine.

He touched her cheek and she wanted to lean into his palm. Instead, acutely aware of the wide-open parlor door and the guards outside, she kept her distance. She would be in his arms soon enough.

This night's event was the most daring thing she'd ever done. The risk was worth the reward. Only four days remained before her mother's ultimatum came due. If she didn't know by then whom to marry, she would be forced into Gideon's arms. She cringed at the very idea of that vile merchant touching her. One way or another, she would *never* allow that to happen.

This plan had to succeed.

Thyel was her last and only hope. For the past several weeks, she had tried to entice many of the men who courted her to overstep their boundaries. To prove they would put her needs above their fears. All alleged to be deeply in love with her but the moment she tested them, each feared to displease the queen more than pleasing Tamara.

All, that is, except Thyel. He'd enthusiastically agreed to do as she asked.

In fact, it was he who came up with tonight's plan. Her guard was to be drugged by doctored wine. All that remained was to set the time of the tryst. She was about to ask Thyel that very important question when a knock interrupted.

Bevan stood uncertainly in the open doorway.

"May I speak with Aunt Tamara?" he asked in his tentative way.

"I'm busy." Tension spiked her suspicions. *Had her mother sent him to spy?*

"It's important." Bevan stared at Thyel, chin unusually stubborn. "I have to speak with my aunt. Now."

Odd to hear her normally reticent nine-year-old nephew sound insistent but she didn't have time today, nor was she in the mood to humor him. She was about to tell him to go annoy his sister instead when Thyel touched her shoulder.

"Yes?" she asked, startled.

"Perhaps you should speak with the young prince. We can finish our conversation in a short while. I've some arrangements to make yet and will return to tell you of my success."

He bowed to Bevan before heading for the door.

Tamara folded her arms. "You've gained my undivided attention, Bevan. What do you want?"

Once Thyel was out of earshot, Bevan said, "I don't like that m.m.m...man."

As Bevan's amazing magical ability continued to blossom, he'd been steadily gaining the appearance and authority of his grandfather, but he'd also gained a stutter.

She'd thought he'd conquered that speech malady last year. Or so Skye had said. As he'd overcome being mute for the first four years of his life. Something must be upsetting him.

"In case you haven't heard," she said, "I have four days left to choose my mate. That choice is mine alone. Not yours. *Not* the queen's." She picked up her cup of chocolate. "Why do you want to talk to me, anyway? If you've a problem, why not annoy your sister with it? The issue is magical, right?"

He nodded.

"Then I'm not the one to help, am I?" She took a sip.

"You're the only one." Bevan shut the parlor doors. "I think we m.m.m...may be in trouble."

"*We?* Do you mean you, me, or our family?"

"You, m.m.m...me, our family, perhaps all of r.r.r...Ryca."

Tamara had to laugh. He spoke in such a dire tone, as if the world were about to end. She put her cup down and stepped out onto the balcony. *This is where I stood with Father before he died.* She hugged herself, willing her strumming nerves to hush. She normally avoided this area of the castle, but Bevan had made her so nervous she'd forgotten and come out here. A chill wind made the hairs on her arms quiver.

Why couldn't he leave her alone? She was about to agree to lay with Thyel to test his loyalty. Who had time for family matters before a momentous event like that? Too much at stake to waste time on imagined problems. "Your Aunt Saira saved our world five years ago," she said. "There's no one left to threaten us. Well, threaten Ryca, anyway. Mother seems to enjoy threatening me."

She gave Bevan, who'd followed her out onto the balcony a teasing smile to lighten his mood. "Unless you've come to save me from my current threat, little nephew, we've nothing to talk about."

He shook his head solemnly. "We are in danger." His shoulders just cleared the tall railing as he peered in the direction of Tibor. The city lay like a slumbering giant, with the twin towers and enjoining arch, its shoulder blades.

"I see what you mean," Tamara said. "Look at all those Horsemen with flaming swords and trolls swarming over the city. Run, sound the alarm!"

Bevan gave her a tolerant look that reminded her uncannily of her father. "Is that all you see, Aunt Tamara? What about the dragon swooping down with flaming breath or screaming in fury? Don't you see and hear that, too?"

The comment rendered her speechless. "How could you..." she began when he interrupted.

"You have information I need. Only you can help avert world-wide d.d.d...disaster."

The boy was beginning to frighten her. "I have no magical talent. Thank you for reminding me of that unfairness. If there's really a disaster looming, speak to Saira, or Anna, or your sister. Anyone who can really help you."

Having said that, she believed he was upset about something. "Would you like me to come with you?"

"No. Why will you not l.l.l...listen? It's all tied to your dreams. You spent time with Grandfather on his last day. Tell m.m.m...me about what he did. Everything. Please? It's important."

What did that horrible day have to do with anything? The recollection of her precious time spent with her father and all the horror that followed returned to scorch her.

She shook her head, wanting to block out that day. She backed away until the cold metal railing dug into her back. "Go away."

She folded her arms and forced her voice to sound hard and firm. "I can't help you. I won't. I want nothing to do with anything Father was involved in. Leave me be!"

Tears welled but anger swept away her grief.

"Aunt Tamara." Bevan tugged at her sleeve. "Please, what did you and Grandfather speak about?"

She snatched her arm back. "Nothing."

Everyone in her family knew talking to her about her father was forbidden.

"I might have discovered one of Grandfather's spells," Bevan continued. "Except it isn't working properly. Something's wrong with it. I need to know how he crafted it. Please. Where did he go? Did he say anything about his spell?"

Tamara ground her teeth to keep her temper in check. "Bevan, I don't want to remember anything about my father."

"B.b.b...but..."

"Go. Away."

"Grandmother said you two spent the whole day together."

Tamara cringed. She had been an adoring puppy, seeing no ill in him. Thinking him indestructible. What a fool she'd been. He'd been vulnerable and weak, like any man.

A knock came and then the door opened to reveal Thyel. "All done?"

"Yes," Tamara replied with utter relief.

Bevan said, "No."

"Yes," she insisted, striding up to Thyel's side. "I don't remember that day, Bevan. I can't help you. I know nothing about his magic. Saira may be able to do something about your distorted spell. She's good at fixing things."

"What distorted spell?" Thyel asked.

"Bevan was …" Tamara began.

"N.n.n…nothing important," the boy interrupted.

She sent him a frowning glance. First, he wanted to talk. Now, he had nothing to say?

"I'll come back later, when we can be alone," Bevan said as he left the room. "M.m.m…maybe in an hour. I will discuss this with Aunt Saira. She might be able to talk to you."

"Don't hold your breath," Tamara called after him.

As Thyel shut the door, Tamara sighed resignedly. Yes, that's exactly what she needed next, her sister and nephew combining forces to torture her about her knowledge of her father. She'd have to ensure she wasn't so easy to find in an hour. She turned to Thyel. "Let's go for a ride."

"Of course." Thyel kissed her hand, sending out shivers of anticipation about tonight. "This is our day. We can do anything you wish." He then rubbed her forehead with a forefinger. A pulse leaped inside her temple and all went dark.

When she opened her eyes next, her father lowered his hand that had been touching her temple. He had also been holding hands with Jarrod, who was connected to Fane and from him to Skye. She guessed by their unbroken link, they'd all seen what her father must have when he touched her forehead.

Jarrod looked profoundly sympathetic and Fane concerned. Skye on the other hand, when she met Tamara's gaze, showed the first hint of true dislike.

Tamara could find no words to defend herself. She deserved her niece's wrath. She had not only ignored Bevan, but likely put him in the path of danger.

Her cheeks heated with shame. How could she have acted like that? Had it been the first time, or had she been mean-spirited every day since being released? In the midst of her turmoil, another stunning thought intruded.

"Bevan never told me about a tall white-haired man coming to challenge him," Tamara whispered.

"You were under a misdirection spell," her father said. "We must find Thyel." All King and Commander, his voice whipped out the order.

"Misdirection? Thyel be-spelled me?" Could these revelations get worse? He can work Light?

"More like twisting Light into Darkness," her father said.

"You couldn't have known." Jarrod's arm went around her in support.

Tamara was stricken. "I didn't trust my family, yet I trusted him, an enemy."

"Blinders are made not just by spells, Tamara, but from our own fears." Her father's gentle tone made her feel worse.

"This brings us back to our original question," Jarrod said. "Could Thyel be Tamarisk's missing kin?"

"Yes," the king said. "I tasted Tamarisk's magical scent on you."

A burning rage took over Tamara's shame. Thyel had used her. She'd allowed it.

Just then Halla winged overhead, landing gracefully nearby. The wind of her descent bent branches and flattened grass. In her jaws, she carried a dead deer that she expertly tossed to Kiron, who caught and gobbled up the morsel. Halla then turned to Tamara.

It's my fault that Bevan's missing, Tamara whispered in anguish.

WE FIND BOY, came Halla's calm answer. *ALL WELL.*

All not well! We're stranded in this strange land. I'm probably responsible for Ryca's history unraveling. For the Erovians disappearances!

BE CALM, Halla fluttered her wings looking anything but calm. *WHAT MUST WE DO?*

The answer was simple. *Find Thyel!*

YES, came Halla's fervent response. *HE BAD TO MY TAMARA.*

She shrugged on her chainmaille and reached for her sword sheath and remembered she'd lost the weapon fighting Denton. Dropping that, she raced toward Halla. Ignoring the hot tears streaming down her cheeks and calls from her friends and family, she swiftly climbed up. *Did you see Thyel on your flight?*

NOT LOOK FOR EVIL ONE.

Even Halla had known better than to trust him.

Fane was the first to reach Halla's side, though the others were fast on his heels. "Does she know where Thyel has gone? Is that where you're going?"

"No," she called down. "But I'll find him."

"Tamara," her father said. "None of this is your fault. I was fooled by Tamarisk. It's hard to know whom to trust when magic is involved."

Unable to stand his sympathy, Tamara shook her head.

"We'll help you search." Fane raced toward Kiron. The bronze knelt to allow him to climb.

"Wait for me." Skye ran to join Fane.

Tamara winced. With this last revelation, she had finally killed her niece's trust. She swallowed the hurt and gestured for Halla to begin her flight.

Halla rose into the air. Tamara spared a heartbreaking glance at Skye, who avoided eye contact and refused to acknowledge her in any way.

• • • •

KEEGAN'S HAND AT JARROD'S elbow restrained him from following Tamara. "We've grave matters to discuss about your historians. Allow Tam to deal with this Thyel. I do not envy his future at her hands, do you?"

He gave the king a concerned look and then nodded his head in agreement. Skye climbed aboard Kiron and sat behind Fane. Then a heated discussion took place between them. Finally, the male dragon, too, was airborne, but he flew in the opposite direction to where Halla took Tamara.

Tamara's emotions churned as she clung tight to Halla. He wanted to hold her, to tell her she was loved and deserving of love. He doubted she would believe him.

He turned to his companion and found King Keegan observing him instead of the flyers. He suddenly felt as if he'd been brought before the king to justify his interest in his daughter.

Keegan abruptly headed toward the nearby copse of trees. "Come along."

Jarrod followed, trepidation and excitement warring within him. For so long now, he'd been worried about his people, Ryca's history, his whole reason for existing vanishing like the words in Falcon's Tome. There had been no one he could share his worries with who had the power to resolve the problem. Until now.

"So," Keegan said, "tell me of your intentions toward Tam."

Jarrod's snapped his head up and his startled gaze collided with a determined fatherly stare. "Sir, that kiss…"

"Is irrelevant." Keegan waved a dismissive hand.

"Ah." Jarrod sighed in relief.

"Your obvious reluctance to commit to her is not."

"But..."

"Do you love her?"

Beneath that paternal kingly glare, Jarrod couldn't have lied even if his people were capable of deception. "Yes."

"Good. Let's ensure we are clear about my expectations. I want an invitation to the wedding. I will not be able to attend in person, but be assured, I shall listen to every vow being made."

At the king's words, a clear picture formed in Jarrod's mind of his wedding. It would take place within the tent city of Erov, of course. Since it was a traveling city, they could easily encamp inside the palace, where Tamara's family could attend. She would be robed in a diaphanous...

"Jarrod!"

At Keegan's call, he returned to the present. How strange. He hadn't succumbed to daydreams since he was a boy. "Sir, please understand, I wish to marry Tamara, but I cannot tell her so until I can be certain I will be here to carry through with any marital promise I make to her. I'm unsure if I will even exist tomorrow."

"Let us solve your historian riddle then," Keegan took command of Falcon's Tome.

"Sir," Jarrod began tentatively, wanting to voice a question that had been plaguing him since they arrived on Ashari. "Have you seen my father here?"

Keegan gave him a quick raised-eyebrow look before returning his attention to the book. "No. He's an Erovian and all of you are a tricky breed. I've not quite sorted out your purpose yet."

"Our role is clearly outlined in there," Jarrod said pointing to the tome. "Every Erovian, from childhood, is taught that we are the watchers of events, the historians of Ryca." Though Jarrod spoke with confidence, he was no longer the same man who had stepped through the gate between Ryca and Isa. Falling in love with Tamara had changed his focus. He wanted more than to merely record events. He wanted to be part of the making of history, too.

"Every role undergoes change over time," the king said, as he flicked through the tome. "Has not the recording of history taught your people that?"

"We never change." His every word was spiced with doubt.

"Everyone and everything changes, Jarrod. It is the harmony of life. Without change, all you would have is stagnation and death, which is a reflection of the darker side of Ashari."

Keegan held up his hand and Light appeared in his palm. "This is the source of life. It is what we tap into to create change, what people call 'magic.' Its purpose is to create." He shut his fingers and the Light disappeared. "Without change, nothing exists."

"Sir, Erov has always been the same." Why was he arguing this point? He had changed. A testimony to the king's words.

"Erov has been ever evolving," Keegan said. "It has changed so much you've forgotten where you came from. That discussion is for another time. For now, we must focus on what's happening to your book and to the other Erovians." The king shut the book and tapped the tome's leather bound cover. "Tell me your story."

Jarrod related all that had occurred to bring him, Thyel, Fane, Skye and Tamara on this journey that landed them on Ashari. He was barely finished when a strange sensation crept over him.

He'd felt this same eerie feeling when the historians began to disappear in Erov. As if the world was slowly dying. The idea brought fear hammering at his heart. Had he brought his troubles into this peaceful resting place? "Something's the matter, sir."

"Very perceptive, Chief Councilor," Keegan said, looking around with a frown. "I, too, sense a disturbance in the Light."

· · · ·

TAMARA STROKED HER fingers along Halla's scales as her gaze fell back toward Jarrod's and her father's retreating forms. How quickly the two men had taken to each other. Discovering how Thyel had manipulated her probably sealed any chance she had of earning Jarrod's respect. Was that why he chose to stay with her father? His desertion on top of Skye's brought a lump to her throat.

She wanted him to view her with admiration, yet every action she'd taken so far – ignoring Bevan's call for help, disobeying her mother and allowing Thyel to beguile her – all of it warranted no more than Jarrod's contempt.

JARROD LOVES TAMARA, Halla gave her a worried backward glance. *No*, Tamara replied, *he doesn't.*

JARROD FOOLISH THEN, the green growled. *TAMARA MUCH LOVABLE. HALLA LOVES TAMARA.*

The warmth accompanying that proclamation made her smile. She turned to search with a lighter heart. There were few places to hide in the meadows below. Her gaze scanned for a sign of Thyel's dark brown tunic and black head of hair.

Movement caught her eye, but it wasn't Thyel. It was that lizardy thing again. This time, the beast wasn't hiding. It gazed up at her boldly while hanging precariously to the side of the trunk of a young oak.

Was she imagining things again? She must be, because the idea this thing could have followed her from world to world was too farfetched.

Keeping her eyes pinned on its long billowy green hair, yellowy-green skin, sharp face and wide white eyes, Tamara whispered to Halla, *Do you see what I see?*

Tamara felt the lightest touch of the dragon's mind and then Halla turned her head toward the oak.

YES, SEE LITTLE BEAST. WANT FOR EATING?

"Eeek!" cried the lizard as if it had overheard Halla's mind-talk. How could that be? It scampered off to the other side of the oak.

Halla flew toward the oak and circled low around the copse of trees. Finally, she landed by the tree in question and walked around it. They couldn't spot the little being.

"Let's keep looking for Thyel," Tamara said, frowning. She didn't want to be distracted from her quest. Thyel was dangerous, while the lizard was a mere curiosity. The dragon winged her way into the air. Tamara glanced back toward the oak, but the green lizard did not show itself.

At least now she knew she wasn't imagining it, for Halla, too, had sighted it. Unless what Halla saw was a reflection of what Tamara imagined. Was that possible? She shrugged and looked away. She'd ask her father about it when she returned. If this thing really existed, he would know of it.

Halla suddenly gave a strident cry filled with fear.

Tamara searched for the source of the green's distress. Finding nothing, she focused on Halla's thoughts. There, she pictured Kiron hovering low to the ground with Skye and Fane on his back. Thyel, standing on the ground, was magically wielding a black band lassoed around the bronze's neck to hold him in place. The same cord he'd used on Halla.

Kiron screamed in agony.

Seething with rage, Halla swung about and flew in the direction of the male dragon. Tamara was confused. Fane had got rid of that cord, hadn't he? While hunting for a suitably long vine to tether the two dragons together, Thyel had been absent. If he was capable of casting spells, Light or Dark, he could have somehow retrieved that cord from wherever Fane threw it.

Hurry! she called to the dragon.

They arrived in time to see Kiron land and slump before Thyel.

Fane and Skye rolled free.

Halla dove, inhaling air, readying to spew fire on the man attacking her mate.

Thyel quickly climbed onto the bronze as Halla landed. "Stay back," he warned.

Unable to fire without harming Kiron, Halla snapped.

Thyel drew back his clenched fist and the band around the bronze's throat tightened, pressing into his scales until Kiron coughed.

"Stand down," Tamara said to Halla, gently patting her neck in warning.

The dragon stomped a foot, frustrated by the command but understanding the danger to Kiron.

Thyel's smile stretched wide as he relaxed his fist. The cord loosened and Kiron took a desperate breath. "Welcome, Tamara. Was your reunion with your father pleasant?"

"What do you want?" she asked as Fane and Skye came over to stand beside Halla.

"You have no right to ride Kiron," Fane said.

A glance down showed the lad's face wreathed with matching agony to what shadowed Kiron's features. He must feel every hurt his dragon did, while she, through Halla, only sensed a tiny portion of the bronze's suffering.

"I repeat," she said, "what do you want?"

"I wanted you," he replied.

"Liar! You be-spelled and used me."

He shook his head, smiling. "I see your father's been busy. My spell was merely to make you more amenable, my love. You have a strong mind and I needed to bend it a little."

"Why? What am I to you?"

All his smiles vanished. "You are my doorway to reclaim what should have rightfully been given to me. Your mother was meant to adopt me as her son, and take my father as her husband. Foolishly, she rejected both of us."

"She never even knew you existed," Tamara said.

Thyel's eyes hardened but then he visibly relaxed, shrugging. "Her loss. With my father murdered by your vile lame sister, my next best option was to take you as my wife. It would have brought me into the royal family of Ryca, where I belong."

"You don't belong there, Thyel." Tamara spoke in a mild tone, layering each word with contempt. "You never will, no matter how much you squirm."

"Tamara," Skye whispered fiercely, "this is not helping!"

Thyel laughed. "And you wonder why I want you? We are perfect for each other. You have a feisty temper I admire and a disdain for your family that I respect and mirror. If only the scholarly Jarrod had not distracted you. However, he's no longer an issue."

His smug look sent fear spiraling through Tamara. "What have you done?"

"You'll find out soon enough. I've another matter to tend to. My father tells me the boy prince is free on Melak and is making a nuisance of himself. It's time to end his stay there, permanently."

"No," Skye shouted and ran forward.

Thyel squeezed his fist and Kiron writhed.

Skye stumbled to a halt.

"Never fear, Skye," Thyel said, "you and Fane may accompany me to greet your brother. I'll need Fane's assistance to travel with this beast to Melak and your seeking ability to find the boy."

"I'll never help you," Skye said.

"You will if you want this beast to live," Thyel said.

"We'll come!" Fane shouted, taking Skye's hand.

She shook off his hold. "I won't betray my brother." She gave Fane an apologetic look. "I'm sorry, Fane, I can't."

"Then do it to save your grandfather," Thyel asked. "And Tamara's beloved Jarrod."

"What do you mean?" Tamara asked, heart squeezing in horror. "Speak plainly."

Thyel gestured with his free hand. "My father has gone to capture yours and your lover. He's taking them to the dark side, to give them a taste of his reality."

His gaze returned to Skye. "You have a choice. If you don't help me, you will be responsible for Kiron's death and Fane's. I'll also delay your aunt so she can't race to the others' rescue."

He shrugged with false sympathy. "I cannot guarantee how the Chief Councilor will fare, for those of the flesh cannot survive on the dark side without protection. However, if you come with me, there's a slim chance your grandfather's spirit might escape. What is it to be, Skye?"

She looked at Tamara with shocked eyes. She wanted Tamara to help her decide and Tamara was more than happy to oblige. She knew exactly what needed to be done.

"Bevan's already freed himself once, Skye. He's both smart and powerful. Even if you lead Thyel to him, your brother can defeat Thyel. I'm certain of it. Go with him, and protect Kiron. I'll find my father and Jarrod."

"I can't," Skye said. "I won't give Bevan up."

"A family dilemma. What to do, what to do?" Thyel grinned and tightened his hold making the bronze quiver.

"Please help me, Skye," Fane said. "Don't let him kill Kiron."

Halla spoke to her. Tamara listened and then looked directly at Skye. "Halla says that if Kiron dies, so might Fane. Their connection is too deep to sever."

Tears welled in Skye's eyes and her lips trembled.

Tamara's heart broke for her niece. She'd come on this quest to save her brother and was now being asked to give him up to the man who engineered his kidnapping.

With a cry Skye nodded and she and Fane hurried over to the bronze.

Tamara couldn't stay here any longer. She had to find Jarrod and her father to warn them of danger. She tugged on Halla, but the green refused to move.

NOT LEAVE KIRON, was her stubborn response.

Then Tamara remembered how she had contacted her father while traveling between worlds. She closed her eyes and called to him.

A vision immediately appeared of tortured screams, and a warren of darkness where dark spirits swirled, directing her away from one tiny corner where light blazed. At the center of that bright oasis, her father and Jarrod stood with hands outstretched, fighting to keep the encroaching darkness at bay.

Tamara came back to the present to find Skye sitting on Kiron, between Thyel and Fane. Kiron rose in the air and in the space of one breath, all four were gone.

WE FOLLOW KIRON, Halla commanded.

No, Tamara said. *Their battle. Ours is to free my father and Jarrod.*

KIRON WILL DIE, Halla pleaded.

My father needs me, Tamara insisted. *When he needed me last time, I wasn't there. This time I have to help him and Jarrod.*

Halla shook her head. *KING'S SPIRIT STRONG. HE FREE HIMSELF AND JARROD. SEND JARROD TO YOU. WE HELP KIRON.*

Tamara sat still on the dragon, shuddering with indecision. Her father hadn't been able to save himself the last time Tamarisk attacked him. What about Jarrod?

DECIDE OR TOO LATE FOR KIRON, YOUR FATHER AND JARROD. Halla dropped her head in defeat. *I GO WHERE TAMARA GOES.*

Follow Kiron to Skye and Bevan's aid, or go to the depths of hell to rescue her father and Jarrod. Either way, she would be letting some member of her family down.

With a heavy heart, Tamara made her choice.

Chapter 17

TAMARA SOARED INTO Melak on Halla's back. They arrived in the middle of a deluge. Thunder shuddered in counterpoint to flashes of lightning. Rain pelted her head and shoulders. Tamara caught her breath at the elusive glimpses of the drowning countryside before wet black sheets concealed the view. Within moments, she was thoroughly soaked and shivering.

Too dangerous to remain airborne, she told Halla. *We must land.*

WHERE? Halla's tone was more abrupt than normal.

Lightning ripped across the blackness. Tamara blinked away reflected streaks of light, wondering if that pounding was the buffeting rain, her drumming heart or Halla's thundering pulse hammering against her legs. *Are you all right?*

HALLA LAND, the green replied, flapping hard.

The descent took a long while. Beneath her, Tamara felt the dragon's legs extend, reaching for anything solid. Just as she asked, *Could we be above water?* Halla jerked to a sudden halt, claws scrabbling to hold onto something.

Tamara half slid off the dragon's back and struggled to get her lower limbs back in place, her arms clenched around the scaly neck. Halla had found a perch but was having a hard time balancing.

WEAK BRANCH. Halla sounded petrified.

The branch snapped and they plummeted. The sound of cracking branches was punctuated by a terrified scream, but she wasn't sure if that last sound came from her or Halla.

Their rapid descent ended with another jarring halt. Tamara wrapped her arms fiercely around the dragon, her heart thudding in joy at no longer falling. Only her arms held her in place, for her legs were swinging free.

The ground pulled her downward and her precarious panicked grip on the green's wet scales slipped. *Not to complain, Halla, but we seem to be hanging upside down!*

Halla grasped something higher up and heaved upward, bringing her other foot to join its partner. The bough bent dangerously as she shifted her enormous weight onto it but it held.

The new platform allowed Tamara to sit with her legs straddling the dragon's shoulders again. She collapsed against Halla's neck, relief coursing through her. Though she had often imagined leaping to her death, she wasn't yet ready to face the end of her existence.

Lightning flashed, revealing a giant tropical forest in every direction. The lush greenery seemed never-ending. The canopy concealed the ground and any dangers that lurked beneath.

If this tree they perched on was any indication, the stature of the plants in this world was enormous. Halla might as well be a bird sitting on a limb instead of a dragon that would ordinarily dwarf a tree.

Well, Tamara said, easing apart the bands of panic constricting her chest, *I'd say we've arrived on Melak.*

Halla gave a shiver and stretched her wings before tucking them in with an emphatic *swoosh* that conveyed better than words her opinion of this new world.

Tamara shared the dragon's unease. Not a propitious start to this leg of their journey. How were they to find Kiron, Skye and Fane in all this darkness? Had they made a mistake in coming here instead of going in search of Jarrod and her father? When it came time to decide, she'd known she really had only one acceptable choice.

Her father was already dead, and Jarrod was a man with more mysterious powers than even she knew about. Whereas Skye, along with Fane and Kiron, were under a madman's control. Most important of all, she owed Bevan for letting him down. She couldn't get past that last debt.

Besides, no matter how powerful Bevan was, magic did not function on Melak.

On Ryca, even though she couldn't cast one spell, she had always been able to sense the presence of Light. Frustratingly so. She had felt it within her family, in the time spell that confined her, even in the air she breathed. Like a comforting childhood blanket, Light had always been present, just out of reach.

Here, the world felt empty but for the fury of nature. She shivered.

Halla mimicked the motion and added a warm *THANK YOU FOR COMING TO DEAD PLACE FOR KIRON.*

Tamara patted the dragon's neck. The howling wind and hammering rain made verbal conversation impossible, so she was grateful this magic-dampened place hadn't silenced their mental connection. *I don't see how we'll find him in this weather.*

WAIT FOR DAYLIGHT?

Yes. The delay irked, but what choice did they have? Fly out blindly and get killed? That wouldn't help anyone.

She hoped Thyel, too, would be wise enough to wait out this storm. For Skye and Fane's safety as much as to ensure he didn't get too much of a head start. Assuming they had all arrived at relatively the same location on Melak.

Halla inched along the branch to settle closer to the trunk and invited Tamara to shelter beneath her wing.

Tamara thanked her and scrambled down to do so. She sat with her back against the dragon's warm leg. Her worry for all those whom she loved kept her company. She prayed a new day would bring illumination to the world as well as clarity to her mind. With lightning and thunder muted by Halla's leathery wing, Tamara drifted off to sleep.

Jarrod's hands cupped Tamara's face and turned her toward him. They were on a meadow so pleasant and peaceful that she guessed they were on Ashari. She ran her hand along his smooth dark cheek, and gazed into his black eyes in wonder. His love for her was clear, strong and true. She had never expected to see such devotion, not for her.

"Have you been behaving yourself?" he asked in that deep somber tone she loved.

"I thought you could read my mind."

He chuckled and bent to kiss her but stopped short of meeting her lips. "Tell me you've been good."

"Define good!" she countermanded, closing the distance to finish the kiss, but he pulled back before their lips could connect.

He tilted his head and gave her a stern look. "Not attempting to kill anyone. Not insulting a man's work. Not leaving him when he needs you most."

"Oh," Tamara said, disliking the definition. "Does the kiss depend on my answer?"

That elicited another chuckle. This time, his lips met hers in a sweet melding that quickly delved deeper into a soul-searing union that left her lightheaded. She wrapped her arms around his solid form and moaned her approval of his lovemaking.

"Now you've had your kiss, answer my question," he whispered, his breath brushing across her burning lips. "Have you been behaving yourself?"

"No," she answered and then amended quickly. "But I will, after I've killed Thyel."

She'd barely finished speaking when Jarrod disappeared, leaving her standing alone in the meadow.

"No," she cried out. "Don't leave me."

NOT ALONE. The thought intruded on Tamara's dream. Halla. She ignored the dragon and searched for Jarrod.

COMPANY. The dragon popped into her dream world.

Tamara pushed at Halla. *Go away.*

She tried to walk off but Halla blocked her path with an extended claw. *WAKE! WE HAVE COMPANY!*

Tamara stirred, feeling the aches and pains of lying curled in a tight ball against the dragon. She was still thoroughly soaked and shivering with cold. The dream, however, had cheered her. For a moment, Jarrod had been with her. He was still alive. She was certain of it.

She lazily stretched her cramped left leg and it dropped. Pulse leaping in fright, she snatched her leg back and snapped open her eyes. The entire ordeal of arriving in Melak rushed back. Expecting to find herself in the dark, in the rain, she was astonished to be met by daylight, and an audience.

She caught her breath at the scores of green beings hanging off, swinging on, or spread-eagled over nearby branches as they studied her from the surrounding trees. They were slender, with dense green fur that covered their heads and long tails with a scaly body in-between. Their pointed faces had beautiful wide expressive eyes.

They're like the green thing we saw on Ashari.

NOT FOR EATING, Halla said sagely, eyeing the company with interest.

The thought seemed to startle a flutter among the watchers and Tamara guessed telepathy was a natural means of communication in this Light-dead world. Could she then speak to them, too?

She stood on the branch beside Halla and pictured Skye's long blond hair, Fane's short brown locks and Kiron, much like Halla but larger, bronze and with a recently healed scar on his back.

The lizardy things looked back at her with their wide curious green eyes. Though she hadn't sensed their response, she suspected most had "seen" the pictures she sent.

One stood and placed its little green hands on its hips, its long tail flicking. It had a faint black design etched on its right cheek. She recognized the mark. This was definitely the creature that had spied on her at the Quinlin Temple in Ryca. Had it followed her to Isa, then Ashari, and finally back to here?

Watching it watch her, she gained the impression that "it" was a "he." Not so much from any physical variation in characteristic as much as an internal sense of his presence. Her perception shifted until she sensed each member of her audience – their gender, personality, even their sense of humor. Most seemed lighthearted in nature, though there were the odd dark-humored ones and a few serious spectators.

Her attention returned to her green-skinned shadow. How had he managed to follow her from world to world?

What do you want? she asked.

A vision of the black cord Thyel had used to trap Kiron and bind him to his will flashed in her mind.

"The magic-dampening cord," Tamara said to Halla. "They know Thyel has one. Could it be from this world?"

THEY NOT SEEK US.

"Maybe they'll help us, then, since we're both after the same target."

EVIL ONE ELSEWHERE. WHY GREEN THINGS HERE?

"Let's ask." She pictured Thyel with the cord around Kiron's neck arriving in Melak.

Her black-cheeked shadow gestured to a female. There was a flutter of conversation, aloud this time, in high-pitched tones. A female scooted down the tree. Moments later, she returned to hand the leader a vine.

He held it out for Tamara and Halla to see. It was exactly like Thyel's cord. Again, she received a flicker of a vision. This time of Tamarisk, surrounded by several King's Horsemen stepping onto shore from a boat. The men searched the surrounding scenery until they found the black vine.

See that man? Tamara asked Halla.

WHO?

Tamarisk. From a long time ago. So, Tamarisk must have come to Melak. Saira had set off on a voyage to the other side of Ryca, hoping to enter Melak through a natural inter-world boundary. Had Tamarisk done the same? "Could these Melakeans travel using boundaries between various realms?"

ASK.

Before Tamara had formulated her question, a series of ethereal doorways flashed into her mind. She scowled. If they could read her so easily, could she reciprocate the experience?

The idea of intentionally invading another's mind against their will in order to steal their thoughts made her queasy, even if they had shown no such restraint toward her. The concept felt invasive, unnatural, or at the least, impolite. Still, how else could she find out what they wanted. She needed a bargaining chip to get them to help her.

As quietly as she could, she shared her dilemma with Halla.

I TRY?

Tamara was relieved. Halla had no such moral aversion. She made a mental note to have a discussion with the green about this subject later. For now, she said, *Would you, please?*

She watched the dragon stare at the lizards, who stared back at the dragon. The silence stretched and then Halla said, *WON'T SHARE.*

You mean you can't read them?

NOT LET ME.

They can stop you?

BLOCK WHEN NOT WANT TO TALK.

Tamara frowned at the crowd, her temper rising. If they didn't want to talk, she and Halla had other things to do.

She climbed up the dragon's back and settled herself between Halla's shoulder blades.

The dragon obligingly spread her wings in preparation for flight and knocked a few Melakeans off their perch.

Several shouted in protest and flailed, trying to find purchase on lower branches.

With a pat, Tamara signaled Halla to go.

The leader from the tree across glared at Tamara.

Halla swooped off the limb and flew below the opposing tree.

A thump behind her startled Tamara. The little black-cheeked lizard had landed on Halla. He grabbed at the dragon's scales for leverage and pulled himself up until he knelt behind Tamara, his little clawed fingers linking into her chainmaille.

She'd never cared for people crowding her. A side effect of being trapped for so many years perhaps. Something she planned to overcome in the near future, with the help of many hugs from her family and closer contact with Jarrod. Those plans, however, did not encompass growing closer to an untrustworthy alien reptilian mind-reader.

She had half a mind to toss him off.

He yelped and crowded even closer, as if expecting her to do that. His claws scraped her skin.

"Ouch!"

Halla turned her head in inquiry.

Tamara leaned sideways so the dragon could spot the stowaway. The dragon's tail whipped around and the interloper plastered himself to Tamara's back, his tail wrapping around her right leg.

OFF? Halla asked Tamara casually.

Before she could respond, Black-Cheek flashed her a series of pictures of Skye, Fane and Thyel riding Kiron as they flew over a forested area. In one of those pictures, Bevan stood on a shore, looking into the horizon – alive and unharmed.

She crowed in happiness and Halla, matching her mood, soared upwards The Melakean hung on.

"If you're coming with us," Tamara told him, "you'll have to earn your passage. Where are Skye and Bevan?"

An urge for Halla to change direction hit her.

The Melakean unwound his tail and loosened his grip. He climbed up her back until he could sit on her shoulder, his rough cheek brushing her ear.

"Move over!" she ordered.

The Melakean grumbled but complied, allowing an inch of space to separate them, but spoilt the effect by wrapping his long furry tail around her neck.

His breath wafted past her cheek like an ill wind. At least he smelled sweet, not sour. The scent reminded her of a mixture of ripe fruits and blossomed flowers. Odd. She would have taken her little stowaway for a meat-eater.

As intrusive as her companion was, Tamara allowed the uncomfortable contact in exchange for finding Skye faster.

On the horizon, clouds gathered and darkness tinted the sky gray. Droplets of rain splattered her nose and cheeks and in the distance, thunder rumbled.

Great. Did it ever stop raining in this world?

The Melakean flashed a picture of a cloudless blue sky with the underbrush bathed in sunshine.

Would she ever get used to having everyone she encountered living inside her head? To think she'd been worried about her mother running her life. *Huh!*

Her companion chuckled, if that little hissing noise coming from between his teeth was laughter.

The dragon changed direction again. Tamara couldn't tell if it had been Halla's idea or the Melakean's – it hadn't been hers.

Halla roared. An answering call came from Kiron in the distance. In moments, the bronze swung around the side of a mountain with Fane on his back. The two dragons circled each other and Fane waved wildly. Soon they flew side by side so the riders could talk.

Tamara was so thrilled to see these two, it took her a moment to realize Skye was missing. "Where is she?"

"Thyel has her. We were searching for them, when we heard Halla."

"What happened?" Tamara asked, fear crowding closer than the Melakean.

"Thyel's cord stopped working. He must have expected that because he grabbed Skye and threatened to break her neck if we didn't drop him off."

Tamara's blood roiled. No matter what Jarrod cautioned, she would have killed Thyel if he had been in her line of sight.

"She fought back," Fane said. "When we landed, Thyel dragged her off into the woods." He nodded to the little green lizard. "Who, or what, is that?"

"Our local guide," Tamara thought the lizard had been unusually quiet and attentive as he, too, listened to Fane's story. "Not a helpful sort." She gave Black-Cheek a searching side glance. Would he assist them in finding Skye?

The Melakean showed her Bevan again by the shore.

She gave a resigned sigh. Bevan was the one they had come for and he was also Thyel's target. Finding her nephew might put them ahead of the game.

Turning to Fane she outlined her plan.

Fane nodded and spoke to Kiron. Halla, receiving her instructions from the Melakean, obligingly followed a route that Tamara assumed would take them toward the sea.

They had flown for only a short span of time before the clouds opened up. Lightning littered the sky with flashes of heat that threatened to sear them.

A strike almost touched Halla's extended left wing.

Too dangerous to go on? she asked Halla.

The green nodded emphatically and winged her way lower to get away from the dark clouds. Kiron followed her lead. That maneuver had no appreciable effect as their flight path took them closer to the eye of the storm. It grew darker, making flying difficult.

Black-Cheek's directions never faltered, however, until Tamara asked him to find them a safe place to land. Then she was given another picture of Bevan, once again bathed in sunshine beneath a clear sky.

Tamara's suspicions grew about the validity of that image. The clouds didn't seem localized and if they were indeed heading for Bevan, how could they be going deeper into the rain when he was standing in sunshine?

Down, she said to Halla.

The dragon faltered and then headed downward in counterpoint to a high-pitched protest from the Melakean. Kiron effortlessly followed Halla's lead, and the two searched the canopy below for a hint of clear ground.

Tamara made a judgment call, deciding her stowaway probably didn't wish to die any more than she did. *Halla, just land. Pretend the tree-covered ground is a clearing.*

Halla dove. Tamara's stomach lurched as the trees sped to meet them. Kiron gave one startled call and then followed his mate.

Excellent. Two suicidal dragons that won't question my wild decisions.

The Melakean reacted to their fast descent with a high-pitched scream and then, miraculously, Halla veered at the last moment and flew toward a clearing that had been hidden by a grove of overgrown trees. Kiron swerved smoothly in her wake.

Halla landed with a hard bump that jolted Tamara forward in her seat and sent the Melakean rolling down to her lap. The dragon ran beneath a wide canopy and away from the pounding rain. The covering which was daunting from overhead, now acted as a wonderful shield.

Tamara breathed a sigh of relief as the pelting rain eased up and then stopped peppering them with raindrops. The sounds of the storm remained, pattering on leaves as the wind tore at branches. High above, rapid bursts of thunder echoed.

"Get off me," Tamara pushed the untrustworthy Melakean away. He grabbed hold of some scales to keep from tumbling off the dragon. "Time for some straight talk."

Tamara slid to the ground and waited for Fane to join her.

"Good call." Fane shook the wetness out of his hair and clothes like a shaggy dog. "How did you know your green friend would help us?"

"He wants something. He wouldn't get it if we all died during landing."

"A search by foot might be better, in any case," Fane said, looking around. "The canopy effectively hides all movement down here. That's how we lost sight of Skye and Thyel."

"Movement is not the only thing the canopy hid." Tamara looked around in shock. From above, the ground had seemed to be an unending line of green, lush plant growth in all directions. From below, a different picture emerged.

The large, stronger, older trees making up the canopy concealed the devastation below. Sections of the ground looked rotten, smaller trees were toppled or uprooted. There was hardly any undergrowth and what there was appeared brittle and dying. She tentatively touched one of the large upright trees. Its bark crumbled beneath her touch, revealing a rotting, molding trunk.

She turned to the Melakean to ask him what was wrong with this land and found he was still on Halla and appeared displeased. Smarting at her trick? She was a little surprised he hadn't read her plan in her mind, since he previously had shown no problem invading her thoughts.

FRIGHTENED. Halla looked over at her unwelcome rider who now studied the clearing with a frown.

Of what? Tamara asked with annoyance. *This is his world and we're the ones who've lost our loved ones.*

She had abandoned Jarrod and her father on Ashari. She mustn't think of that now. There was nothing she could do for them, but she could help Bevan and Skye.

The Melakean's gaze suddenly fixed on her with purpose. As she'd known he would not let them die, she now knew he read her thoughts.

"Fine, so I'm worried about the others. What good does that do you? What do you want from me?"

He resurrected her memory of the day her father had been murdered and, covered in his blood, her mother dragged Tamara and her siblings down the stairs.

She came back to the present with tears in her eyes and saw a mirror of her loss in the Melakean's gaze. They stared at each other in silence, sharing that intimate moment.

"What's wrong?" Fane looked with concern from her to the green hitchhiker.

Tamara wiped away her tears and breathed, allowing that powerful sense of sorrow to fade into the past, where it belonged.

"He's lost something, too," she whispered. "Something precious."

She'd barely finished speaking when images flooded her mind. Fane staggered beside her and the dragons raised their heads, ears up, as if paying attention. They, too, must have been brought into this eloquent communication.

All the bits and pieces she'd been shown fell into place. Tamarisk arriving on Melak with his contingent of Horsemen to steal pieces of a plant. Each strike of their swords against this particular plant, one that grew in vines, rendered a painful tearing in Melak. The guardians of this land came flocking in droves to see who desecrated their world.

Startled by the surge of little green beings, Tamarisk and his men had beaten a hasty retreat to their ship and sailed away toward the horizon with their stolen plunder.

Too late, the Melakeans saw the danger and placed a guard on that beach, where the two worlds overlapped. They meant to ensure no one else would ever cross over to rape their land again.

Years passed, and the threat waned. No other strangers came. The Melakeans returned to their way of life, watching over the world vine. A plant they called the "forgetful one." Though the stolen pieces remained an ever-open wound, the forest adjusted and lived on.

One day another visitor arrived on Melak's shores. This time the locals were prepared to defend their world, with their lives if necessary. Surprisingly, the stranger didn't attack their vine. He instead offered an apology for the past intrusion by his people. He offered two of the stolen vines back, so the forest could heal.

"Thyel," Fane whispered beside Tamara.

"And intending no good." Tamara's suspicions were ripe. "Why didn't you read his intentions as you've been reading mine?"

Silence greeted the question. If she didn't know better, she would have thought Black-Cheek looked contrite.

She glanced at Fane, puzzled.

He looked at their Melakean host with a frown. "I don't think it's normal for them to read minds," he said finally. "Else, they would have known what Tamarisk or Thyel were up to."

She nodded to Black-Cheek. "What happened after Thyel came?" Had his heartfelt apologies been a ruse? She showed a picture of him stealing more of the vines. "Is this what you lost?"

As much as she sympathized with the Melakeans at being duped again, it hardly compared to her father's death. Perhaps they were deeply connected with all the growing things in this world.

The Melakean shook his head and Tamara saw a vision of a beautiful iridescent flower, sprouting out of the soil. Kissed by the sun, it waved gently in the wind. Its petals reflected the sunlight back onto the world. It grew from the heart of the "forgetful" vine, then died, and grew again. Year upon year. Its color was familiar. She'd seen something like that before. The memory was elusive.

The vision the Melakean showed her changed. In the darkness of night, Thyel stood with the Melakeans in a circle, bowing to the plant, as it gracefully, gently died back, shrinking into the ground from which it had come. Before it could wither away completely, Thyel reached out and snapped it from the bed of vines. The world shuddered.

Thyel turned and fled, his stolen flower clutched to his breast, racing toward his ship.

Tamara's heart pounded in horror. Behind him, the ground was littered with limp green Melakeans. Thyel ran, leaping over fallen boulders and trunks, with the desperation of a thief.

By the time the Melakeans recovered, their world had changed. This time worse than ever. Thyel was nowhere to be found. Their flower was no longer on Melak. Then the rains began. Trees died, thunder littered the sky with uncontrolled energy, and they began to perceive each other in ways they had never known possible.

Tamara opened her eyes. Her legs gave way and she fell to the ground. Fane slumped beside her, looking as stunned as she was at the reaction of this world to pulling out of one little flower.

Chapter 18

"THE LIGHTNING IS NOT like it is in our world," Fane whispered. "Here, it's releasing *Light*."

"Magic?" Tamara asked, dumfounded.

"In its rawest form," Fane agreed. "An uncontrolled release. That's why we can still speak with our dragons. Why Melakeans can now talk to each other and us with their minds, when they obviously couldn't with Thyel or Tamarisk in the past."

Tamara looked at him in confusion. "How could stealing one flower cause such a drastic change?"

MAGIC NOT DAMPENED, Halla said.

"That flower must be the source of the magic-dampening effect on this world," Fane said. "Removing it released all the confined *Light*. It's destroying this world. That also explains why Skye's Light ball works in Melak, and why Thyel took her."

"He still plans to use her to find Bevan." Tamara jumped to her feet, anger boiling over.

Fane, too, stood. "After this storm runs its course, we can move quickly to find Skye."

"And Bevan," the green Melakean agreed, in a high-pitched squeaky voice from atop Halla. "To bring back flower."

"What does Bevan have to do with the flower?" Tamara asked.

The Melakean frowned, and Tamara received a series of impressions of Bevan speaking to the green Melakeans, of him coming to see Tamara, of his suspicions about Thyel. As fast as Black-Cheek had picked up her language, he still struggled to put into words what he could better communicate with images.

She tried to comprehend what those images meant. "I think he's saying Bevan suspected what Thyel might have done."

Fane nodded and approached Kiron, who immediately lowered his forehead for a scratch. Fane obliged, speaking thoughtfully, "That's the impression I get, too. Why didn't the prince stop Thyel or tell his mother or grandmother of his suspicions?"

"Nor does it explain why he sought me out." Tamara rubbed at her temple where a headache was throbbing. The more they talked this out, the more complicated the problem became. That reminded her of the headache she had when her mother discovered her in Thyel's room and had him removed to be deported.

Her head had been aching violently then, too. Could it be related to the mind spell placed on her? Her father had removed Thyel's spell, so why was her head hurting now? "How is Bevan involved in this?"

Without answering, Black-Cheek glanced toward the forest. He sent her an image of the holy flower, blooming and then plucked. Once out of the ground, it drooped and transformed into an iridescent ribbon.

Tamara slammed the gates of her mind shut before the Melakean gleaned her thoughts.

He stared at her wide-eyed, as if realizing she blocked him. Halla, too, cocked her head, looking worried, no doubt sensing the connection between them had closed.

"Bevan," Black-Cheek said in his high piercing voice, pointing to his head. "Show you here." The gesture had an enticing quality, as if tempting her to lower her defenses.

With strict control, Tamara faced Fane. Getting Bevan and Skye back safely depended on how well she protected her mind from intrusion. No more slip ups! She had a secret and if she finally succeeded in keeping everyone out of her head, that tiny bit of knowledge might save all those she loved.

"How do you suppose Bevan got to Melak?" she asked Fane, carefully redirecting the subject.

He shrugged watching her carefully. "After Prince Bevan approached you, Thyel might have used the flower to stifle the prince's magic and brought him to Melak."

"No, he didn't," Tamara said with certainty. "First, that would bring the flower back here after Thyel had gone to all the trouble to steal it." She couldn't tell him the second reason. "He must have used another of those vines his father stole."

"But magic works on Melak now," Fane said. "Shouldn't that mean Prince Bevan could have returned home?"

Tamara gestured to the Melakean. "Ask him that."

Fane did.

After a moment of silence, she said, "What did he say?"

"Didn't you see it?"

"My head hurts and that is blocking his shared visions. Tell me."

Fane's eyebrow rose with blatant skepticism but he obliged. "He showed me the trees of Melak, still alive, though damaged and dying. This world could be in a transition stage with the release of magic."

Tamara glanced at the upright giant trees shielding the world from the smaller ones decomposing below. The sky thundered as if in protest. This world did embody all the signs of change: chaos, anger and uncertainty.

"With the flower gone, the vines die," Fane continued, focusing on the one thing Tamara had overlooked in her surroundings. "They are the magical links of this world. Just as the strength of this lightning storm waxes, without the flower, the vines' ability to suppress magic wanes."

"Which suggests the vines worked enough to trap Bevan and bring him here," she said, "but couldn't hold him for long."

"Exactly." Tamara said but Fane hadn't yet realized the half of it. She ignored the agitated gestures from Black-Cheek and focused on Fane.

"If Thyel left Bevan here, tied but unharmed, with the power of the vines weakened, my nephew could have freed himself. This Melakean has been showing us Bevan walking free along a beach."

"If Bevan's free, and can access magic, why is he still here?"

Tamara sighed with impatience. Every answer produced more questions. She studied the upset little Melakean, but his closed face told her he was finished answering questions.

Well, she wasn't finished asking them. They had already caught him lying once. What if he'd been lying all along? What if Bevan wasn't free? What if the Melakeans kept him captive?

She took a step toward Halla, ready to shake Black-Cheek until he confessed everything. She even contemplated enlisting Halla's roasting abilities as persuasion.

One glance at her murderous face and Black-Cheek let out a high-pitched screech and scrambled off the dragon.

Tamara skirted Halla's legs to reach him but he raced toward the woods. Kiron whipped his long tail toward Black-Cheek. The agile Melakean leaped over that obstruction and vanished into the dark while Tamara crashed into the tail and tumbled over.

Cursing, she scrambled to her feet and, ignoring the pain in her left shin from the collision, took off limping after the little Melakean. She finally stopped when she lost sight of his scurrying form in the darkness.

Fane came to a panting halt beside her.

"He has Bevan," she said. "I know it."

"Could he be hoping for a trade? The prince for the flower?"

"I'll give him a flower," Tamara muttered, opening her mind enough to send a picture of her strangling the Melakean and wrapping his precious flower around his neck.

A high-pitched squeak from deep in the forest suggested the fleeing Melakean had received her projection.

"Wait until I get my hands on you next," she shouted.

"Right." Fane gave her a nervous look. "If he wanted to trade, wouldn't he have offered by now? Why hide the fact he has the prince? And if not for trade, why would the Melakeans be holding the prince captive?"

"He wants us to find the flower for him. He was probably leading us to Thyel, not Bevan." Shoulders slumped in defeat, she retreated toward the dragons.

Tamara gestured at the lightning and thunder littering the sky. "This world is filled with magic, Fane. Yet I can't wield any of it to find either Skye or Bevan. How unfair is that?"

At his compassionate look, she turned away. As long as she could remember, she had bemoaned her father's extraordinary ability to work Light, reflected in abundance by everyone in her family but her. She thought she had overcome that old bitterness. Apparently not, for the injustice still ate away deep inside. Mind-speak simply wasn't an adequate substitute.

Halla gave her an encouraging nudge as she approached. The loving gesture broke through her resentment and she gently petted the dragon. "I wouldn't trade my ability to speak with you for any other talent, Halla."

Her love for this dragon astonished her. Halla showed her how to connect with another soul, how not to push love away. Yet, without the use of real magic, how were they to find Skye and Bevan in this strange land? They could search for all eternity, rove the sky from one end to the other and never catch a glimpse of what lay hidden beneath the canopy.

The dark clouds shuddered under another lightning strike, illuminating the wet world with bright, startling clarity.

The energy of that strike reverberated through her like an electric shock. Saira, Anna and her mother casually tapped into that energy to work their spells. On Melak, Light was being released in its raw form, more powerful and dangerous, but still the source of all magic.

"What's the matter?" Fane asked. "You've thought of something, haven't you?"

She glanced at him broodingly, allowing her thoughts free rein to graze along a path she instinctively sensed could offer rich fare.

Fane had been born with the ability to mind-speak to Kiron, and only Kiron. A one-to-one union that was intrinsic to his being. Born and bred into him. There could be no other such pairing.

She turned to Halla, who blinked her golden eyes with utter trust. The connection she shared with the green dragon felt as intrinsic as Fane's was with Kiron, with one important difference.

"I saw Halla in my dreams while still in Ryca," she said. "Across worlds. How could that be?"

"I remember you mentioning that. From all I've learned, it's impossible to bond with a dragon until the physical meeting occurs. The connection begins visually, then proceeds through touch and scent and grows stronger over time. I've never heard of a bond across worlds."

"I sensed Halla before I even knew dragons still existed." Her thoughts, as wild as the lightning-filled sky, drew her gaze from Halla to Kiron.

The bronze dragon returned her stare with an aloof gaze.

Ever since meeting Jarrod and realizing he could read her thoughts, she'd been careful to try and hide her mind from him. Then, when Halla easily stole into her thoughts, she'd built stronger walls to keep the green out. Not with any particular success, but she'd been working on it, and had managed to hold herself back to some degree. Just now she had shut both Halla and the Melakean out. What if she didn't try to hold herself back?

An implausible idea took hold then. "What if my bonding with Halla isn't like yours, Fane, but comes from magic? Of wielding *Light*, without me even realizing it?"

As the possibility of what Tamara suggested opened his mind, Fane's shocked glance slid to Kiron. "There's one way to test that theory."

Tamara, too, turned to the bronze.

Kiron silently stared back.

Can you hear me? she asked.

The bronze leaned forward and nudged Tamara back. *LONG TIME*, he replied in a bold rumbling tone.

Feeling as stunned as Fane looked, she asked, *How long?*

LONG, Halla replied, rubbing her face against Kiron's snout. *AFTER HE FREED ME FROM CAVE, KIRON TOLD ME WHERE YOU WERE ON ISA.*

ALL KNOW, the bronze added casually.

"Who is *all*?" Tamara asked, forgetting to mind-talk.

ALL DRAGONS, the bronze answered. *WHY THEY CAME TO WATCH BLACK'S CHALLENGE. HALLA NOW VALUED MORE THAN AS DAUGHTER TO QUEEN'S LINE. AFTER BONDING WITH YOU, SHE IS QUEEN OF ISA. QUEEN'S MATE RULES ISA. SO BLACK DESPERATE TO KILL ME.*

He said the last with a touch of pride and Halla used her tail to playfully tap him.

"That explains why the black came after us even though Kiron had wounded him," Fane said. "I'd wondered about our audience."

"I don't understand," Tamara said. "Did you or Halla tell the rest of the dragons about me? How did they find out?"

Kiron gave her a long-suffering look that made her smile despite her frustration. It reminded her of the look her mother often gave her when Queen Mamosia thought Tamara had said or done something particularly dense. Like on the night she caught her daughter in Thyel's bed.

Halla took pity and said, *ALL DRAGONS HEAR YOU*. At Tamara's continued blank look, Halla expanded her wings to show off her reflective color and then tucked them in, adding with studied patience, *QUEEN ONLY BOND WITH QUEEN. TAMARA IS QUEEN OF DRAGONS.*

. . . .

KEEGAN'S WARNING THAT the Light was being affected sent Jarrod's pulse racing. To his untrained eye, everything seemed normal. The grass was green. The sky was as blue as ever, without a cloud to mar the day's perfection. He trusted Keegan's spiritual insight more than his vision.

"Tamara? Skye and Fane? Could they be in trouble?" He should have gone with them.

The king was staring at a point straight ahead and spoke in a voice layered with unease. "We are the ones in trouble, Jarrod."

As the king finished speaking, the world shifted. One moment Jarrod stood at the edge of a green meadow. The next, the world had vanished. It was the only way he could describe what he experienced. There was a sense of absolute emptiness: no sights, no sounds, no sense of touch or taste. Not even a stray scent of a flower or grass.

He wanted to scream just to hear his voice but was terrified of hearing nothing. Panic had him whirling, except every direction looked the same. Empty.

Stop panicking. Be calm and think. Had he been transported into the void? Or was he simply unable to see anything? No, not true. Below him, something glowed. Falcon's Tome!

He picked up the book and opened it. Light flashed from the book. The illuminated pages were filled, margin-to-margin, with colorful drawings and dark neatly written script.

Jarrod flicked through the pages, peace settling in him as he recognized the tales his people had recorded over the ages. It was all back. Not a single word missing. No blank pages. He wanted to shout for joy, jump up and down and scream a heartfelt, *Thank you,* to whoever had enacted this miracle.

He paused, squashing his swelling excitement. Something was different about Falcon's Tome. There was some writing in it he'd never seen before. In the front of the book, there were pages he'd never read.

"How can this be?" he asked aloud, not excepting an answer or even to hear his words.

"How can it not be?" Keegan replied nearby. "The book's finally returned home."

He swung around but couldn't identify anything resembling the king. Jarrod had distinctly heard him speak though. Which meant he still had ears to hear the king, eyes to see the tome, even if the rest of his body had vacated the premises. "Sir, you're here, too?"

"If we give our minds time to adjust, we should, theoretically, be able to see each other as well as hear ourselves," Keegan said in a thoughtful tone. "Our senses are too attuned to the world of the living, Jarrod. Even on the light side of Ashari, perception is patterned to mimic the living world, to remind us of where we'd visited, of where we'd loved and lost. Any wonder we can't 'see' the dark side, where such luxuries are forbidden, where those who return here are made to pay the price for not appreciating the gift of being born."

Jarrod digested that explanation and then asked, "How did we come to be here?"

"We were pulled in, rather rudely, I would add."

"And 'here' is the dark side?"

"If I properly understand the working of Light, and I've only been studying it intently since my death, the dark side is the Place of Chaos, where Light was first shaped and formed."

"Formed?" Jarrod asked, astonished. "Into what?"

"Us. People, places, things," Keegan said. "'Life' as we know it was formed from this dark mass."

Jarrod blinked and a shape appeared beside him. The king! He was a glow – a distorted, ethereal being. Jarrod's hand moved through him as if he passed his palm over campfire flames.

"What's happened to you?" Jarrod asked, and then looked at himself. "To us?"

"Light and form do not exist here, Jarrod. This is the place of the beginning. Be careful and stay close. We must not allow ourselves to become lost among the others who inhabit this plane or we may never get home."

"Can we? Go home? You said earlier no one returns from the dark place." He felt himself shatter as he said those fretful words. His body began to lose its cohesiveness.

"Hold on!" Keegan said in a sharp tone. "Do not let despair take hold or you will be lost."

Jarrod mentally pulled himself together and felt a whoosh as if what was left of his form mimicked his imagining. He glanced at the tome. It remained in his grip. "How is it I hold Falcon's Tome when I have no hands."

"Our thoughts and emotions control our actions here. Stay focused. I suspect the key to leaving lies within your unique book, Jarrod. Don't lose it."

Jarrod imagined himself gripping the book tighter and the book moved toward him as if he had clenched the hard-covered tome to his chest. "Why were we brought here, sir? Who did this to us?"

"No time for questions. I've no taste to remain where I was dropped. Follow me."

"If we are still alive," Jarrod muttered, but curbed his despair before it literally tore him apart. He hugged his tome and hurried after the floating version of the king.

For what seemed an eternity, they moved about in silence, yet it didn't feel as if they went anywhere. This place had no landmarks, no points of reference that showed here was different from there. He doubted the king was any wiser about their whereabouts. Keegan, however, epitomized purpose and that produced a comforting presence. Jarrod blindly kept pace with him, intent on escaping whatever had delivered them into this insubstantial hell.

Jarrod didn't know when he first perceived more of this world. One moment he was alone but for an eerie spark of light ahead that was Keegan. Next, he was one among millions.

He could no longer identify the king.

Keegan! he sent out a call coated in desperation.

Here, came the startlingly close answer. *Ignore them.*

Who are they?

Locals. The response was tinged with such dry humor, a hysterical laugh fought to burst out of Jarrod. The king's warm touch now led him. He followed, feeling claustrophobic and in complete sympathy with Tamara's qualms about closed-in places. *Do they sense us? Hear my projected thoughts?*

They're a part of this darkness, more so than us, who should never have been brought here. As it was difficult for us to adjust to this realm, it might be hard for them to perceive us. That should work to our benefit.

How so?

Whoever brought us here might also be having difficulty detecting us.

Finally, Jarrod understood Keegan's urgency to move away from where they'd been deposited. If he'd had shoulders, they would have collapsed in relief.

At least temporarily, Keegan amended his reassuring statement.

Jarrod's tension spiked again. By Keegan's erratic movement, he suspected the king wanted to not only lose their kidnapper, but this crowd, too. Yet, the further they went, the more teeming the surroundings felt, as if he were in the midst of market day, with people bustling about, bumping each other from stall to stall.

This way. Keegan drew Jarrod in another direction.

The crowds didn't thin out but Jarrod was glad simply to move about. Stillness felt akin to being buried alive. *How do you know so much about this place, sir?*

The dead are allowed to learn much, Keegan said as he wove among the crowd. *The secret to life is written in the winds, Jarrod. This is true on Ryca as well as on Ashari. However, on Ryca, people are too distracted by the 'things' around us and our concerns about what we want, to pay attention to unseen truths. On Ashari, many focus on what we've lost instead of where we came from.*

Not you? Jarrod asked.

Especially me. A moment does not go by when I do not reflect on all whom I lost so prematurely. I'm a determined man, Jarrod. It came to me one day that if I could study how life began, I might find a way to...

The abrupt end to the king's speech provoked Jarrod's curiosity. *Find a way to do what, sir?*

Keegan did not respond and Jarrod wondered if he'd been presumptuous in asking.

They continued on for a while in silence. Then the king spoke. *I wanted to find a way to return to my Mamosia.*

The answer, and the longing behind the words, touched Jarrod. He recognized the feeling, for he had sensed it often in the presence of the queen. Even so many years after the death of her husband, Queen Mamosia still grieved, and still hoped that one day she would see the love of her life again.

As a historian, it was his role to record events, and mark the reasons behind people's actions. He had often thought that was why he, and other Erovians, had been given the gift of empathy – to intuitively read people's emotions.

Yet, he'd never been able to entirely separate himself from the feelings he gained from his subjects. Other Erovians acknowledged those same passions and recorded the whys behind actions without becoming involved in people's lives. Jarrod always felt the urge to help, to offer support, to ease people's sorrows.

In truth, that had been why he became so involved with Saira's quest. So much so, he had bowed to her demands that he help and had assisted her in rescuing her family instead of merely recording the event. Instead of regretting his part in that play, Jarrod secretly rejoiced in his role.

In your studies, did you discover any hint of how to get back to Ryca? he asked the king.

No, Keegan said in a regretful voice.

The answer crushed Jarrod's slight hopes of them escaping this dark place.

There's always a way, Keegan added, some of his redoubtable spirit returning. *I simply haven't discovered it yet. As for our current dilemma, why we were brought here might hold the clue to us gaining our freedom.*

Please explain.

Nothing in life happens without a reason. It's all about healing, either by soothing a scarred wound or burning a gaping one closed.

I hope it's the former, Jarrod replied, not liking the sound of being an open wound that needed to be burned closed.

That remains to be seen, Keegan said. *The trick is, why you're here may be different from why I'm here.*

How so?

The king paused and when he finally replied, he did so aloud. "Because you, Jarrod, are an Erovian."

Jarrod drew back shocked that Keegan had given away their presence.

"Jarrod," a nearby voice repeated.

"Erovian?" several others said, sounding surprised.

"Jarrod, Erovian, Jarrod, Erovian." The chant spread.

The crowd closed about Jarrod, touching when there was nothing to touch, inciting his panic. Where Keegan's touch had seemed warm, these beings felt icy cold.

Why did you do that? he asked the king. He felt as if Keegan had put a boot to his backside and shoved him into an arena of hungry lions. *We're never going to lose them now.*

If anyone's safe here, it's you, Keegan calmly replied.

The more Jarrod pushed the spirits away, the closer they drew, as if they'd discovered a new toy that must be prodded and tested. *How am I safer?*

If I understand our history correctly, your ancestors, like mine, were once one of them. Unlike the rest of humanity, the first Erovian left of his own accord.

He wanted to shout at Keegan to stop speaking in riddles. It was as if in coming into this bizarre realm, the king had learned a foreign tongue. Clutching the tome to his chest like a shield, Jarrod said, *Speak plainly.*

This is the place of Beginning, Jarrod. From which Ryca, and all the other worlds, were crafted. Where all people, all animals, all dragons even, were born.

Jarrod's whole being vibrated with recognition of Keegan's words as truth.

"The first Erovian, Falcon, stepped out of this dark mass to create life," Keegan continued, but this time aloud, "and then he set up the inhabitants of Erov as life's guardians."

A shiver spun through Jarrod like a whirlwind.

"Falcon," a local moaned, as if it, too, reacted to the king's statement.

"One of us, gone, never to return," another said.

"Not never," a new voice, nearby, interjected. "Jarrod is here. He has brought Erov home."

A collective sigh sounded and then a chant began. "Jarrod is here. Erov has returned."

Chapter 19

OPEN YOUR BOOK, Keegan said, *and read. Start at the beginning. Time both you and these dark ones remembered the truth of what happened after your ancestor, Falcon, left this realm.*

Jarrod opened Falcon's Tome.

"Read!" The dark ones commanded.

Jarrod looked at the first page filled with words he'd never seen. "From Darkness came Light. From Light came Substance. From Substance came Flesh. Then Flesh was returned to Darkness and Light."

Each word resounded like thunderbolts.

"Yes!" cried the dark ones. "We are darkness!"

"We were once Light!" the rest shouted and Jarrod heard astonishment in those voices.

Jarrod looked up. He had a rapt audience.

"We were darkness. We became Light!"

"There must be no Light," a voice boomed in the distance. "Light is abomination. Light was crafted by twisting darkness. All light must be consumed...brought back into our dark fold."

Jarrod hugged the book to his chest as if to protect the words. A band of Light shot out from inside the book and encircled him as if binding him to the tome. Then something sharp struck his chest, tumbling him backwards into the embrace of the cold dark ones that surrounded him. The book had acted as a shield, protecting him from the pounding he would have otherwise received.

"Who attacks Jarrod?" a dark one asked, sounding as shocked as Jarrod felt. "He must be protected."

Where the book had shielded him with a band of light, now dark coldness surrounded him like an ice field. Bolt after bolt struck at him. Each time the dark shielding grew thicker, as if these dark ones banded together to guard him.

Keegan? Jarrod murmured silently, afraid for the king, but also concerned he might bring attention to Keegan. What if he wasn't equally shielded?

I'm fine, the king replied in the barest of whispers. *Read on. You've struck a nerve. Don't let go of it.*

Jarrod tugged the book away from where it was plastered to his chest. The banding of Light tying him to the tome lengthened but did not break. He was about to carry on reading when he noticed something else odd. "Eyes are looking back at me from inside the book."

"Eyes looking back!" the crowd repeated.

Don't distract them, Keegan urged. *Just read.*

Ignoring the audience from inside the book was difficult, but Jarrod did his best to focus on the words. "Falcon crafted Light from Darkness. Falcon shifted Light and formed Substance. Falcon shaped Substance to bring forth Flesh. Falcon returned Flesh to Darkness and Light."

"LIES!" The distant voice boomed.

"Truth!" The chorus replied. "We were once Light. We were once Flesh. We are returned to Darkness."

Excellent, Keegan mind-whispered. *There's definitely discontent in the fold. We may yet be returned to our world.*

"Falcon formed the Circle," Jarrod read, as fascinated by the words in the tome as his audience. "From Falcon came the Erovians. The Erovians were made Guardians of the Light. Historians of the Circle. Restorers of Balance."

Jarrod looked at Keegan, understanding and doubt fighting for supremacy. *How could we have forgotten we are the Guardians of the Light? Is this true?*

You are reading from Falcon's Tome. Has it ever contained anything false? Is it capable of lies?

Questions crowded inside Jarrod. He could understand and accept the Erovians were meant to be Guardians of the Light. Restorers of Balance? That did not imply a hands-off approach to life.

Those words sounded as if Erov was meant to fix things when magic went wrong. As it had when Tamarisk used his influence on Keegan's brother to ban magic on Ryca. It meant that in Jarrod helping Saira defeat Tamarisk, he hadn't been going against the role of his people, he had been doing exactly what his people were meant to do.

"Guardians of the Light," the dark ones intoned. "Historians of the Circle. Restorers of Balance. Why are you here? Why have you come home?"

"I summoned him," the distant voice said. "Like Falcon, I formed Flesh from Darkness and set forth as Tamarisk to return all Light back to Darkness. The guardian interfered with my sacred mission. My Light was prematurely returned to Darkness. I have brought the guardian home to account for his actions. To receive retribution. Release him to face my justice!"

Who speaks? Jarrod whispered to Keegan.

Our kidnapper, Keegan replied, sounding shockingly gleeful. *He seems unhappy with your role in helping my Saira stop him from ripping Light from Ryca. Serves him right, for if he is in some part Tamarisk, then he is responsible for sending me to Ashari, prematurely. Jarrod, this could work to our benefit.* He added aloud, "Who are you to interfere with Falcon's child?"

That was unhelpful! Jarrod said, alarmed by the way Keegan kept throwing him back into the lion's den.

"Who interferes with Falcon's child?" a dark one nearby asked.

"I did," the distant voice replied. "I am your god."

The silence following that proclamation was profound.

"We are Chaos," a quiet voice then said tentatively from right beside Jarrod. "Chaos has no god."

"Chaos has no god," the chorus chanted.

"I am your god. I have been your god through all of time."

Jarrod heard worry in that deep tone and felt a little encouraged. The fact the dark ones protecting him had not released their shield was even more comforting.

"I am your god," the distant voice insisted. "From me you were torn by Falcon the Damned. I know what we need."

"Chaos has no need," Jarrod's dark neighbor replied.

"Chaos has no need," the chorus chanted.

"We must be one again," the distant voice insisted. "We must not be dispersed, divided, disconnected."

"We are Chaos," Jarrod's neighbor argued. "We are dispersed. We are divided. We are disconnected."

Jarrod wanted to clap him on his back in cheerful support but caution impeded.

"We are Light and we are Darkness," the chorus added.

"We need no god," his dark neighbor said.

"We need no god," the chorus chanted. "We need you no more."

"NO!" cried the lone voice in the distance, now sounding truly terrified.

Suddenly, the dark bands of coldness protecting Jarrod vanished. He was left with the Light of Falcon's Tome holding him steady. A pregnant hush descended.

Jarrod sensed emptiness settle around him and Keegan. In one instant, all the dark ones had vanished, including his vocal dark neighbor.

He looked toward Keegan's dim glow in worry. *What's happening?*

For once, the king appeared speechless.

Then the dark beings returned, buzzing like locusts.

"Send the guardian back." His dark neighbor said. "Brought here in blunder. Debt yet to be repaid."

"Send back the guardian," the chorus repeated.

"And my companion?" Jarrod asked quickly, worried Keegan would otherwise end up like the self-proclaimed God of Chaos.

"And his companion," the locals replied and began to chant, speaking quicker and louder. "Flesh returned to Darkness. Darkness consumed Flesh. Flesh came from Substance. Now Darkness returns Substance to Flesh. Light once infused Substance. Light is put back into Substance."

The voices paused as if for a collective breath.

Jarrod remembered the eyes watching him from inside Falcon's Tome. His suspicions blossomed about to whom those eyes belonged.

He turned to Keegan. "I suppose this is a bad time to bring up my missing historians?"

"Let's hope we're not the ones missing by the time they're finished with us. My only hope is that Tamara, Skye and Bevan are safe." He gave a wistful sigh. "Just once, I'd have given anything to be the father Tamara wanted and go to her when she needs me."

In a booming voice, the chorus interrupted. "Flesh begone from Darkness! For justice has been dispensed."

• • • •

"ALL THIS TIME, *everyone* could read my mind and I didn't know it?" An intense feeling of imposition and horror waged war within Tamara.

"Just all dragons," Fane said and then laughed. At her murderous look, he quickly swallowed the sound.

NOT POLITE TO SPEAK UNTIL SPOKEN TO, Kiron added with studied calm.

Tamara's insides were a vice squeezing her guts. She lost herself, her aloneness. She had become accustomed to the sense of separateness that had cloaked her during her years of confinement. She felt exposed, vulnerable, as if the top of her skull had been ripped open so strangers could peer inside.

It was all too much. She ran into the clearing, allowing rain to pelt her head, face and shoulders. In moments, she was soaked. She stumbled to a halt in the muddy ground and fell to her knees.

Turning her face upward, she voiced her protest to the raping of her privacy. "Nooooo!" Her cry rang out in the night sky, a soulful counterpoint to Light's fury.

Only after the grip on her insides loosened did her mind quiet. She felt no less violated, but was able to breathe again with ease. Feeling better for having released that built-up tension, shoulders down, head bowed, she stood and slowly returned to their shelter.

Her friends looked on with varying degrees of concern.

"Well," Fane said, "now you've let that out, could you see if you can sense where Bevan and Skye are?"

The suggestion set Tamara back. Fane was right. If her "talent" was for communicating without restraint with others, perhaps she could touch Bevan's or Skye's thoughts.

Excitement replaced resentment and Tamara took a deep steadying breath. Closing her eyes, she concentrated on Bevan. Short blond hair. Quite, studious, talented. Up to her shoulder in height. His face was...before she finished the thought, he said, *Aunt Tamara? Is that you?*

A swell of happiness brought tears. *Bevan. Hang on,* she told him. *Not much longer now. We're coming for you.*

She ended, and opened her eyes to smile triumphantly.

Fane let out a loud *Whoop.* Arms swinging in the air, laughing and running in tight circles, he shouted, "Now we're flying with the wind."

Next, she extended her senses in search of Skye and Thyel. She found them instantly. He ran, filled with a sense of impending doom, dragging a stumbling Skye with him.

Grim satisfaction at his panicked state wrapped her in a warm hug. *Run,* she silently urged him. *Run as if retribution were on your trail.*

Tamara? Skye said in shock.

Bevan's all right, she whispered to her niece. *Stay strong until we get to you.*

There was one more person she wanted to contact. For that, she needed a bit more of a push. Looking up at the lightning indiscriminately littering the sky with magic, Tamara reached for that raw energy.

To her amazement, Light responded. Like a night sky filled with stars, it flickered in recognition of her presence. A thousand shooting stars flew toward Tamara and slammed into her chest and spread outward to envelop her. She was swept up in that warm welcoming embrace, like a fierce hug from a long-lost friend.

She cried out in joy, no longer feeling left out, no longer an outsider, no longer alone.

With that loving energy boosting her strength and confidence, like shifting aside a heavy curtain, Tamara edged passed the boundary between worlds and went in search of her father and Jarrod.

Thoroughly frustrated, Tamara snapped her eyes open. "I can't sense them at all."

"Skye and Bevan?" Fane asked.

"I found them. Not Father and Jarrod. They're not on Ashari. I saw the fields and the lake, but they're not there."

"I'm sorry." Fane sounded dazed. "Did you say you reached across into another *world*?"

DRAGONS CAN CROSS REALMS, Kiron said, matter-of-factly. *SO WHY NOT QUEEN OF DRAGONS?*

The fact she could hear Kiron without even trying still amazed Tamara. As did the dragons' insistence she was their queen. Neither of those facts, however, held her attention for long. "Could Jarrod have vanished like the other historians?" Just saying the words made her pulse flutter in horror. She couldn't have lost him.

"We should focus on what we can do." Fane's logical yet sympathetic tone soothed her nerves, a smidgen.

He was right, as usual. Continuing to mentally search for Jarrod and her father would serve no purpose since she had no idea where to look for them. Rescuing Bevan and Skye was within the realm of possibility.

She glanced at the sky. It looked as gloomy as ever but a few patches of blue showed. "Is it wishful thinking or is the storm lessening?"

"It is quieter," Fane agreed. "Not as many lightning strikes. You can now guide us. Shall we risk it?"

With unspoken agreement, they mounted their dragons. It felt good to be doing something.

"Toward Bevan or Skye?" Fane shouted across to her.

A quick check gave the answer. Anna and Saira's vessel had crossed the barrier between worlds and was on the brink of making land. She quickly gave her nephew instruction on where to meet up with them.

Next, she focused on Skye. Her niece's panic was palpable.

"Bevan's fine," she said. "Skye needs us. She and Thyel are headed further inland. We must hurry. She's hurt." She pointed to the right where mountains rose past the rainforest. "That way."

Fane nodded, his face set in angry lines that warned Thyel had made yet another enemy.

Tamara was furious she'd waited this long to come to Skye's rescue. They flew in silence.

The clouds were indeed dispersing but the air still crackled with the storm's energy. Into the quiet, she scented the stench of burning wood. Plumes of black smoke rose from burnt trees. The landscape was dotted with charred spots and spoke of the devastation the release of Light had done to this world.

Though she still had little sympathy for the Melakeans' role in assisting Thyel or keeping Bevan trapped on this land, Tamara saw the peril they fought.

Fane, too, seemed to take in the ruin with a somber expression. "It isn't right, what Thyel did to Melak."

"What isn't right is how easy it was for him to devastate this world," she replied. "Even if the Melakeans restore their precious flower, what's to prevent someone else from stealing it?"

Yet another troubling question she couldn't answer. "Where do you suppose Thyel's taking Skye?"

"I suspect Princess Skye is the leader." His grin was filled with admiration for the young girl's ingenuity. "Knowing her, she would guide him as far from her brother as she could."

That made sense. Did she lead him in a random direction or somewhere in particular? Then she knew. They were headed to where the flower had first been stolen. She recognized the region from the pictures Black-Cheek had shown them.

Skye was taking Thyel to the site of his plunder. The one place he wouldn't want to go. Where the Melakeans would be sure to skewer him if they captured him nearby.

"Foolish girl," Tamara muttered as her fear mounted. She sent her senses out until they collided with a teeming, furious mob. Hidden within the deep green of the woods, she doubted Thyel realized what awaited him.

"Skye, stop!" She urged Halla ahead.

"What's wrong?" Fane shouted as Kiron increased his speed to catch up.

"She's leading Thyel into an ambush. Herself with him."

Fane's face went ashen, and Kiron responded by howling in protest. Halla joined him in that wail.

Tamara wanted to howl in despair, too. Why hadn't she sensed Skye's plan when she touched her mind?

Because, as usual, I shied away from getting too close.

Her self-accusation only infuriated her more. What if she didn't reach Skye in time to stop the slaughter?

The convergence had already begun. Little green bodies slithered over top branches and stormed under cover of the canopy. They swept toward Skye and Thyel from all directions.

Halla and Kiron flew over a clearing. Below, Thyel, who must have finally realized the trap his furious captive led him into, spun in circles, holding Skye like a shield.

The encircling trees were filled with Melakeans. Many dropped to the ground. They looked too enraged to care who they hurt in reaching the one responsible for the destruction of their world.

One blast of Halla's fiery breath could take out Thyel but Skye would be caught in the crossfire. As livid as Tamara was with the Melakeans, she couldn't order Halla to take out the encroaching mass either. It would be pure butchery of innocents and both she and Halla knew it.

"What can we do?" she asked Fane in desperation.

"Land." Grim-faced, Fane directed his bronze to do just that.

Halla followed. The giant beasts bore down on top of the Melakeans and accomplished the one thing Tamara needed most. It caught the surging crowd's attention and stopped their forward momentum. They scattered to get out of the way of claws reaching for purchase.

Skye gazed up at Tamara, one eye bruised, nose bloody and lips pressed thin. Niece gave aunt a glance mixed with equal amounts of relief and defiance.

Tamara kept her face shuttered, unwilling to forgive Skye for such a foolish act. She swung to lock gazes with Thyel, instead.

He sent her a warm, relieved smile. "Timely, my love."

Halla tucked her wings in and lowered her head. The look of utter hatred in the dragon's eyes had him scrambling backwards practically brushing against the Melakeans.

He held Skye between him and the fuming Halla issuing hot smoke from her nostrils.

Someone walloped his thigh with a big stick.

Thyel viciously kicked back, sending several Melakeans flying, while the rest retreated out of boot range.

"Let her go," Tamara ordered from Halla's back.

"Skye and I have become close friends." Thyel kept a tight hold around his prisoner's midriff. "She doesn't want to leave."

"I'm happy to die with you," Skye answered. "Tell Halla to roast him. Do it!"

Tamara's heart melted at the terror and pain her niece must have gone through to sink her to this desperate state. "I'm sorry, Skye. I can't."

"I knew it," Thyel said. "You do care for me. You know I never meant you any harm, Tamara. I only wanted you to love me. I still do."

"That would be a little difficult, Thyel," Tamara said in a mild tone, while seething inside. "I've fallen in love with someone else. Besides, by the time these good folks whose world you've ruined are finished with you, there won't be much left to love." She tilted her head toward several Melakeans who were abandoning their sticks in favor of rocks.

Thyel's eyes narrowed, his anger flashing before raw fear swamped it. "Surely you don't intend to let these savages kill me? If you do, you'll be sentencing your niece to death, be sure of that. Then they'll go after Bevan, if he isn't dead already. You should be mad at them. They're the ones who took the boy prince."

"Liar." A rock flew through the air and struck Thyel on his forehead.

He jerked back and a bead of blood trickled down to wet his eyebrow.

A Melakean stepped out of the crowd.

Tamara recognized Black-Cheek and her eyes narrowed with lingering anger.

As if he sensed her resentment, Black-Cheek took a cautious step back toward his fellows. Without sympathy for his plight, they shoved him forward and planted a rock into his fist.

Making a show of bravery, he tossed the rock up and down, his gaze flicking between Thyel to Tamara. "The evil one told us the prince had hidden the flower. That by enticing him to Melak, we could weaken him and force him to give the flower back. He lied then, and he lies now."

"But you did take Bevan," Tamara said in a tone laced with fury.

The green dragon turned to study him.

Black-Cheek swallowed and blinked rapidly. He missed catching his rock on the next throw, and it barely missed landing on his foot. "Only to retrieve our flower, Princess," he said, sounding shaken. "That's all we want. We have no quarrel with the prince or anyone else." He glanced at Thyel. "Except this one. We want him to pay for what he did."

Tamara turned back to Thyel with a raised eyebrow.

Thyel looked worried. "Surely you wouldn't leave me to my death, my love?" Though he spoke with entreaty, a blade slipped out of his sleeve and he raised it to Skye's throat.

Tamara's heart skipped and then thumped in rapid terror. She wanted to jump off Halla and run to Skye's rescue.

FANE SAYS STAY, Kiron mind-spoke.

Tamara froze. Fane no longer sat astride his bronze.

I'm not alone in this fight. Fane and Halla and Kiron were here with her. For her. Without a single doubt she trusted in whatever Fane planned. For a young lad, he had a smart head on his shoulders.

On that realization, followed another extraordinary thought. *Nothing will ever again be just my fight.* She was torn between crying in terror and laughing with joy.

What she needed to do now was stall for time and keep Thyel's attention firmly on her. With that goal in mind, Tamara maintained eye contact with Thyel, prepared to entice, entreat or enrage him to hold his attention.

"Let Skye go," she said with casual nonchalance, "and perhaps we can deal."

"I will, my love," he replied, looking encouraged. "I promise. After we lose this mob. Let me ride with you."

Halla reared her head in distaste and the mob inched forward with a protesting howl.

Thyel's hand jerked as if in fear. The blade nicked Skye's neck and a trail of blood oozed out.

Fear spiked in Tamara but she couldn't risk checking on Fane's whereabouts. Was he close enough to wrestle Skye away from Thyel?

Feigning serenity, Tamara gently stroked the agitated green's neck, calming herself as much as the dragon. "Halla is unlikely to allow you anywhere near her again."

An image of her sitting on Halla and speaking to Thyel flashed in her mind. Tamara blinked in surprise. That image hadn't come from Kiron or Black-Cheek. The angle was all wrong. It had also held the distinct flavor of Jarrod's mind-talk!

The image disappeared as quickly as it populated her thoughts. It took monumental self-control to ignore looking for the source of that beloved mind-touch.

On the periphery of her vision, the crowd stirred, as if the Melakeans were being shoved aside by someone moving among them. Couldn't be Jarrod doing it, or he would have towered over the short Melakeans.

An Erovian trick? Despite their dramatically darker skin and hair color, his people had lived and worked in Ryca for centuries without Rycans being aware of the Erovians' presence.

The fact he was not only alive but also here and coming to her aid had Tamara's toes curling in astonishment and joy. Her mouth pressed into a thin line to keep her delighted smile from bursting out.

Thyel's attention swung from the furious crowd, to the snorting Halla, and finally to Tamara confronting him, apparently. His flitting gaze flew in all the wrong directions, unaware of his impending doom. *Good!*

At one more turn of Thyel's attention away from her, Tamara took the opportunity to wink in reassurance at Skye. Her niece blinked back in surprise.

Thyel turned back to Tamara. "If you take us away from here, I'll help you look for Bevan on our way off this blighted world."

"No!" Skye said.

Thyel's gaze swung away from Tamara, but instead of returning to the crowd, he glanced at Kiron, from whose shoulders Fane was alarmingly absent.

Eyes filled with disbelief, Thyel clenched the blade.

"Don't!" Tamara shouted. She scrambled off Halla's back and landed on the hard-packed ground with a jolt. She ran toward Thyel. Before she could reach him, the knife in his hand vanished. As he was staring in astonishment at his empty hand, someone jerked Skye away from his hold. Fane took that opportunity to barrel into Thyel.

The crowd of Melakeans scrambled back, shouting encouragement to Fane as the two males rolled on the ground punching and shoving each other.

Tamara spotted Jarrod on the sidelines, looking as solid and handsome as ever, holding Skye out of harm's way. She made a mental note to ask about his invisibility another time. For now, she spared Jarrod a short loving glance.

He returned it with warm eyes that embraced her mentally and tantalizingly promised more later.

Before she could follow that enticing train of thought another intruded. If Jarrod snatched Skye away, who took Thyel's knife?

Chapter 20

FANE AND THYEL ROLLED near Black-Cheek and the little Melakean kicked out with his bare foot, striking Thyel squarely in the head where a rock had struck earlier. Thyel winced and it gave Fane the chance to get a solid blow to his opponent's chin.

The crowd cheered.

Skye shouted, "Kill him, Fane!"

Jarrod had his hands full keeping Skye from joining in the fray.

The normally diffident Fane didn't look as if he needed help. He seemed to enjoy thrashing Thyel. Pumped by his apparent fierce thirst for payback, and perhaps by his connection to Kiron, Fane was an equal match to his larger opponent. *Good for you, Fane.*

Then Tamara spotted her father. He watched the spectacle with an animated expression. In his hand, he casually twirled Thyel's blade.

Avoiding the combatants, she ran to her father. This time her arms didn't go through him as they had on Ashari and he staggered back, laughing. She asked in wonder, "How?"

"Explanations after the fight?" he suggested with a mischievous grin.

A hiss from the crowd and a cry of alarm from Skye swung Tamara's attention back to Thyel and Fane. Thyel was poised to thrash him with a thick branch.

Tamara pushed away to leap to Fane's aid but Keegan pulled her back.

Before her objection left her lips, Kiron sent a spume of flames right across from where she stood. The blaze struck Thyel, branch and all. The blast of hot burning air had Tamara reeling back into her father's arms, cringing from the acrid stench of brimstone.

Thyel's screams silenced the mob's shouts and Skye's cries. Utter silence descended except for the crackle and snap of the sustained flames scorching skin, tearing through muscles and melting organs until the unrelenting flames reached bones. They glowed red and orange before being charred black and gray. The air stank of roasted meat and marrow.

Still lying on the ground, Fane stared wide-eyed and silent until the flames receded and like snowfall, ashes sprinkled onto his chest and legs. Only then did he scramble to his feet.

"Thank you, Papa," Tamara whispered, the first to speak, grateful for his quick thinking in pulling her back. She was stunned at how close she'd come to getting seared alongside Thyel.

Keegan's eyes looked suspiciously bright as he said, "You're welcome. Glad I could be here to help you."

A loud jubilant roar from Kiron swung her attention to the dragon. Halla gave her mate an affectionate shove with her snout that he returned with a proud caress, before leaning forward to lick Fane.

Tamara's nerves, strung tight as a drum since Thyel first kidnapped Skye, collapsed. She would likely have fallen but for her father's steady support. She wanted to go to Fane but Skye was already at his side, fiercely hugging him. Then Skye kissed him resoundingly on his lips.

Tamara hid her smile. Fane had just saved Skye's life. Fought Thyel for her. No doubt Kiron scorching Thyel to cinders was also a reflection of Fane's anger. Fane was her savior. What young woman wouldn't be affected by all of that? Skye had met her first hero.

Keegan loudly cleared his throat.

Fane, looking thoroughly flushed, quickly pushed Skye away and gave her grandfather, his king, a nervous look and a credible bow.

Skye couldn't seem to stop grinning as she clung to Fane's arm as if she meant to stay there for a lifeline.

"Father, are you truly here?" Tamara whispered, breaking the tension.

He drew her close and kissed the top of her head. "Does that feel real enough for you?"

"But how?"

"It's a long story. Mostly it's thanks to Jarrod."

"It wasn't me, sir," Jarrod came over. "It was Falcon's Tome. Seems my people have a history we've forgotten." He shook his head as if realizing the irony. Historians losing track of their past.

"And the missing Erovians?" Fane asked, coming up to them with Skye. "Did you discover what happened to them?"

Jarrod held out his hand and the tome simply appeared.

Tamara stared in wonder. Not only could Jarrod call the book at will, but the tome no longer looked like a raggedy old thing, with pages falling out, and held together with a vine. Falcon's Tome was a thick volume, impressively leather-bound, with engravings on the cover that shone in a rainbow of colors.

"They were in here," Jarrod said with excitement. "When I read from the missing pages, the missing historians found me. Once the king and I were recreated," he held up his hand to silence the ensuing questions, "when we were remade into substance, the historians reappeared beside us. We left them on Ashari while we came here to look for all of you."

"Until the problem in Ryca is resolved," Keegan put in, "there's no point in sending them home. They'd again be affected by the Melakean flower that interferes with magic. Seems Erovians are magic personified."

"Flower," Black-Cheek jumped into the conversation. He stomped over to stand before Tamara, fists back on his hips, spearing her with a stubborn glare. "Queen dragon says you have it."

Tamara gave Halla a surly look over her shoulder. The green returned with a limpid glance, blinking her golden eyes with innocence.

"Tamara!" Keegan's stern fatherly tone commanded her attention. "Give the lizard back his flower."

She crossed her arms and sent the Melakean a challenging look. "First, explain how you plan to protect your treasure the next time someone wants to take it."

"We savvy now," the little Melakean touched his forehead with a pointed finger. "Not trust peoples again."

"I'm peoples," Tamara pointed out. "I mean, I'm a person."

"Yes. We not trust you."

She rolled her eyes at his faulty logic. He trusted her and the rest of her party enough to return his flower and leave Melak without causing further problems. Exactly the type of wrong thinking that had landed these Melakeans in trouble in the first place. "Why do you deserve this precious flower if you can't take proper care of it?"

Her family and friends groaned in unison.

All except for Jarrod, who grinned with enjoyment as he watched her. She suspected he'd delved into her mind again and understood her reasoning.

"Tamara!" Skye came over to stand beside the little Melakean. "Give him back his flower. Can you not see his world is dying? This isn't something to plague him about, no matter how much you enjoy doing that to your family."

Jarrod chuckled aloud at that and her father, too, seemed to find the comment amusing.

"Your aunt is right, Skye." Fane picked bits of dust and slivers of cracked bone out of his clothes as he spoke. "The Melakeans must be able to safeguard their flower. It's too important to plant in the ground and hope no one will pluck it."

"Exactly," Tamara said. "Thank you, Fane."

"We guard it!" Black-Cheek insisted and his people shouted in strident assertion of that sentiment.

"What did you have in mind, Tamara?" Her father's words cut through the unhappy chatter.

"Once the flower is back on Melak, magic will again be dead here," Tamara patiently explained. "You will need a non-magical form of protection or intrinsically magical beings to assist you."

In response to Tamara's suggestion, the Melakeans thoughtfully studied the only, intrinsically magical beings on their world – the two dragons.

Halla and Kiron's sheer size attested to their defensive capabilities.

Halla nudged Tamara, giving her tacit agreement to her unvoiced, unplanned and unanticipated proposal to move permanently to Melak. Halla, it seemed, had no wish to return to Isa and its volatile politics.

AGREED, Kiron said, *IF FANE IS WILLING, WE WILL STAY AND GUARD MELAK.*

Fane glanced at Tamara with a raised eyebrow. "Never to return home?"

"We can return any time we want, with dragons at our disposal," Tamara said. "That is, if we're invited to stay," she added with a challenging look at the little Melakeans. "We could make this world our home. Unless Fane's too attached to the Quinlin Towers and, um, other attractions on Ryca to leave?"

Skye, who had been listening with great interest, took the young man's hand. "Your master would probably love to visit here, Fane. You said this was the one world he'd never dared explore. It would be a great way to end a dragon rider's career. I'd like to visit with you. We'll have to check with my parents and grandmother." She sent a quick smile to Keegan. "And my grandfather."

"What would we do here?" Fane said. "Our presence might be enough protection for the Melakeans, but it isn't enough for me. I need a purpose, a reason to be here, something meaningful to do. Living with my master, alone, taking care of him was fine once, but not anymore. During this journey, I outgrew the joys of an isolated life."

"Dragon riders need apprentices," Skye said. "Now you're a full-fledged dragon rider, why not acquire an apprentice of your own?"

Fane frowned and then his eyes widened as if an extraordinary idea had occurred. He looked at Tamara with hope rising. "Could we start a dragon riding school on Melak? Matching rider to dragon could happen on Isa, then the apprentices brought here for training. It would ensure that rebellious dragons couldn't obstruct the lessons of fledgling dragons and their riders. Remove the threat of giants interfering in the training."

"A fine idea," Tamara agreed. With Bevan found, she, too, suddenly craved a new purpose, other than annoying her mother. She sent Jarod a tentative invitation. To claim her. To build a home with her on Melak.

She held her breath, wondering if she had earned the right to ask for his love. He'd once said his traveling city was bound to Ryca. How would he feel about leaving there?

The sensual images he sent in response, swept a heat wave up her cheeks.

What about Erov? she asked him silently, still unsure.

I am Erov, he said with quiet confidence. *We are not a place, but guardians of all places, and I am yours.*

"Then it's agreed," Tamara took Jarrod's hand.

"Agreed to what?" Keegan asked.

"I intend to marry Tamara," Jarrod raised her hand for a kiss.

Skye whooped and ran over to hug them both.

"I don't recall anyone asking my permission." Keegan's gaze swung from Tamara to Jarrod. "It is customary to ask the father before stealing his daughter."

"Sir..." Jarrod began.

"The answer's no," Keegan replied.

"But…"

"No."

"Papa!"

"Absolutely not."

"Why not?" Tamara asked in exasperation.

"Because I have just returned to your life and I'm not ready to let go yet. He'll have to wait." The king held his hand in the air, palm down, tilting it back and forth. "Maybe for a year or two."

Tamara found that despite his blatantly unreasonable stance, she couldn't stop smiling. Even Skye burst out laughing, though Jarrod looked as if he were about to argue with his king. Then his face relaxed and Tamara guessed he'd read her certainty about her father's true intentions to relent soon.

It was wonderful to believe her father had missed her, too. He gave her a hug then.

With a happy cry, Skye joined them.

"We not agreed to plan." Black-Cheek stomped his foot, calling Tamara's attention back to the Melakeans.

Tamara relented and broadcast to Black-Cheek and the rest of the Melakeans the whereabouts of the flower. She'd given them her best advice. What they chose to do was up to them.

In a wink, several of the Melakeans disappeared and then returned. Black-Cheek held the iridescent ribbon she'd left in Thyel's old room in the castle.

Tamara looked at the ribbon, finally allowing herself to think clearly about it. Ever since she guessed what that ribbon represented, she had hidden it from her thoughts, afraid Black-Cheek would steal it from her mind.

Now she gave herself permission to remember Thyel presenting the ribbon to her on the night he tried to bed her. She shivered at how thrilled she'd been with the colorful offering. The insensitive fiend. As if she would ever want something that could destroy not only Ryca but also Melak.

"That's the flower?" Skye asked in a stunned whisper.

Tamara nodded. "Thyel gifted it to me."

A Melakean dug a hole and Black-Cheek inserted the ribbon into the ground. Immediately the slender flat piece of shimmering ribbon expanded and grew upward, its roots burrowing into the ground. The ribbon turned a greenish brown and sprouted branches and leaves. They all shuffled backwards as the giant vine expanded. Iridescent multi-petaled flowers spilled out on all the limbs, all the way to the very top.

To think she'd tied that ribbon around her head. No wonder it had given her such a headache. It had probably been profoundly offended at being used as a hair ribbon.

Giving a collective sigh, the Melakeans edged closer until each one in turn could hug their sacred plant. Then each Melakean walked over to pat a dragon, as if in approval of Tamara's plan, before disappearing into the surrounding woods.

With his people obviously satisfied with the impromptu strategy for the dragons to serve as Melak's future protectors, Black-Cheek gave a grunt that could have been either approval or disgust, and stomped away.

"What, no 'thank you'?" Tamara called after him.

"No thanks to you," he shouted back.

Fane smiled at her. "He'll make a good neighbor."

"Not," Tamara said and grinned back.

"With that flower gone from Ryca," Keegan said, "my spell should be working well again, protecting the Light. It'll be safe to return home. Shall we go pick up your sisters and Bevan? After all you've told me of the boy's magical abilities, I'm curious to meet that young lad."

"He'll be thrilled to meet you, Grandfather." Skye turned to Tamara and took her hand. "Thank you."

Tamara raised an eyebrow in surprise. "For what? Father and Jarrod and Fane were the ones that saved you."

Skye hugged her tight. "Thank you for coming after me."

The words brought tears to Tamara's eyes. She hugged Skye back. "What are friends for if not to watch each other's backs? Besides, if I couldn't save Bevan, I decided I'd at least better bring you home safely to Mother or she would marry me off to Gideon out of spite."

At the reminder of her problems back home, she glanced at Jarrod.

He had a determined set to his jaw.

The bunched muscles of her shoulders instantly relaxed. She and Jarrod were a couple now. The agreeable idea fit her like a well-made coat and bestowed a sense of confidence and pride.

No matter what form of justice her mother or anyone else dreamed up for her in the future, she would never face it alone.

It was close to sunset by the time they all arrived on the two dragons at the seashore. Bevan was seated on the beach speaking with his parents, his Aunt Saira, Tom and an Erovian clothed in a bright cream robe. The ship that brought them was moored in the distance.

Skye was the first to climb down and race to claim a hug from her brother.

Giving Tamara an encouraging hug, he followed Skye at a slower pace with Falcon's Tome in hand. He had much to tell his second-in-command about their past and Erov's purpose.

Tamara descended from Halla last, allowing her family and friends to greet each other, to exclaim over King Keegan's unexpected appearance and all talk at once trying to hear about each other's adventures.

Anna looked over suddenly and noticing Tamara lingering beside Halla. She took Saira's hand and tugged her toward Tamara.

"I'm sorry I didn't listen to Bevan when he came for my help, Anna," Tamara said softly.

"You kept my Skye safe," Anna said and hugged her. "Thank you!"

Tamara relished her youngest sister's hug. Anna gave the best ones. Even better than their mother's.

Finally pulling away, she turned to Saira with a contrite expression. "Would you please tell Tom that I lost his sword but I promise to clean and mend his clothes and chainmaille before returning them? And I'm sorry I've been so inhospitable to both of you since you rescued me."

Saira smiled her warm acceptance and the three sisters joined in a happy family embrace under the light of the three moons.

· · · ·

THE RETURN OF THE KING of Ryca to his castle occurred in the dead of night, without any fanfare or reception.

The startled guards at the queen's door were silenced with one gesture of the king's finger against his lips. The original plan had been for the men to stay outside while the women went in to prepare the queen. Then Bevan came in with them because Skye refused to let him out of her sight. The king also followed them in because he said he didn't trust Tamara not to overset his wife.

On Tamara's insistence, he finally agreed to stay hidden behind the bed curtains, so he wouldn't frighten the slumbering queen.

They quietly stepped into the dark bedchamber and Saira limped up to the large four-poster bed first. She shifted a section of the curtains aside to sit on the mattress and gently shook her mother's hand.

"Saira!" Mamosia sat up. "Oh, thank the Light you're safe. Bevan?"

"I'm here." Bevan came around to wave to his grandmother.

The queen pulled him closer and enveloped him in a ferocious hug, rocking back and forth. "Oh Bevan. You won't understand this, but losing you felt like losing *him* all over. You mustn't ever run away like that again. Promise me?"

"He didn't run away, Mother." Tamara came up to the side of the bed and pushed the curtains open just a little more.

Her mother looked surprised, then teary. Quickly enough, her gaze cooled and she wiped away a stray tear. "So, Saira found you, too. I'm glad you're back safe. We will talk more in the morning."

"But it's the night of the full moons, Mother," Tamara said. "Don't you want to know who I've picked for my mate? This is the night the ultimatum runs out, isn't it?"

"Tamara, can't this wait?" Skye reached for her aunt's hand.

Tamara pulled away, her focused gaze trained on her mother. All the threats of Gideon and the terror he represented, which the queen had wielded like a spiked whip, returned with a vengeance. At this moment, retribution tasted sweeter than honey.

"I don't care if you did help Saira recover Bevan," her mother said in a hard voice, not releasing the squirming boy from her grasp, "you will not marry Thyel. I forbid it."

Tamara sympathized with Bevan's long-suffering look but she wasn't ready to release her mother from her grip yet.

She shifted out of Skye's painful pinching hold and swished opened the curtains at the bottom of the bed. "Mother, I've changed my mind about Thyel. I've chosen someone else."

"Who is it?" the queen asked. "Tell me and get it over with. I see the challenge in your eyes and know I'm not going to like the answer."

"Are you bracing yourself?" Tamara raised an eyebrow, before moving to the far side of the bed, ready to open the final curtain, behind which her father would no longer be able to hide. *Coward.*

She gave him a wicked grin and he rolled his eyes at her theatrics.

"Speak." Her mother looked with suspicion at all her children and grandchildren who couldn't seem to stop smiling or laughing around her.

Tamara held the edge of the final curtain, "Well, actually, I don't need your permission to marry the man I've picked. I've received someone else's blessing."

"My dear child," her mother said, in a frosty tone. "I don't care whose blessing you've received. Without my approval, there will be NO marriage."

Keegan reached past Tamara and whipped the curtain aside. "I've told you since she was a child, Mamosia, never let this one goad you into a fight. Her lack of compassion has apparently blossomed in my absence."

The queen stared at him with wide-eyes and open mouth.

Saira squeezed her mother's hand and whispered, "Mam, he's really back. This is not a dream or a sham."

Before she finished speaking, Mamosia, Queen of Ryca, a woman who had staunchly and single-handedly defended her family against a murderous brother-in-law and courageously outwitted a mad sorcerer, sank onto her pillow in a dead faint.

Released from her grip, Bevan scrambled off the bed.

His sister took his place. Skye tenderly stroked her grandmother's forehead. "We should have been gentler."

"Everybody out." Keegan's tone brooked no argument. "I need no witnesses for this part of my homecoming."

Before Tamara could leave, he snagged her by her elbow and said in a harsh tone, "If you ever torment your mother like that again, you'll answer to me."

Tamara couldn't contain her smile at that old familiar rebuke and leaned in to kiss his cheek. "Yes, Papa," she said in her meekest voice. She tugged free of his grip and raced away before the swipe of his hand could connect with her backside.

Outside the door, she ran full tilt into Jarrod.

"What did the queen say?" He sounded worried.

"She never told her." Without a backward glance, Saira strode passed them down the corridor with Tom. "Too busy giving Mother grief to mention your proposal."

"I don't believe your behavior sometimes," Skye added in a paternal voice as she followed her parents out the door. She had such a tight grip on her brother's wrist, Tamara doubted Bevan would be permitted to leave her side for a week. Maybe not even for a month.

The nine-year-old grinned at Tamara over his shoulder and mind-spoke, *That was fun.*

Skye gave him a frowning glare and tugged him along.

Keegan slammed the door shut on all of them.

"I see your relationship with your family is back to normal," Jarrod observed.

As they headed downstairs, word spread of the king's return through the castle populace. Despite the lateness of the hour, people stirred and talked and ran from room to room.

Tamara led Jarrod down the stairs and along the length of a portrait gallery toward her chamber. She wanted some private time to talk about Erov and her role among his people.

All Erovians were scholars while Tamara wasn't exactly studious. Already, she was thinking up ways to distract him from his work. What if the Erovians considered her too flighty a mate for their Chief Councilor?

At sight of a familiar tapestry on the wall, she tugged Jarrod behind it and opened the hidden panel. Once inside the narrow passageway, the panel shut tight, enclosing them in darkness.

Jarrod took advantage of the proximity to pull her close. "By the way, we're not waiting two years to marry," he said in a resolute voice, hands roaming from her shoulders to waist, as if he intended to lay claim on every inch of her right then and there.

The walls closed in around Tamara. Her pulse shot up like a geyser and she chuckled against Jarrod's seeking lips.

"What is so amusing?" He sounded out of breath and provoked. "I'm serious. We'll move to Melak today if necessary. Your parents can't follow us there."

"At the moment, my legs couldn't carry me to bed, let alone another world, Jarrod."

He pulled back, his restless hands turning comforting. "Are closed-in places still a problem?"

"My heart is definitely racing," she whispered against the underside of his chin and the side of his throat. Inhaling deeply, she decided she was becoming addicted to his scent. "But not because of tiny spaces."

"Ah," Jarrod sounded pleased. "To be safe, will you allow me to show you our new home on Melak?"

"Right now? But we just returned."

"I promise, we'll be back in time for supper."

In a moment, he'd whisked her away.

Would she ever get used to traveling like this? Jarrod's newly discovered ability to go wherever he pleased, even between worlds, made her feel freer even than flying Halla.

They arrived beside an oasis in the midst of a desert. A small bright blue tent was set up by the edge of a pool.

"This isn't Melak," Tamara said, with suspicion. Had he taken her to Erov after all? She wasn't ready to meet his people yet. She wanted to be dressed properly. Saira had said they loved color and bangles and flowing gowns. She needed time to change out of her trousers, tunic and chainmaille.

"This is Melak," Jarrod insisted, sounding excited. "I discovered this area on the other side of the mountain range while waiting for you to finish speaking with your mother. Melak is actually similar in terrain to Ryca."

Ah, there was his scholarly tone. If he broke into a lecture, she intended to kiss him. She sent a mental hello to Halla, informing her she was back on Melak.

BUILDING NEST WITH KIRON, Halla replied. *EXPECT EGGS TO HATCH BY SPRING. KIRON AND I ARE COLLECTING QUINLIN STONES FOR YOU AND FANE.*

"Thank you!" Tamara said, touched.

Jarrod bowed deeply and gave one of his flourishing arm gestures as he invited her to step inside his tent. A hot breeze blew the front flaps open.

With a delighted cry, Tamara ran in and discovered lavishly decorated rooms extending in every direction.

And there were hundreds of people inside!

She came to a startled halt, stunned by the richness of the Erovians' clothing, their dark skin coloring, and the extraordinary smiles they beamed her way, each of which was matched with a projected image of a warm welcoming hug.

Her throat clogged with a grateful heart, she turned to Jarrod. His people didn't judge her at all. Instead, they seemed glad to meet her.

He raised her hand for a long lingering kiss. "I pledge with my life that you will never feel trapped or alone, Tamara. Welcome home, my queen."

THE END

••••

IF YOU LOVE FANTASY with a historical flavor, you're sure to enjoy the historical fantasy series, The Cauldron Effect, set during the Regency period (early 1800s). Book 1 of The Cauldron Effect is **Coven at Callington**, where a newly graduated coven protectress receives her first assignment–find a missing warlock boy. When she meets a handsome church guard, an enemy of witches, on the same mission, things get complicated. You can read more about their fascinating and fiery encounter here: https://www.shereenvedam.com/witches-warlocks

••••

IF YOU ENJOYED THIS story, please consider leaving a short review for this book wherever you purchased it. The review will help other readers decide if this book is worth their time

••••

SIGN UP TO SHEREEN'S Newsletter to learn about her new releases: https://www.subscribepage.com/c9u7e6

Thank you for reading!

Don't miss out!

Visit the website below and you can sign up to receive emails whenever Shereen Vedam publishes a new book. There's no charge and no obligation.

https://books2read.com/r/B-A-POZG-ILEZ

BOOKS 2 READ

Connecting independent readers to independent writers.

Did you love *Hushed*? Then you should read *Coven at Callington*[1] by Shereen Vedam!

[2]

A kidnapped child. A witch on the warpath. A church guard in crisis. In 1815, Thomas Drake Saint-Clair, Earl of Braden, a Guard of the Green Cross, is tasked by his archbishop to rescue a missing boy and return him to his warlock father. The order lands Braden in the middle of an unholy war between witches and warlocks and shoves him headlong past a sacred line he'd sworn never to cross.Newly confirmed Coven Protectress, Merryn Pendraven, rushes to rescue a witch's son. She's convinced the same evil warlock who was responsible for her younger brother's death is behind this kidnapping, too. She has no intention of letting this vile villain get away with the same crime, twice.When Merryn discovers Braden is also on the case, she's tempted to join forces. Yet, how can she truly trust him when her aunt has warned that Braden's second secret charge is to destroy their coven? Finding love in this cauldron of trouble might prove to be Merryn's

---

1. https://books2read.com/u/38r6rB

2. https://books2read.com/u/38r6rB

deadliest mission and Braden's complete undoing. *If you liked A Discovery of Witches or Dr. Strange and Mr. Norrell, you'll love Coven at Callington, an anime-inspired witchy tale that will whisk you away on a rip-roaring Regency ride.* **Scroll up and pick up your copy now.**

Read more at www.shereenvedam.com.

Also by Shereen Vedam

Harrington Bay Mystery
Sage It Out
Missing You

Outside the Circle Mystery
To Capture Love
Death Takes a Detour
Death Shifts Gears
Death Smells Disaster
Death Swipes Right
Death Comes Up Short

Tales of Ryca
Hidden
Hushed

The Cauldron Effect
Coven at Callington
Warlock from Wales
Love Spell in London

Standalone
Tales of Ryca: The Complete Series
Torn
The Cauldron Effect: The Complete Series
Believe
Innocent

Watch for more at www.shereenvedam.com.

About the Author

Once upon a time, USA Today bestselling author Shereen Vedam read fantasy and romance novels to entertain herself. Now she writes heartwarming tales braided with threads of magic and love and mystery elements woven in for good measure.

Shereen's a fan of resourceful women, intriguing men, and happily-ever-after endings. If her stories whisk you away to a different realm for a few hours, then Shereen will have achieved one of her life goals.

Please consider leaving a review wherever you purchased this book.

Read more at www.shereenvedam.com.